The Borough Treasurer

By J. S. Fletcher

Originally published in 1921

The Borough Treasurer

© 2012 Resurrected Press
www.ResurrectedPress.com

Published by Intrepid Ink, LLC

Intrepid Ink, LLC provides full publishing services to authors of fiction and non-fiction books, eBooks and websites. From editing to formatting, to publishing, to marketing, Intrepid Ink gets your creative works into the hands of the people who want to read them.
Find out more at www.IntrepidInk.com.

ISBN 13: 978-1-937022-39-6

Printed in the United States of America

Foreword

Many British mysteries have been set in London, in neighborhoods both mean and posh. Others have been set along the bleak coast of Cornwall or on the moors of Devonshire. The university towns of Oxford and Cambridge have seen their share of fictional crime. But it has been left to J. S. Fletcher to bring murder and mayhem to the small towns and rural countryside of England's north country, in particular his native Yorkshire.

Though he occasionally set his mysteries in London or other parts of the country, it was his beloved Yorkshire moors and dales and the small towns nestled in them that served as the settings for some of his best works. And rightly so, for Fletcher was not only a popular writer of mysteries, but he was a keen observer of the local customs and dialect as well as a highly regarded writer on the history of the region.

Yorkshire is a world apart from southern England and particularly the bustle of London. The natives speak an obscure dialect only barely recognizable as English. They have an air of superiority over their southern countrymen who the feel do not understand the real world of farming and manufacturing and hard work and honest dealings. Reading Fletcher's works, one senses he shares this opinion.

The setting of *The Borough Treasurer*, as in many of Fletcher's novels is a small town, in this case Highmarket, a place of about five thousand residents and situated not too far from the coast. Like many small towns, it social and political life is dominated by a few wealthy men, in this case Mallalieu and Cotherstone who run a construction company and serve as mayor and treasurer respectively of the borough of Highmarket. And, as in most small towns, everybody knows everybody and everybody's business. Reputation is everything, and one's stature in the community depends not so much on personal wealth as on the networks of trust and association built up over a life time.

But even small towns can hold secrets, and where there are secrets, there is blackmail. And where there is blackmail, murder is sure to follow.

The Borough Treasuer, as in many British mysteries, is a story then of secrets, blackmail, and murder. It is a story well told, where the secrets are revealed one by one as are the clues. But, where Fletcher excels, is in his depiction of this world of the north country. He understands from first hand knowledge the attitudes and relationships that exist in such small towns and the surrounding countryside. Most importantly, he understands the language, which he recreates not only in the dialog, but even occasionally in the prose.

J. S. Fletcher, unfortunately is not as well read today as he deserves. He has become, in the words of one critic, "that forgotten Yorkshireman." But, in the first part of the twentieth century he was one of the most popular of mystery writers and author of over a hundred books in that genre. It is then, with great pleasure, that Resurrected Press brings its readers this new edition of *The Borough Treasurer*.

About the Author

Joseph Smith Fletcher (1863-1935) was a journalist and the author of over 200 books. Born in Halifax, West Yorkshire, he studied law before turning to journalism. His earlier works were either histories or historical fiction, and he was made a fellow of the Royal Historical Society. He didn't start writing mysteries until 1914, though before he died he had written over 100 in the genre.

Greg Fowlkes
Editor-In-Chief
Resurrected Press
www.ResurrectedPress.com

TABLE OF CONTENTS

1. BLACKMAIL

Half way along the north side of the main street of Highmarket an ancient stone gateway, imposing enough to suggest that it was originally the entrance to some castellated mansion or manor house, gave access to a square yard, flanked about by equally ancient buildings. What those buildings had been used for in other days was not obvious to the casual and careless observer, but to the least observant their present use was obvious enough. Here were piles of timber from Norway; there were stacks of slate from Wales; here was marble from Aberdeen, and there cement from Portland: the old chambers of the grey buildings were filled to overflowing with all the things that go towards making a house—ironwork, zinc, lead, tiles, great coils of piping, stores of domestic appliances. And on a shining brass plate, set into the wall, just within the gateway, were deeply engraven the words: *Mallalieu and Cotherstone, Builders and Contractors.*

Whoever had walked into Mallalieu & Cotherstone's yard one October afternoon a few years ago would have seen Mallalieu and Cotherstone in person. The two partners had come out of their office and gone down the yard to inspect half a dozen new carts, just finished, and now drawn up in all the glory of fresh paint. Mallalieu had designed those carts himself, and he was now pointing out their advantages to Cotherstone, who was more concerned with the book-keeping and letter-writing side of the business than with its actual work. He was a big, fleshy man, Mallalieu, midway between fifty and sixty, of a large, solemn, well-satisfied countenance, small, sly eyes, and an expression of steady watchfulness; his attire was always of the eminently respectable sort, his linen fresh and glossy; the thick gold chain across his ample front, and the silk hat which he invariably wore, gave him an unmistakable air of prosperity. He stood now, the silk hat cocked a little to one side, one hand under the tail of his broadcloth coat, a pudgy finger of the other pointing to some new feature of the mechanism of the new carts, and he looked the personification of self-satisfaction and smug content.

"All done in one action, d'ye see, Cotherstone?" he was saying. "One pull at that pin releases the entire load. We'd really ought to have a patent for that idea."

Cotherstone went nearer the cart which they were examining. He was a good deal of a contrast to his partner—a slightly built, wiry man, nervous and quick of movement; although he was Mallalieu's junior he looked older, and the thin hair at his temples was already whitening. Mallalieu suggested solidity and almost bovine sleekness; in Cotherstone, activity of speech and gesture was marked well-nigh to an appearance of habitual anxiety. He stepped about the cart with the quick action of an inquisitive bird or animal examining something which it has never seen before.

"Yes, yes, yes!" he answered. "Yes, that's a good idea. But if it's to be patented, you know, we ought to see to it at once, before these carts go into use."

"Why, there's nobody in Highmarket like to rob us," observed Mallalieu, good-humouredly. "You might consider about getting—what do they call it?—provisional protection?—for it."

"I'll look it up," responded Cotherstone. "It's worth that, anyhow."

"Do," said Mallalieu. He pulled out the big gold watch which hung from the end of his cable chain and glanced at its jewelled dial. "Dear me!" he exclaimed. "Four o'clock—I've a meeting in the Mayor's parlour at ten past. But I'll look in again before going home."

He hurried away towards the entrance gate, and Cotherstone, after ruminative inspection of the new carts, glanced at some papers in his hand and went over to a consignment of goods which required checking. He was carefully ticking them off on a list when a clerk came down the yard.

"Mr. Kitely called to pay his rent, sir," he announced. "He asked to see you yourself."

"Twenty-five—six—seven," counted Cotherstone. "Take him into the private office, Stoner," he answered. "I'll be there in a minute."

He continued his checking until it was finished, entered the figures on his list, and went briskly back to the counting-house near the gateway. There he bustled into a room kept sacred to himself and Mallalieu, with a cheery greeting to his visitor—an elderly man who had recently rented from him a small house on the outskirts of the town.

"Afternoon, Mr. Kitely," he said. "Glad to see you, sir—always glad to see anybody with a bit of money, eh? Take a chair, sir—I hope you're satisfied with the little place, Mr. Kitely?"

The visitor took the offered elbow-chair, folded his hands on the top of his old-fashioned walking-cane, and glanced at his landlord with a half-humorous, half-quizzical expression. He was an elderly, clean-shaven, grey-haired man, spare of figure, dressed in rusty black; a wisp of white neckcloth at his throat gave him something of a clerical appearance: Cotherstone, who knew next to nothing about him, except that he was able to pay his rent and taxes, had already set him down as a retired verger of some cathedral.

"I should think you and Mr. Mallalieu are in no need of a bit of money, Mr. Cotherstone," he said quietly. "Business seems to be good with you, sir."

"Oh, so-so," replied Cotherstone, off-handedly. "Naught to complain of, of course. I'll give you a receipt, Mr. Kitely," he went on, seating himself at his desk and taking up a book of forms. "Let's see—twenty-five pounds a year is six pound five a quarter—there you are, sir. Will you have a drop of whisky?"

Kitely laid a handful of gold and silver on the desk, took the receipt, and nodded his head, still watching Cotherstone with the same half-humorous expression.

"Thank you," he said. "I shouldn't mind."

He watched Cotherstone produce a decanter and glasses, watched him fetch fresh water from a filter in the corner of the room, watched him mix the drinks, and took his own with no more than a polite nod of thanks. And Cotherstone, murmuring an expression of good wishes, took a drink himself, and sat down with his desk-chair turned towards his visitor.

"Aught you'd like doing at the house, Mr. Kitely?" he asked.

"No," answered Kitely, "no, I can't say that there is."

There was something odd, almost taciturn, in his manner, and Cotherstone glanced at him a little wonderingly.

"And how do you like Highmarket, now you've had a spell of it?" he inquired. "Got settled down, I suppose, now?"

"It's all that I expected," replied Kitely. "Quiet— peaceful. How do you like it?"

"Me!" exclaimed Cotherstone, surprised. "Me?—why, I've had—yes, five-and-twenty years of it!"

Kitely took another sip from his glass and set it down. He gave Cotherstone a sharp look.

"Yes," he said, "yes—five-and-twenty years. You and your partner, both. Yes—it'll be just about thirty years since I first saw you. But—you've forgotten."

Cotherstone, who had been lounging forward, warming his hands at the fire, suddenly sat straight up in his chair. His face, always sharp seemed to grow sharper as he turned to his visitor with a questioning look.

"Since—what?" he demanded.

"Since I first saw you—and Mr. Mallalieu," replied Kitely. "As I say, you've forgotten. But—I haven't."

Cotherstone sat staring at his tenant for a full minute of speechlessness. Then he slowly rose, walked over to the

door, looked at it to see that it was closed, and returning
to the hearth, fixed his eyes on Kitely.

"What do you mean?" he asked.

"Just what I say," answered Kitely, with a dry laugh.
"It's thirty years since I first saw you and Mallalieu.
That's all."

"Where?" demanded Cotherstone.

Kitely motioned his landlord to sit down. And
Cotherstone sat down—trembling. His arm shook when
Kitely laid a hand on it.

"Do you want to know where?" he asked, bending close
to Cotherstone. "I'll tell you. In the dock—at Wilchester
Assizes. Eh?"

Cotherstone made no answer. He had put the tips of
his fingers together, and now he was tapping the nails of
one hand against the nails of the other. And he stared
and stared at the face so close to his own—as if it had
been the face of a man resurrected from the grave. Within
him there was a feeling of extraordinary physical
sickness; it was quickly followed by one of inertia, just as
extraordinary. He felt as if he had been mesmerized; as if
he could neither move nor speak. And Kitely sat there, a
hand on his victim's arm, his face sinister and purposeful,
close to his.

"Fact!" he murmured. "Absolute fact! I remember
everything. It's come on me bit by bit, though. I thought I
knew you when I first came here—then I had a feeling
that I knew Mallalieu. And—in time—I remembered—
everything! Of course, when I saw you both—where I did
see you—you weren't Mallalieu & Cotherstone. You
were——"

Cotherstone suddenly made an effort, and shook off
the thin fingers which lay on his sleeve. His pale face
grew crimson, and the veins swelled on his forehead.

"Confound you!" he said in a low, concentrated voice.
"Who are you?"

Kitely shook his head and smiled quietly.

"No need to grow warm," he answered. "Of course, it's excusable in you. Who am I? Well, if you really want to know, I've been employed in the police line for thirty-five years—until lately."

"A detective!" exclaimed Cotherstone.

"Not when I was present at Wilchester—that time," replied Kitely. "But afterwards—in due course. Ah!—do you know, I often was curious as to what became of you both! But I never dreamed of meeting you—here. Of course, you came up North after you'd done your time? Changed your names, started a new life—and here you are! Clever!"

Cotherstone was recovering his wits. He had got out of his chair by that time, and had taken up a position on the hearthrug, his back to the fire, his hands in his pockets, his eyes on his visitor. He was thinking—and for the moment he let Kitely talk.

"Yes—clever!" continued Kitely in the same level, subdued tones, "very clever indeed! I suppose you'd carefully planted some of that money you—got hold of? Must have done, of course—you'd want money to start this business. Well, you've done all this on the straight, anyhow. And you've done well, too. Odd, isn't it, that I should come to live down here, right away in the far North of England, and find you in such good circumstances, too! Mr. Mallalieu, Mayor of Highmarket—his second term of office! Mr. Cotherstone, Borough Treasurer of Highmarket—now in his sixth year of that important post! I say again—you've both done uncommonly well—uncommonly!"

"Have you got any more to say?" asked Cotherstone.

But Kitely evidently intended to say what he had to say in his own fashion. He took no notice of Cotherstone's question, and presently, as if he were amusing himself with reminiscences of a long dead past, he spoke again, quietly and slowly.

"Yes," he murmured, "uncommonly well! And of course you'd have capital. Put safely away, of course, while you were doing your time. Let's see—it was a Building Society that you defrauded, wasn't it? Mallalieu was treasurer, and you were secretary. Yes—I remember now. The amount was two thous——"

Cotherstone made a sudden exclamation and a sharp movement—both checked by an equally sudden change of attitude and expression on the part of the ex-detective. For Kitely sat straight up and looked the junior partner squarely in the face.

"Better not, Mr. Cotherstone!" he said, with a grin that showed his yellow teeth. "You can't very well choke the life out of me in your own office, can you? You couldn't hide my old carcase as easily as you and Mallalieu hid those Building Society funds, you know. So—be calm! I'm a reasonable man—and getting an old man."

He accompanied the last words with a meaning smile, and Cotherstone took a turn or two about the room, trying to steady himself. And Kitely presently went on again, in the same monotonous tones:

"Think it all out—by all means," he said. "I don't suppose there's a soul in all England but myself knows your secret—and Mallalieu's. It was sheer accident, of course, that I ever discovered it. But—I know! Just consider what I do know. Consider, too, what you stand to lose. There's Mallalieu, so much respected that he's Mayor of this ancient borough for the second time. There's you—so much trusted that you've been Borough Treasurer for years. You can't afford to let me tell the Highmarket folk that you two are ex-convicts! Besides, in your case there's another thing—there's your daughter."

Cotherstone groaned—a deep, unmistakable groan of sheer torture. But Kitely went on remorselessly.

"Your daughter's just about to marry the most promising young man in the place," he said. "A young fellow with a career before him. Do you think he'd marry her if he knew that her father—even if it is thirty years ago—had been convicted of——"

"Look you here!" interrupted Cotherstone, through set teeth. "I've had enough! I've asked you once before if you'd any more to say—now I'll put it in another fashion. For I see what you're after—and it's blackmail! How much do you want? Come on—give it a name!"

"Name nothing, till you've told Mallalieu," answered Kitely. "There's no hurry. You two can't, and I shan't, run away. Time enough—I've the whip hand. Tell your partner, the Mayor, all I've told you—then you can put your heads together, and see what you're inclined to do. An annuity, now?—that would suit me."

"You haven't mentioned this to a soul?" asked Cotherstone anxiously.

"Bah!" sneered Kitely. "D'ye think I'm a fool? Not likely. Well—now you know. I'll come in here again tomorrow afternoon. And—you'll both be here, and ready with a proposal."

He picked up his glass, leisurely drank off its remaining contents, and without a word of farewell opened the door and went quietly away.

2. CRIME—AND SUCCESS

For some moments after Kitely had left him, Cotherstone stood vacantly staring at the chair in which the blackmailer had sat. As yet he could not realize things. He was only filled with a queer, vague amazement about Kitely himself. He began to look back on his relations with Kitely. They were recent—very recent, only of yesterday, as you might say. Kitely had come to him, one day about three months previously, told him that he had come to these parts for a bit of a holiday, taken a fancy to a cottage which he, Cotherstone, had to let, and inquired its rent. He had mentioned, casually, that he had just retired from business, and wanted a quiet place wherein to spend the rest of his days. He had taken the cottage, and given his landlord satisfactory references as to his ability to pay the rent—and Cotherstone, always a busy man, had thought no more about him. Certainly he had never anticipated such an announcement as that which Kitely had just made to him—never dreamed that Kitely had recognized him and Mallalieu as men he had known thirty years ago.

It had been Cotherstone's life-long endeavour to forget all about the event of thirty years ago, and to a large extent he had succeeded in dulling his memory. But Kitely had brought it all back—and now everything was fresh to him. His brows knitted and his face grew dark as he thought of one thing in his past of which Kitely had spoken so easily and glibly—the dock. He saw himself in that dock again—and Mallalieu standing by him. They were not called Mallalieu and Cotherstone then, of course. He remembered what their real names were—he remembered, too, that, until a few minutes before, he had certainly not repeated them, even to himself, for many a long year. Oh, yes—he remembered everything—he saw it all again. The case had excited plenty of attention in Wilchester at the time—Wilchester, that for thirty years had been so far away in thought and in actual distance that it might have been some place in the Antipodes. It was not a nice case—even now, looking back upon it from his present standpoint, it made him blush to think of. Two better-class young working-men, charged with embezzling the funds of a building society to which they had acted as treasurer and secretary!—a bad case. The Court had thought it a bad case, and the culprits had been sentenced to two years' imprisonment. And now Cotherstone only remembered that imprisonment as one remembers a particularly bad dream. Yes—it had been real.

His eyes, moody and brooding, suddenly shifted their gaze from the easy chair to his own hands—they were shaking. Mechanically he took up the whisky decanter from his desk, and poured some of its contents into his glass—the rim of the glass tinkled against the neck of the decanter. Yes—that had been a shock, right enough, he muttered to himself, and not all the whisky in the world would drive it out of him. But a drink—neat and stiff— would pull his nerves up to pitch, and so he drank, once, twice, and sat down with the glass in his hand—to think still more.

That old Kitely was shrewd—shrewd! He had at once hit on a fact which those Wilchester folk of thirty years ago had never suspected. It had been said at the time that the two offenders had lost the building society's money in gambling and speculation, and there had been grounds for such a belief. But that was not so. Most of the money had been skilfully and carefully put where the two conspirators could lay hands on it as soon as it was wanted, and when the term of imprisonment was over they had nothing to do but take possession of it for their own purposes. They had engineered everything very well—Cotherstone's essentially constructive mind, regarding their doings from the vantage ground of thirty years' difference, acknowledged that they had been cute, crafty, and cautious to an admirable degree of perfection. Quietly and unobtrusively they had completely disappeared from their own district in the extreme South of England, when their punishment was over. They had let it get abroad that they were going to another continent, to retrieve the past and start a new life; it was even known that they repaired to Liverpool, to take ship for America. But in Liverpool they had shuffled off everything of the past—names, relations, antecedents. There was no reason why any one should watch them out of the country, but they had adopted precautions against such watching. They separated, disappeared, met again in the far North, in a sparsely-populated, lonely country of hill and dale, led there by an advertisement which they had seen in a local newspaper, met with by sheer chance in a Liverpool hotel. There was an old-established business to sell as a going concern, in the dale town of Highmarket: the two ex-convicts bought it. From that time they were Anthony Mallalieu and Milford Cotherstone, and the past was dead.

During the thirty years in which that past had been dead, Cotherstone had often heard men remark that this world of ours is a very small one, and he had secretly laughed at them. To him and to his partner the world had been wide and big enough. They were now four hundred miles away from the scene of their crime. There was nothing whatever to bring Wilchester people into that northern country, nothing to take Highmarket folk anywhere near Wilchester. Neither he nor Mallalieu ever went far afield—London they avoided with particular care, lest they should meet any one there who had known them in the old days. They had stopped at home, and minded their business, year in and year out. Naturally, they had prospered. They had speedily become known as hard-working young men; then as good employers of labour; finally as men of considerable standing in a town of which there were only some five thousand inhabitants. They had been invited to join in public matters— Mallalieu had gone into the Town Council first; Cotherstone had followed him later. They had been as successful in administering the affairs of the little town as in conducting their own, and in time both had attained high honours: Mallalieu was now wearing the mayoral chain for the second time; Cotherstone, as Borough Treasurer, had governed the financial matters of Highmarket for several years. And as he sat there, staring at the red embers of the office fire, he remembered that there were no two men in the whole town who were more trusted and respected than he and his partner—his partner in success ... and in crime.

But that was not all. Both men had married within a few years of their coming to Highmarket. They had married young women of good standing in the neighbourhood; it was perhaps well, reflected Cotherstone, that their wives were dead, and that Mallalieu had never been blessed with children. But Cotherstone had a daughter, of whom he was as fond as he was proud; for her he had toiled and contrived, always intending her to be a rich woman. He had seen to it that she was well educated; he had even allowed himself to be deprived of her company for two years while she went to an expensive school, far away; since she had grown up, he had surrounded her with every comfort. And now, as Kitely had reminded him, she was engaged to be married to the most promising young man in Highmarket, Windle Bent, a rich manufacturer, who had succeeded to and greatly developed a fine business, who had already made his mark on the Town Council, and was known to cherish Parliamentary ambitions. Everybody knew that Bent had a big career before him; he had all the necessary gifts; all the proper stuff in him for such a career. He would succeed; he would probably win a title for himself—a baronetcy, perhaps a peerage. This was just the marriage which Cotherstone desired for Lettie; he would die more than happy if he could once hear her called Your Ladyship. And now here was—this!

Cotherstone sat there a long time, thinking, reflecting, reckoning up things. The dusk had come; the darkness followed; he made no movement towards the gas bracket. Nothing mattered but his trouble. That must be dealt with. At all costs, Kitely's silence must be purchased—aye, even if it cost him and Mallalieu one-half of what they had. And, of course, Mallalieu must be told—at once.

A tap of somebody's knuckles on the door of the private room roused him at last, and he sprang up and seized a box of matches as he bade the person without to enter. The clerk came in, carrying a sheaf of papers, and Cotherstone bustled to the gas.

"Dear me!" he exclaimed. "I've dropped off into a nod over this warm fire, Stoner. What's that—letters?"

"There's all these letters to sign, Mr. Cotherstone, and these three contracts to go through," answered the clerk. "And there are those specifications to examine, as well."

"Mr. Mallalieu'll have to see those," said Cotherstone. He lighted the gas above his desk, put the decanter and the glasses aside, and took the letters. "I'll sign these, anyhow," he said, "and then you can post 'em as you go home. The other papers'll do tomorrow morning."

The clerk stood slightly behind his master as Cotherstone signed one letter after the other, glancing quickly through each. He was a young man of twenty-two or three, with quick, observant manners, a keen eye, and a not handsome face, and as he stood there the face was bent on Cotherstone with a surmising look. Stoner had noticed his employer's thoughtful attitude, the gloom in which Cotherstone sat, the decanter on the table, the glass in Cotherstone's hand, and he knew that Cotherstone was telling a fib when he said he had been asleep. He noticed, too, the six sovereigns and the two or three silver coins lying on the desk, and he wondered what had made his master so abstracted that he had forgotten to pocket them. For he knew Cotherstone well, and Cotherstone was so particular about money that he never allowed even a penny to lie out of place.

"There!" said Cotherstone, handing back the batch of letters. "You'll be going now, I suppose. Put those in the post. I'm not going just yet, so I'll lock up the office. Leave the outer door open—Mr. Mallalieu's coming back."

He pulled down the blinds of the private room when Stoner had gone, and that done he fell to walking up and down, awaiting his partner. And presently Mallalieu came, smoking a cigar, and evidently in as good humour as usual.

"Oh, you're still here?" he said as he entered. "I— what's up?"

He had come to a sudden halt close to his partner, and he now stood staring at him. And Cotherstone, glancing past Mallalieu's broad shoulder at a mirror, saw that he himself had become startlingly pale and haggard. He looked twenty years older than he had looked when he shaved himself that morning.

"Aren't you well?" demanded Mallalieu. "What is it?"

Cotherstone made no answer. He walked past Mallalieu and looked into the outer office. The clerk had gone, and the place was only half-lighted. But Cotherstone closed the door with great care, and when he went back to Mallalieu he sank his voice to a whisper.

"Bad news!" he said. "Bad—bad news!"

"What about?" asked Mallalieu. "Private? Business?"

Cotherstone put his lips almost close to Mallalieu's ear.

"That man Kitely—my new tenant," he whispered. "He's met us—you and me—before!"

Mallalieu's rosy cheeks paled, and he turned sharply on his companion.

"Met—us!" he exclaimed. "Him! Where?—when?"

Cotherstone got his lips still closer.

"Wilchester!" he answered. "Thirty years ago. He— knows!"

Mallalieu dropped into the nearest chair: dropped as if he had been shot. His face, full of colour from the keen air outside, became as pale as his partner's; his jaw fell, his mouth opened; a strained look came into his small eyes.

"Gad!" he muttered hoarsely. "You—you don't say so!"

"It's a fact," answered Cotherstone. "He knows everything. He's an ex-detective. He was there—that day."

"Tracked us down?" asked Mallalieu. "That it?"

"No," said Cotherstone. "Sheer chance—pure accident. Recognized us—after he came here. Aye—after all these years! Thirty years!"

Mallalieu's eyes, roving about the room, fell on the decanter. He pulled himself out of his chair, found a clean glass, and took a stiff drink. And his partner, watching him, saw that his hands, too, were shaking.

"That's a facer!" said Mallalieu. His voice had grown stronger, and the colour came back to his cheeks. "A real facer! As you say—after thirty years! It's hard—it's blessed hard! And—what does he want? What's he going to do?"

"Wants to blackmail us, of course," replied Cotherstone, with a mirthless laugh. "What else should he do? What could he do? Why, he could tell all Highmarket who we are, and——"

"Aye, aye!—but the thing is here," interrupted Mallalieu.

"Supposing we do square him?—is there any reliance to be placed on him then? It 'ud only be the old game—he'd only want more."

"He said an annuity," remarked Cotherstone, thoughtfully. "And he added significantly, that he was getting an old man."

"How old?" demanded Mallalieu.

"Between sixty and seventy," said Cotherstone. "I'm under the impression that he could be squared, could be

satisfied. He'll have to be! We can't let it get out—I can't,
any way. There's my daughter to think of."

"D'ye think I'd let it get out?" asked Mallalieu. "No!—
all I'm thinking of is if we really can silence him. I've
heard of cases where a man's paid blackmail for years
and years, and been no better for it in the end."

"Well—he's coming here tomorrow afternoon some
time," said Cotherstone. "We'd better see him—together.
After all, a hundred a year—a couple of hundred a year—
'ud be better than—exposure."

Mallalieu drank off his whisky and pushed the glass
aside.

"I'll consider it," he remarked. "What's certain sure is
that he'll have to be quietened. I must go—I've an
appointment. Are you coming out?"

"Not yet," replied Cotherstone. "I've all these papers
to go through. Well, think it well over. He's a man to be
feared."

Mallalieu made no answer. He, like Kitely, went off
without a word of farewell, and Cotherstone was once
more left alone.

3. MURDER

When Mallalieu had gone, Cotherstone gathered up the papers which his clerk had brought in, and sitting down at his desk tried to give his attention to them. The effort was not altogether a success. He had hoped that the sharing of the bad news with his partner would bring some relief to him, but his anxieties were still there. He was always seeing that queer, sinister look in Kitely's knowing eyes: it suggested that as long as Kitely lived there would be no safety. Even if Kitely kept his word, kept any compact made with him, he would always have the two partners under his thumb. And for thirty years Cotherstone had been under no man's thumb, and the fear of having a master was hateful to him. He heartily wished that Kitely was dead—dead and buried, and his secret with him; he wished that it had been anywise possible to have crushed the life out of him where he sat in that easy chair as soon as he had shown himself the reptile that he was. A man might kill any poisonous insect, any noxious reptile at pleasure—why not a human blood-sucker like that?

He sat there a long time, striving to give his attention to his papers, and making a poor show of it. The figures danced about before him; he could make neither head nor tail of the technicalities in the specifications and estimates; every now and then fits of abstraction came over him, and he sat drumming the tips of his fingers on his blotting-pad, staring vacantly at the shadows in the far depths of the room, and always thinking—thinking of the terrible danger of revelation. And always, as an under-current, he was saying that for himself he cared naught—Kitely could do what he liked, or would have done what he liked, had there only been himself to think for. But—Lettie! All his life was now centred in her, and in her happiness, and Lettie's happiness, he knew, was centred in the man she was going to marry. And Cotherstone, though he believed that he knew men pretty well, was not sure that he knew Windle Bent sufficiently to feel sure that he would endure a stiff test. Bent was ambitious—he was resolved on a career. Was he the sort of man to stand the knowledge which Kitely might give him? For there was always the risk that whatever he and Mallalieu might do, Kitely, while there was breath in him, might split.

A sudden ringing at the bell of the telephone in the outer office made Cotherstone jump in his chair as if the arresting hand of justice had suddenly been laid on him. In spite of himself he rose trembling, and there were beads of perspiration on his forehead as he walked across the room.

"Nerves!" he muttered to himself. "I must be in a queer way to be taken like that. It won't do!—especially at this turn. What is it?" he demanded, going to the telephone. "Who is that?"

His daughter's voice, surprised and admonitory, came to him along the wire.

"Is that you, father?" she exclaimed. "What are you doing? Don't you remember you asked Windle, and his friend Mr. Brereton, to supper at eight o'clock. It's a quarter to eight now. Do come home!"

Cotherstone let out an exclamation which signified annoyance. The event of the late afternoon had completely driven it out of his recollection that Windle Bent had an old school-friend, a young barrister from London, staying with him, and that both had been asked to supper that evening at Cotherstone's house. But Cotherstone's annoyance was not because of his own forgetfulness, but because his present abstraction made him dislike the notion of company.

"I'd forgotten—for the moment," he called. "I've been very busy. All right, Lettie—I'm coming on at once. Shan't be long."

But when he had left the telephone he made no haste. He lingered by his desk; he was slow in turning out the gas; slow in quitting and locking up his office; he went slowly away through the town. Nothing could have been further from his wishes than a desire to entertain company that night—and especially a stranger. His footsteps dragged as he passed through the market-place and turned into the outskirts beyond.

Some years previously to this, when they had both married and made money, the two partners had built new houses for themselves. Outside Highmarket, on its western boundary, rose a long, low hill called Highmarket Shawl; the slope which overhung the town was thickly covered with fir and pine, amidst which great masses of limestone crag jutted out here and there. At the foot of this hill, certain plots of building land had been sold, and Mallalieu had bought one and Cotherstone another, and on these they had erected two solid stone houses, fitted up with all the latest improvements known to the building trade. Each was proud of his house; each delighted in welcoming friends and acquaintances there— this was the first night Cotherstone could remember on which it was hateful to him to cross his own threshold. The lighted windows, the smell of good things cooked for supper, brought him no sense of satisfaction; he had to make a distinct effort to enter and to present a face of welcome to his two guests, who were already there, awaiting him.

"Couldn't get in earlier," he said, replying to Lettie's half-anxious, half-playful scoldings. "There was some awkward business turned up this evening—and as it is, I shall have to run away for an hour after supper—can't be helped. How do you do, sir?" he went on, giving his hand to the stranger. "Glad to see you in these parts—you'll find this a cold climate after London, I'm afraid."

He took a careful look at Bent's friend as they all sat down to supper—out of sheer habit of inspecting any man who was new to him. And after a glance or two he said to himself that this young limb of the law was a sharp chap—a keen-eyed, alert, noticeable fellow, whose every action and tone denoted great mental activity. He was sharper than Bent, said Cotherstone, and in his opinion, that was saying a good deal. Bent's ability was on the surface; he was an excellent specimen of the business man of action, who had ideas out of the common but was not so much given to deep and quiet thinking as to prompt doing of things quickly decided on. He glanced from one to the other, mentally comparing them. Bent was a tall, handsome man, blonde, blue-eyed, ready of word and laugh; Brereton, a medium-sized, compact fellow, dark of hair and eye, with an olive complexion that almost suggested foreign origin: the sort, decided Cotherstone, that thought a lot and said little. And forcing himself to talk he tried to draw the stranger out, watching him, too, to see if he admired Lettie. For it was one of Cotherstone's greatest joys in life to bring folk to his house and watch the effect which his pretty daughter had on them, and he was rewarded now in seeing that the young man from London evidently applauded his friend's choice and paid polite tribute to Lettie's charm.

"And what might you have been doing with Mr. Brereton since he got down yesterday?" asked Cotherstone. "Showing him round, of course?"

"I've been tormenting him chiefly with family history," answered Bent, with a laughing glance at his sweetheart. "You didn't know I was raking up everything I could get hold of about my forbears, did you? Oh, I've been busy at that innocent amusement for a month past—old Kitely put me up to it."

Cotherstone could barely repress an inclination to start in his chair; he himself was not sure that he did not show undue surprise.

"What!" he exclaimed. "Kitely? My tenant? What does he know about your family? A stranger!"

"Much more than I do," replied Bent. "The old chap's nothing to do, you know, and since he took up his abode here he's been spending all his time digging up local records—he's a good bit of an antiquary, and that sort of thing. The Town Clerk tells me Kitely's been through nearly all the old town documents—chests full of them! And Kitely told me one day that if I liked he'd trace our pedigree back to I don't know when, and as he seemed keen, I told him to go ahead. He's found out a lot of interesting things in the borough records that I never heard of."

Cotherstone had kept his eyes on his plate while Bent was talking; he spoke now without looking up.

"Oh?" he said, trying to speak unconcernedly. "Ah!— then you'll have been seeing a good deal of Kitely lately?"

"Not so much," replied Bent. "He's brought me the result of his work now and then—things he's copied out of old registers, and so on."

"And what good might it all amount to?" asked Cotherstone, more for the sake of talking than for any interest he felt. "Will it come to aught?"

"Bent wants to trace his family history back to the Conquest," observed Brereton, slyly. "He thinks the original Bent came over with the Conqueror. But his old man hasn't got beyond the Tudor period yet."

"Never mind!" said Bent. "There were Bents in Highmarket in Henry the Seventh's time, anyhow. And if one has a pedigree, why not have it properly searched out? He's a keen old hand at that sort of thing, Kitely. The Town Clerk says he can read some of our borough charters of six hundred years ago as if they were newspaper articles."

Cotherstone made no remark on that. He was thinking. So Kitely was in close communication with Bent, was he?—constantly seeing him, being employed by him? Well, that cut two ways. It showed that up to now he had taken no advantage of his secret knowledge and might therefore be considered as likely to play straight if he were squared by the two partners. But it also proved that Bent would probably believe anything that Kitely might tell him. Certainly Kitely must be dealt with at once. He knew too much, and was obviously too clever, to be allowed to go about unfettered. Cost what it might, he must be attached to the Mallalieu-Cotherstone interest. And what Cotherstone was concentrating on just then, as he ate and drank, was—how to make that attachment in such a fashion that Kitely would have no option but to keep silence. If only he and Mallalieu could get a hold on Kitely, such as that which he had on them——

"Well," he said as supper came to an end, "I'm sorry, but I'm forced to leave you gentlemen for an hour, at any rate—can't be helped. Lettie, you must try to amuse 'em until I come back. Sing Mr. Brereton some of your new songs. Bent—you know where the whisky and the cigars are—help yourselves—make yourselves at home."

"You won't be more than an hour, father?" asked Lettie.

"An hour'll finish what I've got to do," replied Cotherstone, "maybe less—I'll be as quick as I can, anyway, my lass."

He hurried off without further ceremony; a moment later and he had exchanged the warmth and brightness of his comfortable dining-room for the chill night and the darkness. And as he turned out of his garden he was thinking still further and harder. So Windle Bent was one of those chaps who have what folk call family pride, was he? Actually proud of the fact that he had a pedigree, and could say who his grandfather and grandmother were?— things on which most people were as hazy as they were indifferent. In that case, if he was really family-proud, all the more reason why Kitely should be made to keep his tongue still. For if Windle Bent was going on the game of making out that he was a man of family, he certainly would not relish the prospect of uniting his ancient blood with that of a man who had seen the inside of a prison. Kitely!—promptly and definitely—and for *good!*—that was the ticket.

Cotherstone went off into the shadows of the night— and a good hour had passed when he returned to his house. It was then ten o'clock; he afterwards remembered that he glanced at the old grandfather clock in his hall when he let himself in. All was very quiet in there; he opened the drawing-room door to find the two young men and Lettie sitting over a bright fire, and Brereton evidently telling the other two some story, which he was just bringing to a conclusion.

" ... for it's a fact, in criminal practice," Brereton was saying, "that there are no end of undiscovered crimes— there are any amount of guilty men going about free as the air, and——"

"Hope you've been enjoying yourselves," said Cotherstone, going forward to the group. "I've been as quick as I could."

"Mr. Brereton has been telling us most interesting stories about criminals," said Lettie. "Facts—much stranger than fiction!"

"Then I'm sure it's time he'd something to refresh himself with," said Cotherstone hospitably. "Come away, gentlemen, and we'll see if we can't find a drop to drink and a cigar to smoke."

He led the way to the dining-room and busied himself in bringing out some boxes of cigars from a cupboard while Lettie produced decanters and glasses from the sideboard.

"So you're interested in criminal matters, sir?" observed Cotherstone as he offered Brereton a cigar. "Going in for that line, eh?"

"What practice I've had has been in that line," answered Brereton, with a quiet laugh. "One sort of gets pitchforked into these things, you know, so——"

"What's that?" exclaimed Lettie, who was just then handing the young barrister a tumbler of whisky and soda which Bent had mixed for him. "Somebody running hurriedly up the drive—as if something had happened! Surely you're not going to be fetched out again, father?"

A loud ringing of the bell prefaced the entrance of some visitor, whose voice was heard in eager conversation with a parlourmaid in the hall.

"That's your neighbour—Mr. Garthwaite," said Bent.

Cotherstone set down the cigars and opened the dining-room door. A youngish, fresh-coloured man, who looked upset and startled, came out of the hall, glancing round him inquiringly.

"Sorry to intrude, Mr. Cotherstone," he said. "I say!— that old gentleman you let the cottage to—Kitely, you know."

"What of him?" demanded Cotherstone sharply.

"He's lying there in the coppice above your house—I stumbled over him coming through there just now," replied Garthwaite. "He—don't be frightened, Miss Cotherstone—he's—well, there's no doubt of it—he's dead! And——"

"And—what?" asked Cotherstone. "What, man? Out with it!"

"And I should say, murdered!" said Garthwaite. "I— yes, I just saw enough to say that. Murdered—without a doubt!"

4. THE PINE WOOD

Brereton, standing back in the room, the cigar which Cotherstone had just given him unlighted in one hand, the glass which Lettie had presented to him in the other, was keenly watching the man who had just spoken and the man to whom he spoke. But all his attention was quickly concentrated on Cotherstone. For despite a strong effort to control himself, Cotherstone swayed a little, and instinctively put out a hand and clutched Bent's arm. He paled, too—the sudden spasm of pallor was almost instantly succeeded by a quick flush of colour. He made another effort—and tried to laugh.

"Nonsense, man!" he said thickly and hoarsely. "Murder? Who should want to kill an old chap like that? It's—here, give me a drink, one of you—that's—a bit startling!"

Bent seized a tumbler which he himself had just mixed, and Cotherstone gulped off half its contents. He looked round apologetically.

"I—I think I'm not as strong as I was," he muttered. "Overwork, likely—I've been a bit shaky of late. A shock like that——"

"I'm sorry," said Garthwaite, who looked surprised at the effect of his news. "I ought to have known better. But you see, yours is the nearest house——"

"Quite right, my lad, quite right," exclaimed Cotherstone. "You did the right thing. Here!—we'd better go up. Have you called the police?"

"I sent the man from the cottage at the foot of your garden," answered Garthwaite. "He was just locking up as I passed, so I told him, and sent him off."

"We'll go," said Cotherstone. He looked round at his guests. "You'll come?" he asked.

"Don't you go, father," urged Lettie, "if you're not feeling well."

"I'm all right," insisted Cotherstone. "A mere bit of weakness—that's all. Now that I know what's to be faced—" he twisted suddenly on Garthwaite—"what makes you think it's murder?" he demanded. "Murder! That's a big word."

Garthwaite glanced at Lettie, who was whispering to Bent, and shook his head.

"Tell you when we get outside," he said. "I don't want to frighten your daughter."

"Come on, then," said Cotherstone. He hurried into the hall and snatched up an overcoat. "Fetch me that lantern out of the kitchen," he called to the parlourmaid. "Light it! Don't you be afraid, Lettie," he went on, turning to his daughter. "There's naught to be afraid of—now. You gentlemen coming with us?"

Bent and Brereton had already got into their coats: when the maid came with the lantern, all four men went out. And as soon as they were in the garden Cotherstone turned on Garthwaite.

"How do you know he's murdered?" he asked. "How could you tell?"

"I'll tell you all about it, now we're outside," answered Garthwaite. "I'd been over to Spennigarth, to see Hollings. I came back over the Shawl, and made a short cut through the wood. And I struck my foot against something—something soft, you know—I don't like thinking of that! And so I struck a match, and looked, and saw this old fellow—don't like thinking of that, either. He was laid there, a few yards out of the path that runs across the Shawl at that point. I saw he was dead—and as for his being murdered, well, all I can say is, he's been strangled! That's flat."

"Strangled!" exclaimed Bent.

"Aye, without doubt," replied Garthwaite. "There's a bit of rope round his neck that tight that I couldn't put my little finger between it and him! But you'll see for yourselves—it's not far up the Shawl. You never heard anything, Mr. Cotherstone?"

"No, we heard naught," answered Cotherstone. "If it's as you say, there'd be naught to hear."

He had led them out of his grounds by a side-gate, and they were now in the thick of the firs and pines which grew along the steep, somewhat rugged slope of the Shawl. He put the lantern into Garthwaite's hand.

"Here—you show the way," he said. "I don't know where it is, of course."

"You were going straight to it," remarked Garthwaite. He turned to Brereton, who was walking at his side. "You're a lawyer, aren't you?" he asked. "I heard that Mr. Bent had a lawyer friend stopping with him just now—we hear all the bits of news in a little place like Highmarket. Well—you'll understand, likely—it hadn't been long done!"

"You noticed that?" said Brereton.

"I touched him," replied Garthwaite. "His hand and cheek were—just warm. He couldn't have been dead so very long—as I judged matters. And—here he is!"

He twisted sharply round the corner of one of the great masses of limestone which cropped out amongst the trees, and turned the light of the lantern on the dead man.

"There!" he said in a hushed voice. "There!"

The four men came to a halt, each gazing steadily at the sight they had come to see. It needed no more than a glance to assure each that he was looking on death: there was that in Kitely's attitude which forbade any other possibility.

"He's just as I found him," whispered Garthwaite. "I came round this rock from there, d'ye see, and my foot knocked against his shoulder. But, you know, he's been dragged here! Look at that!"

Brereton, after a glance at the body, had looked round at its surroundings. The wood thereabouts was carpeted—thickly carpeted—with pine needles; they lay several inches thick beneath the trunks of the trees; they stretched right up to the edge of the rock. And now, as Garthwaite turned the lantern, they saw that on this soft carpet there was a great slur—the murderer had evidently dragged his victim some yards across the pine needles before depositing him behind the rock. And at the end of this mark there were plain traces of a struggle— the soft, easily yielding stuff was disturbed, kicked about, upheaved, but as Brereton at once recognized, it was impossible to trace footprints in it.

"That's where it must have been," said Garthwaite. "You see there's a bit of a path there. The old man must have been walking along that path, and whoever did it must have sprung out on him there—where all those marks are—and when he'd strangled him dragged him here. That's how I figure it, Mr. Cotherstone."

Lights were coming up through the wood beneath them, glancing from point to point amongst the trees. Then followed a murmur of voices, and three or four men came into view—policemen, carrying their lamps, the man whom Garthwaite had sent into the town, and a medical man who acted as police surgeon.

"Here!" said Bent, as the newcomers advanced and halted irresolutely. "This way, doctor—there's work for you here—of a sort, anyway. Of course, he's dead?"

The doctor had gone forward as soon as he caught sight of the body, and he dropped on his knees at its side while the others gathered round. In the added light everybody now saw things more clearly. Kitely lay in a heap—just as a man would lie who had been unceremoniously thrown down. But Brereton's sharp eyes saw at once that after he had been flung at the foot of the mass of rock some hand had disarranged his clothing. His overcoat and under coat had been torn open, hastily, if not with absolute violence; the lining of one trousers pocket was pulled out; there were evidences that his waistcoat had been unbuttoned and its inside searched:

everything seemed to indicate that the murderer had also been a robber.

"He's not been dead very long," said the doctor, looking up. "Certainly not more than three-quarters of an hour. Strangled? Yes!—and by somebody who has more than ordinary knowledge of how quickly a man may be killed in that way! Look how this cord is tied—no amateur did that."

He turned back the neckcloth from the dead man's throat, and showed the others how the cord had been slipped round the neck in a running-knot and fastened tightly with a cunning twist.

"Whoever did this had done the same thing before— probably more than once," he continued. "No man with that cord round his neck, tightly knotted like that, would have a chance—however free his hands might be. He'd be dead before he could struggle. Does no one know anything about this? No more than that?" he went on, when he had heard what Garthwaite could tell. "Well, this is murder, anyway! Are there no signs of anything about here?"

"Don't you think his clothing looks as if he had been robbed?" said Brereton, pointing to the obvious signs. "That should be noted before he's moved."

"I've noted that, sir," said the police-sergeant, who had bent over the body while the doctor was examining it. "There's one of his pockets turned inside out, and all his clothing's been torn open. Robbery, of course—that's what it's been—murder for the sake of robbery!"

One of the policemen, having satisfied his curiosity stepped back and began to search the surroundings with the aid of his lamp. He suddenly uttered a sharp exclamation.

"Here's something!" he said, stooping to the foot of a pine-tree and picking up a dark object. "An old pocket-book—nothing in it, though."

"That was his," remarked Cotherstone. "I've seen it before. He used to carry it in an inner pocket. Empty, do you say?—no papers?"

"Not a scrap of anything," answered the policeman, handing the book over to his sergeant, and proceeding to search further. "We'd best to see if there's any footprints about."

"You'd better examine that path, then," said Garthwaite. "You'll find no prints on all this pine-needle stuff—naught to go by, anyway—it's too thick and soft. But he must have come along that path, one way or another—I've met him walking in here of an evening, more than once."

The doctor, who had exchanged a word or two with the sergeant, turned to Cotherstone.

"Wasn't he a tenant of yours?" he asked. "Had the cottage at the top of the Shawl here. Well, we'd better have the body removed there, and some one should go up and warn his family."

"There's no family," answered Cotherstone. "He'd naught but a housekeeper—Miss Pett. She's an elderly woman—and not likely to be startled, from what I've seen of her."

"I'll go," said Bent. "I know the housekeeper." He touched Brereton's elbow, and led him away amongst the trees and up the wood. "This is a strange affair!" he continued when they were clear of the others. "Did you hear what Dr. Rockcliffe said?—that whoever had done it was familiar with that sort of thing!"

"I saw for myself," replied Brereton. "I noticed that cord, and the knot on it, at once. A man whose neck was tied up like that could be thrown down, thrown anywhere, left to stand up, if you like, and he'd be literally helpless, even if, as the doctor said, he had the use of his hands. He'd be unconscious almost at once— dead very soon afterwards. Murder?—I should think so!— and a particularly brutal and determined one. Bent!— whoever killed that poor old fellow was a man of great strength and of—knowledge! Knowledge, mind you!—he knew the trick. You haven't any doubtful character in Highmarket who has ever lived in India, have you?"

"India! Why India?" asked Bent.

"Because I should say that the man who did that job has learned some of the Indian tricks with cords and knots," answered Brereton. "That murder's suggestive of Thuggeeism in some respects. That the cottage?" he went on, pointing to a dim light ahead of him. "This housekeeper, now?—is she the sort who'll take it quietly?"

"She's as queer a character as the old fellow himself was," replied Bent, as they cleared the wood and entered a hedge-enclosed garden at the end of which stood an old-fashioned cottage. "I've talked to her now and then when calling here—I should say she's a woman of nerve."

Brereton looked narrowly at Miss Pett when she opened the door. She carried a tallow candle in one hand and held it high above her head to throw a light on the callers; its dim rays fell more on herself than on them. A tall, gaunt, elderly woman, almost fleshless of face, and with a skin the colour of old parchment, out of which shone a pair of bright black eyes; the oddity of her appearance was heightened by her head-dress—a glaring red and yellow handkerchief tightly folded in such a fashion as to cover any vestige of hair. Her arms, bare to the elbow, and her hands were as gaunt as her face, but Brereton was quick to recognize the suggestion of physical strength in the muscles and sinews under the parchment-like skin. A strange, odd-looking woman altogether, he thought, and not improved by the fact that she appeared to have lost all her teeth, and that a long, sharp nose and prominent chin almost met before her sunken lips.

"Oh, it's you, is it, Mr. Bent?" she said, before either of the young men could speak. "Mr. Kitely's gone out for his regular bedtime constitution—he will have that, wet or fine, every night. But he's much longer than usual, and——"

She stopped suddenly, seeing some news in Bent's face, and her own contracted to a questioning look.

"Is there aught amiss?" she asked. "Has something happened him? Aught that's serious? You needn't be afraid to speak, Mr. Bent—there's naught can upset or frighten me, let me tell you—I'm past all that!"

"I'm afraid Mr. Kitely's past everything, too, then," said Bent. He looked steadily at her for a moment, and seeing that she understood, went on. "They're bringing him up, Miss Pett—you'd better make ready. You won't be alarmed—I don't think there's any doubt that he's been murdered."

The woman gazed silently at her visitors; then, nodding her turbaned head, she drew back into the cottage.

"It's what I expected," she muttered. "I warned him— more than once. Well—let them bring him, then."

She vanished into a side-room, and Bent and Brereton went down the garden and met the others, carrying the dead man. Cotherstone followed behind the police, and as he approached Bent he pulled him by the sleeve and drew him aside.

"There's a clue!" he whispered. "A clue, d'ye hear—a strong clue!"

5. THE CORD

Ever since they had left the house at the foot of the pine wood, Brereton had been conscious of a curious psychological atmosphere, centring in Cotherstone. It had grown stronger as events had developed; it was still stronger now as they stood outside the dead man's cottage, the light from the open door and the white-curtained window falling on Cotherstone's excited face. Cotherstone, it seemed to Brereton, was unduly eager about something—he might almost be said to be elated. All of his behaviour was odd. He had certainly been shocked when Garthwaite burst in with the news—but this shock did not seem to be of the ordinary sort. He had looked like fainting—but when he recovered himself his whole attitude (so, at any rate, it had seemed to Brereton) had been that of a man who has just undergone a great relief. To put the whole thing into a narrow compass, it seemed as if Cotherstone appeared to be positively pleased to hear—and to find beyond doubt—that Kitely was dead. And now, as he stood glancing from one young man to the other, his eyes glittered as if he were absolutely enjoying the affair: he reminded Brereton of that type of theatre-goer who will insist on pointing out stage effects as they occur before his eyes, forcing his own appreciation of them upon fellow-watchers whose eyes are as keen as his own.

"A strong clue!" repeated Cotherstone, and said it yet again. "A good 'un! And if it's right, it'll clear matters up."

"What is it?" asked Bent. He, too, seemed to be conscious that there was something odd about his prospective father-in-law, and he was gazing speculatively at him as if in wonder. "What sort of a clue?"

"It's a wonder it didn't strike me—and you, too—at first," said Cotherstone, with a queer sound that was half a chuckle. "But as long as it's struck somebody, eh? One's as good as another. You can't think of what it is, now?"

"I don't know what you're thinking about," replied Bent, half impatiently.

Cotherstone gave vent to an unmistakable chuckle at that, and he motioned them to follow him into the cottage.

"Come and see for yourselves, then," he said. "You'll spot it. But, anyway—Mr. Brereton, being a stranger, can't be expected to."

The three men walked into the living-room of the cottage—a good-sized, open-raftered, old-fashioned place, wherein burnt a bright fire, at either side of which stood two comfortable armchairs. Before one of these chairs, their toes pointing upwards against the fender, were a pair of slippers; on a table close by stood an old lead tobacco-box, flanked by a church-warden pipe, a spirit decanter, a glass, and a plate on which were set out sugar and lemon—these Brereton took to be indicative that Kitely, his evening constitutional over, was in the habit of taking a quiet pipe and a glass of something warm before going to bed. And looking round still further he became aware of an open door—the door into which Miss Pett had withdrawn—and of a bed within on which Kitely now lay, with Dr. Rockcliffe and the police-sergeant bending over him. The other policemen stood by the table in the living-room, and one of them—the man who had picked up the pocket-book—whispered audibly to Cotherstone as he and his companions entered.

"The doctor's taking it off him," he said, with a meaning nod of his head. "I'll lay aught it's as I say, Mr. Cotherstone."

"Looks like it," agreed Cotherstone, rubbing his hands. "It certainly looks like it, George. Sharp of you to notice it, though."

Brereton took this conversation to refer to the mysterious clue, and his suspicion was confirmed a moment later. The doctor and the sergeant came into the living-room, the doctor carrying something in his hand which he laid down on the centre table in full view of all of them. And Brereton saw then that he had removed from the dead man's neck the length of grey cord with which he had been strangled.

There was something exceedingly sinister in the mere placing of that cord before the eyes of these living men. It had wrought the death of another man, who, an hour before, had been as full of vigorous life as themselves; some man, equally vigorous, had used it as the instrument of a foul murder. Insignificant in itself, a mere piece of strongly spun and twisted hemp, it was yet singularly suggestive—one man, at any rate, amongst those who stood looking at it, was reminded by it that the murderer who had used it must even now have the fear of another and a stronger cord before him.

"Find who that cord belongs to, and you may get at something," suddenly observed the doctor, glancing at the policemen. "You say it's a butcher's cord?"

The man who had just whispered to Cotherstone nodded.

"It's a pig-killer's cord, sir," he answered. "It's what a pig-killer fastens the pig down with—on the cratch."

"A cratch?—what's that?" asked Brereton, who had gone close to the table to examine the cord, and had seen that, though slender, it was exceedingly strong, and of closely wrought fibre. "Is it a sort of hurdle?"

"That's it, sir," assented the policeman. "It is a sort of hurdle—on four legs. They lay the pig on it, don't you see, and tie it down with a cord of this sort—this cord's been used for that—it's greasy with long use."

"And it has been cut off a longer piece, of course," said the doctor. "These cords are of considerable length, aren't they?"

"Good length, sir—there's a regular coil, like," said the man. He, too, bent down and looked at the length before him. "This has been cut off what you might call recent," he went on, pointing to one end.

"And cut off with a sharp knife, too."

The police sergeant glanced at the doctor as if asking advice on the subject of putting his thoughts into words.

"Well?" said the doctor, with a nod of assent. "Of course, you've got something in your mind, sergeant?"

"Well, there is a man who kills pigs, and has such cords as that, lives close by, doctor," he answered. "You know who I mean—the man they call Gentleman Jack."

"You mean Harborough," said the doctor. "Well—you'd better ask him if he knows anything. Somebody might have stolen one of his cords. But there are other pig-killers in the town, of course."

"Not on this side the town, there aren't," remarked another policeman.

"What is plain," continued the doctor, looking at Cotherstone and the others, "is that Kitely was strangled by this rope, and that everything on him of any value was taken. You'd better find out what he had, or was likely to have, on him, sergeant. Ask the housekeeper."

Miss Pett came from the inner room, where she had already begun her preparations for laying out the body. She was as calm as when Bent first told her of what had occurred, and she stood at the end of the table, the cord between her and her questioners, and showed no emotion, no surprise at what had occurred.

"Can you tell aught about this, ma'am?" asked the sergeant. "You see your master's met his death at somebody's hands, and there's no doubt he's been robbed, too. Do you happen to know what he had on him?"

The housekeeper, who had her arms full of linen, set her burden down on a clothes-horse in front of the fire before she replied. She seemed to be thinking deeply, and when she turned round again, it was to shake her queerly ornamented head.

"Well, I couldn't say exactly," she answered. "But I shouldn't wonder if it was a good deal—for such as him, you know. He did carry money on him—he was never short of money ever since I knew him, and sometimes he'd a fair amount in his pockets—I know, of course, because he'd pull it out, loose gold, and silver, and copper, and I've seen him take bank-notes out of his pocket-book. But he'd be very like to have a good deal more than usual on him tonight."

"Why?" asked the sergeant.

"Because he'd been to the bank this morning to draw his pension money," replied Miss Pett. "I don't know how much that would be, any more than I know where it came from. He was a close man—he'd never tell anybody more than he liked, and he never told me aught about that. But I do know it was what you'd call a fair amount—for a man that lives in a cottage. He went to the bank this noon—he always went once a quarter—and he said this afternoon that he'd go and pay his rent to Mr. Cotherstone there—"

"As he did," muttered Cotherstone, "yes—he did that."

"Well, he'd have all the rest of his money on him," continued the housekeeper. "And he'd have what he had before, because he'd other money coming in than that pension. And I tell you he was the sort of man that carried his money about him—he was foolish that way. And then he'd a very valuable watch and chain—he told me they were a presentation, and cost nearly a hundred pounds. And of course, he'd a pocket-book full of papers."

"This pocket-book?" asked the sergeant.

"Aye, that's it, right enough," assented Miss Pett. "But he always had it bursting with bits of letters and papers. You don't mean to say you found it empty? You did?—very well then, I'm no fool, and I say that if he's been murdered, there's been some reason for it altogether apart from robbing him of what money and things he had on him! Whoever's taken his papers wanted 'em bad!"

"About his habits, now?" said the sergeant, ignoring Miss Pett's suggestion. "Did he go walking on the Shawl every night?"

"Regular as clock-work," answered the housekeeper. "He used to read and write a deal at night—then he'd side away all his books and papers, get his supper, and go out for an hour, walking round and about. Then he'd come in, put on his slippers—there they are, set down to warm for him—smoke one pipe, drink one glass of toddy—there's the stuff for it—and go to bed. He was the regularest man I ever knew, in all he did."

"Was he out longer than usual tonight?" asked Bent, who saw that the sergeant had no more to ask. "You seemed to suggest that, when we came."

"Well, he was a bit longer," admitted Miss Pett. "Of course, he varied. But an hour was about his time. Up and down and about the hill-side he'd go—in and out of the coppices. I've warned him more than once."

"But why?" asked Brereton, whose curiosity was impelling him to take a part in this drama. "What reason had you for warning him?"

Miss Pett turned and looked scrutinizingly at her last questioner. She took a calm and close observation of him and her curious face relaxed into something like a smile.

"I can tell what you are, mister," she said. "A law gentleman! I've seen your sort many a time. And you're a sharp 'un, too! Well—you're young, but you're old enough to have heard a thing or two. Did you never hear that women have got what men haven't—instinct?"

"Do you really tell me that the only reason you had for warning him against going out late at night was—instinct?" asked Brereton. "Come, now!"

"Mostly instinct, anyhow," she answered. "Women have a sort of feeling about things that men haven't—leastways, no men that I've ever met had it. But of course, I'd more than that. Mr. Kitely, now, he was a townsman—a London man. I'm a countrywoman. He didn't understand—you couldn't get him to understand—

that it's not safe to go walking in lonely places in country districts like this late at night. When I'd got to know his habits, I expostulated with him more than once. I pointed out to him that in spots like this, where there's naught nearer than them houses at the foot of the hill one way, and Harborough's cottage another way, and both of 'em a good quarter of a mile off, and where there's all these coverts and coppices and rocks, it was not safe for an elderly man who sported a fine gold watch and chain to go wandering about in the darkness. There's always plenty of bad characters in country places who'd knock the King himself on the head for the sake of as much as Mr. Kitely had on him, even if it was no more than the chain which every Tom and Dick could see! And it's turned out just as I prophesied. He's come to it!"

"But you said just now that he must have been murdered for something else than his valuables," said Brereton.

"I said that if his papers were gone, somebody must have wanted them bad," retorted Miss Pett. "Anyway, what's happened is just what I felt might happen, and there he is—dead. And I should be obliged to some of you if you'd send up a woman or two to help me lay him out, for I can't be expected to do everything by myself, nor to stop in this cottage alone, neither!"

Leaving the doctor and a couple of policemen to arrange matters with the housekeeper, the sergeant went outside, followed by the others. He turned to Cotherstone.

"I'm going down to Harborough's cottage, at the other end of the Shawl," he said. "I don't expect to learn aught much there—yet—but I can see if he's at home, anyway. If any of you gentlemen like to come down——"

Bent laid a hand on Cotherstone's arm and turned him in the direction of his house.

"Brereton and I'll go with the sergeant," he said. "You must go home—Lettie'll be anxious about things. Go down with him, Mr. Garthwaite—you'll both hear more later."

To Brereton's great surprise, Cotherstone made no objection to this summary dismissal. He and Garthwaite went off in one direction; the others, led by the observant policeman who had found the empty pocket-book and recognized the peculiar properties of the cord, turned away in another.

"Where's this we're going now?" asked Brereton as he and Bent followed their leaders through the trees and down the slopes of the Shawl.

"To John Harborough's cottage—at the other end of the hill," answered Bent. "He's the man they spoke of in there. He's a queer character—a professional pig-killer, who has other trades as well. He does a bit of rat-catching, and a bit of mole-catching—and a good deal of poaching. In fact, he's an odd person altogether, not only in character but in appearance. And the curious thing is that he's got an exceedingly good-looking and accomplished daughter, a really superior girl who's been well educated and earns her living as a governess in the town. Queer pair they make if you ever see them together!"

"Does she live with him?" asked Brereton.

"Oh yes, she lives with him!" replied Bent. "And I believe that they're very devoted to each other, though everybody marvels that such a man should have such a daughter. There's a mystery about that man—odd character that he is, he's been well bred, and the folk hereabouts call him Gentleman Jack."

"Won't all this give the girl a fright?" suggested Brereton. "Wouldn't it be better if somebody went quietly to the man's cottage?"

But when they came to Harborough's cottage, at the far end of the Shawl, it was all in darkness.

"Still, they aren't gone to bed," suddenly observed the policeman who had a faculty for seeing things. "There's a good fire burning in the kitchen grate, and they wouldn't leave that. Must be out, both of 'em."

"Go in and knock quietly," counselled the sergeant.

He followed the policeman up the flagged walk to the cottage door, and the other two presently went after them. In the starlight Brereton looked round at these new surroundings—an old, thatched cottage, set in a garden amongst trees and shrubs, with a lean-to shed at one end of it, and over everything an atmosphere of silence.

The silence was suddenly broken. A quick, light step sounded on the flagged path behind them, and the policemen turned their lamps in its direction. And Brereton, looking sharply round, became aware of the presence of a girl, who looked at these visitors wonderingly out of a pair of beautiful grey eyes.

6. THE MAYOR

Here, then, thought Brereton, was Gentleman Jack's daughter—the girl of whom Bent had just been telling him. He looked at her narrowly as she stood confronting the strange group. A self-possessed young woman, he said to himself—beyond a little heightening of colour, a little questioning look about eyes and lips she showed no trace of undue surprise or fear. Decidedly a good-looking young woman, too, and not at all the sort of daughter that a man of queer character would be supposed to have— refined features, an air of breeding, a suggestion of culture. And he noticed that as he and Bent raised their hats, the two policemen touched their helmets—they were evidently well acquainted with the girl, and eyed her with some misgiving as well as respect.

"Beg pardon, miss," said the sergeant, who was obviously anything but pleased with his task. "But it's like this, d'you see?—your father, now, does he happen to be at home?"

"What is it you want?" she asked. And beginning a glance of inquiry at the sergeant she finished it at Bent. "Has something happened, Mr. Bent?" she went on. "If you want my father, and he's not in, then I don't know where he is—he went out early in the evening, and he hadn't returned when I left the house an hour ago."

"I daresay it's nothing," replied Bent. "But the fact is that something has happened. Your neighbour at the other end of the wood—old Mr. Kitely, you know—he's been found dead."

Brereton, closely watching the girl, saw that this conveyed nothing to her, beyond the mere announcement. She moved towards the door of the cottage, taking a key from her muff.

"Yes?" she said. "And—I suppose you want my father to help? He may be in—he may have gone to bed."

She unlocked the door, walked into the open living-room, and turning up a lamp which stood on the table, glanced around her.

"No," she continued. "He's not come in—so——"

"Better tell her, Mr. Bent," whispered the sergeant. "No use keeping it back, sir—she'll have to know."

"The fact is," said Bent, "Mr. Kitely—we're afraid—has been murdered."

The girl turned sharply at that; her eyes dilated, and a brighter tinge of colour came into her cheeks.

"Murdered!" she exclaimed. "Shot?"

Her eyes went past Bent to a corner of the room, and Brereton, following them, saw that there stood a gun, placed amongst a pile of fishing-rods and similar sporting implements. Her glance rested on it for only the fraction of a second; then it went back to Bent's face.

"I'd better tell you everything," said Bent quietly. "Mr. Kitely has been strangled. And the piece of cord with which it was done is—so the police here say—just such a piece as might have been cut off one of the cords which your father uses in his trade, you know."

"We aren't suggesting aught, you know, Miss Avice," remarked the sergeant. "Don't go for to think that—at present. But, you see, Harborough, he might have one o' those cords hanging about somewhere, and—do you understand?"

The girl had become very quiet, looking steadily from one man to the other. Once more her eyes settled on Bent.

"Do you know why Kitely was killed?" she asked suddenly. "Have you seen any reason for it?"

"He had been robbed, after his death," answered Bent. "That seems absolutely certain."

"Whatever you may say, you've got some suspicion about my father," she remarked after a pause. "Well—all I can say is, my father has no need to rob anybody—far from it, if you want the truth. But what do you want?"

she continued, a little impatiently. "My father isn't in, and I don't know where he is—often he is out all night."

"If we could just look round his shed, now?" said the sergeant. "Just to see if aught's missing, like, you know. You see, miss——"

"You can look round the shed—and round anywhere else," said Avice. "Though what good that will do—well, you know where the shed is."

She turned away and began taking off her hat and coat, and the four men went out into the garden and turned to the lean-to shed at the end of the cottage. A tiled verandah ran along the front of cottage and shed, and the door of the shed was at its further end. But as the sergeant was about to open it, the policeman of the observant nature made his third discovery. He had been flashing the light of his bull's-eye lamp over his surroundings, and he now turned it on a coil of rope which hung from a nail in the boarded wall of the shed, between the door and the window.

"There you are, gentlemen!" he said, lifting the lamp in one hand and pointing triumphantly to a definite point of the coiled cord with the index finger of the other. "There! Cut clean, too—just like the bit up yonder!"

Brereton pressed forward and looked narrowly at what the man was indicating. There was no doubt that a length of cord had been freshly cut off the coil, and cut, too, with an unusually sharp, keen-bladed knife; the edges of the severance were clean and distinct, the separated strands were fresh and unsoiled. It was obvious that a piece of that cord had been cut from the rest within a very short time, and the sergeant shook his head gravely as he took the coil down from its nail.

"I don't think there's any need to look round much further, Mr. Bent," he said. "Of course, I shall take this away with me, and compare it with the shorter piece. But we'll just peep into this shed, so as to make his daughter believe that was what we wanted: I don't want to frighten her more than we have done. Naught there, you see," he went on, opening the shed door and revealing a whitewashed interior furnished with fittings and articles of its owner's trade. "Well, we'll away—with what we've got."

He went back to the door of the cottage and putting his head inside called gently to its occupant.

"Well?" demanded Avice.

"All right, miss—we're going," said the sergeant. "But if your father comes in, just ask him to step down to the police-station, d'you see?—I should like to have a word or two with him."

The girl made no answer to this gentle request, and when the sergeant had joined the others, she shut the door of the cottage, and Brereton heard it locked and bolted.

"That's about the strangest thing of all!" he said as he and Bent left the policemen and turned down a by-lane which led towards the town. "I haven't a doubt that the piece of cord with which Kitely was strangled was cut off that coil! Now what does it mean? Of course, to me it's the very surest proof that this man Harborough had nothing to do with the murder."

"Why?" asked Bent.

"Why? My dear fellow!" exclaimed Brereton. "Do you really think that any man who was in possession of his senses would do such a thing? Take a piece of cord from a coil—leave the coil where anybody could find it—strangle a man with the severed piece and leave it round the victim's neck? Absurd! No—a thousand times no!"

"Well—and what then?" asked Bent.

"Ah! Somebody cut that piece off—for the use it was put to," answered Brereton. "But—who?"

Bent made no reply for a while. Then, as they reached the outskirts of the town, he clapped a hand on his companion's arm.

"You're forgetting something—in spite of your legal mind," he said. "The murderer may have been

interrupted before he could remove it. And in that case—
—"

He stopped suddenly as a gate opened in the wall of a garden which they were just passing, and a tall man emerged. In the light of the adjacent lamp Bent recognized Mallalieu. Mallalieu, too, recognized him, and stopped.

"Oh, that you, Mr. Mayor!" exclaimed Bent. "I was just wondering whether to drop in on you as I passed. Have you heard what's happened tonight?"

"Heard naught," replied Mallalieu. "I've just been having a hand at whist with Councillor Northrop and his wife and daughter. What has happened, then?"

They were all three walking towards the town by that time, and Bent slipped between Brereton and Mallalieu and took the Mayor's arm.

"Murder's happened," he said. "That's the plain truth of it. You know old Kitely—your partner's tenant? Well, somebody's killed him."

The effect of this announcement on Mallalieu was extraordinary. Bent felt the arm into which he had just slipped his own literally quiver with a spasmodic response to the astonished brain; the pipe which Mallalieu was smoking fell from his lips; out of his lips came something very like a cry of dismay.

"God bless me!" he exclaimed. "You don't say so?"

"It's a fact," said Bent. He stopped and picked up the fallen pipe. "Sorry I let it out so clumsily—I didn't think it would affect you like that. But there it is—Kitely's been murdered. Strangled!"

"Strangled!" echoed Mallalieu. "Dear—dear—dear! When was this, now?"

"Within the hour," replied Bent. "Mr. Brereton here— a friend of mine from London—and I were spending the evening at your partner's, when that neighbour of his, Garthwaite, came running in to tell Mr. Cotherstone that Kitely was lying dead on the Shawl. Of course we all went up."

"Then—you've seen him?" demanded Mallalieu. "There's no doubt about it?"

"Doubt!" exclaimed Bent. "I should think there is no doubt! As determined a murder as ever I heard of. No—there's no doubt."

Mallalieu paused—at the gate of his own house.

"Come in, gentlemen," he said. "Come in just a minute, anyway. I—egad it's struck me all of a heap, has that news! Murder?—there hasn't been such a thing in these parts ever since I came here, near thirty years ago. Come in and tell me a bit more about it."

He led the way up a gravelled drive, admitted himself and his visitors to the house with a latchkey, and turned into a parlour where a fire burned and a small supper-tray was set out on a table beneath a lamp.

"All my folks'll have gone to bed," he said. "They go and leave me a bite of something, you see—I'm often out late. Will you gentlemen have a sandwich—or a dry biscuit? Well, you'll have a drink, then. And so," he went on, as he produced glasses from the sideboard, "and so you were spending the evening with Cotherstone, what?"

"Well, I can't say that we exactly spent all the evening with him," answered Bent, "because he had to go out for a good part of it, on business. But we were with him—we were at his house—when the news came."

"Aye, he had to go out, had he?" asked Mallalieu, as if from mere curiosity. "What time would that be, like? I knew he'd business tonight—business of ours."

"Nine to ten, roughly speaking," replied Bent. "He'd just got in when Garthwaite came with the news."

"It 'ud shock him, of course," suggested Mallalieu. "His own tenant!"

"Yes—it was a shock," agreed Bent. He took the glass which his host handed to him and sat down. "We'd better tell you all about it," he said. "It's a queer affair—Mr. Brereton here, who's a barrister, thinks it's a very queer affair."

Mallalieu nodded and sat down, too, glass in hand. He listened attentively—and Brereton watched him while he listened. A sleek, sly, observant, watchful man, this, said Brereton to himself—the sort that would take all in and give little out. And he waited expectantly to hear what Mallalieu would say when he had heard everything.

Mallalieu turned to him when Bent had finished.

"I agree with you, sir," he said. "Nobody but a fool would have cut that piece of cord off, left it round the man's neck, and left the coil hanging where anybody could find it. And that man Harborough's no fool! This isn't his job, Bent. No!"

"Whose, then?" asked Bent.

Mallalieu suddenly drank off the contents of his glass and rose.

"As I'm chief magistrate, I'd better go down to see the police," he said. "There's been a queer character or two hanging about the town of late. I'd better stir 'em up. You won't come down, I suppose?" he continued when they left the house together.

"No—we can do no good," answered Bent.

His own house was just across the road from Mallalieu's, and he and Brereton said goodnight and turned towards it as the Mayor strode quickly off in the direction of the police-station.

7. NIGHT WORK

From the little colony of new houses at the foot of the Shawl to the police station at the end of the High Street was only a few minutes' walk. Mallalieu was a quick walker, and he covered this distance at his top speed. But during those few minutes he came to a conclusion, for he was as quick of thought as in the use of his feet.

Of course, Cotherstone had killed Kitely. That was certain. He had begun to suspect that as soon as he heard of the murder; he became convinced of it as soon as young Bent mentioned that Cotherstone had left his guests for an hour after supper. Without a doubt Cotherstone had lost his head and done this foolish thing! And now Cotherstone must be protected, safe-guarded; heaven and earth must be moved lest suspicion should fall on him. For nothing could be done to Cotherstone without effect upon himself—and of himself—and of himself Mallalieu meant to take very good care. Never mind what innocent person suffered, Cotherstone must go free.

And the first thing to do was to assume direction of the police, to pull strings, to engineer matters. No matter how much he believed in Harborough's innocence, Harborough was the man to go for—at present. Attention must be concentrated on him, and on him only. Anything—anything, at whatever cost of morals and honesty to divert suspicion from that fool of a Cotherstone!—if it were not already too late. It was the desire to make sure that it was not too late, the desire to be beforehand, that made Mallalieu hasten to the police. He knew his own power, he had a supreme confidence in his ability to manage things, and he was determined to give up the night to the scheme already seething in his fertile brain rather than that justice should enter upon what he would consider a wrong course.

While he sat silently and intently listening to Bent's story of the crime, Mallalieu, who could think and listen and give full attention to both mental processes without letting either suffer at the expense of the other, had reconstructed the murder. He knew Cotherstone—nobody knew him half as well. Cotherstone was what Mallalieu called deep—he was ingenious, resourceful, inventive. Cotherstone, in the early hours of the evening, had doubtless thought the whole thing out. He would be well acquainted with his prospective victim's habits. He would know exactly when and where to waylay Kitely. The filching of the piece of cord from the wall of Harborough's shed was a clever thing—infernally clever, thought Mallalieu, who had a designing man's whole-hearted admiration for any sort of cleverness in his own particular line. It would be an easy thing to do—and what a splendidly important thing! Of course Cotherstone knew all about Harborough's arrangements—he would often pass the pig-killer's house—from the hedge of the garden he would have seen the coils of greased rope hanging from their nails under the verandah roof, aye, a thousand times. Nothing easier than to slip into Harborough's garden from the adjacent wood, cut off a length of the cord, use it—and leave it as a first bit of evidence against a man whose public record was uncertain. Oh, very clever indeed!—if only Cotherstone could carry things off, and not allow his conscience to write marks on his face. And he must help—and innocent as he felt Harborough to be, he must set things going against Harborough—his life was as naught, against the Mallalieu-Cotherstone safety.

Mallalieu walked into the police-station, to find the sergeant just returned and in consultation with the superintendent, whom he had summoned to hear his report. Both turned inquiringly on the Mayor.

"I've heard all about it," said Mallalieu, bustling forward. "Mr. Bent told me. Now then, where's that cord they talk about?"

The sergeant pointed to the coil and the severed piece, which lay on a large sheet of brown paper on a side-table, preparatory to being sealed up. Mallalieu crossed over and made a short examination of these exhibits; then he turned to the superintendent with an air of decision.

"Aught been done?" he demanded.

"Not yet, Mr. Mayor," answered the superintendent. "We were just consulting as to what's best to be done."

"I should think that's obvious," replied Mallalieu. "You must get to work! Two things you want to do just now. Ring up Norcaster for one thing, and High Gill Junction for another. Give 'em a description of Harborough—he'll probably have made for one place or another, to get away by train. And ask 'em at Norcaster to lend you a few plain-clothes men, and to send 'em along here at once by motor—there's no train till morning. Then, get all your own men out—now!—and keep folk off the paths in that wood, and put a watch on Harborough's house, in case he should put a bold face on it and come back—he's impudence enough—and of course, if he comes, they'll take him. Get to all that now—at once!"

"You think it's Harborough, then?" said the superintendent.

"I think there's what the law folks call a prymer facy case against him," replied Mallalieu. "It's your duty to get him, anyway, and if he can clear himself, why, let him. Get busy with that telephone, and be particular about help from Norcaster—we're under-staffed here as it is."

The superintendent hurried out of his office and Mallalieu turned to the sergeant.

"I understood from Mr. Bent," he said, "that that housekeeper of Kitely's said the old fellow had been to the bank at noon today, to draw some money? That so?"

"So she said, your Worship," answered the sergeant. "Some allowance, or something of that sort, that he drew once a quarter. She didn't know how much."

"But she thought he'd have it on him when he was attacked?" asked Mallalieu.

"She said he was a man for carrying his money on him always," replied the sergeant. "We understood from her it was his habit. She says he always had a good bit on him—as a rule. And of course, if he'd drawn more today, why, he might have a fair lot."

"We'll soon find that out," remarked Mallalieu. "I'll step round to the bank manager and rouse him. Now you get your men together—this is no time for sleeping. You ought to have men up at the Shawl now."

"I've left one man at Kitely's cottage, sir, and another about Harborough's—in case Harborough should come back during the night," said the sergeant. "We've two more constables close by the station. I'll get them up."

"Do it just now," commanded Mallalieu. "I'll be back in a while."

He hurried out again and went rapidly down the High Street to the old-fashioned building near the Town Hall in which the one bank of the little town did its business, and in which the bank manager lived. There was not a soul about in the street, and the ringing of the bell at the bank-house door, and the loud knock which Mallalieu gave in supplement to it, seemed to wake innumerable echoes. And proof as he believed himself to be against such slight things, the sudden opening of a window above his head made him jump.

The startled bank-manager, hurrying down to his midnight visitor in his dressing-gown and slippers, stood aghast when he had taken the Mayor within and learned his errand.

"Certainly!" he said. "Kitely was in the bank today, about noon—I attended to him myself. That's the second time he's been here since he came to the town. He called here a day or two after he first took that house from Mr.

Cotherstone—to cash a draft for his quarter's pension. He told me then who he was. Do you know?"

"Not in the least," replied Mallalieu, telling the lie all the more readily because he had been fully prepared for the question to which it was an answer. "I knew naught about him."

"He was an ex-detective," said the bank-manager. "Pensioned off, of course: a nice pension. He told me he'd had—I believe it was getting on to forty years' service in the police force. Dear, dear, this is a sad business—and I'm afraid I can tell you a bit more about it."

"What?" demanded Mallalieu, showing surprise in spite of himself.

"You mentioned Harborough," said the bank-manager, shaking his head.

"Well?" said Mallalieu. "What then?"

"Harborough was at the counter when Kitely took his money," answered the bank-manager. "He had called in to change a five-pound note."

The two men looked at each other in silence for a time. Then the bank-manager shook his head again.

"You wouldn't think that a man who has a five-pound note of his own to change would be likely, to murder another man for what he could get," he went on. "But Kitely had a nice bit of money to carry away, and he wore a very valuable gold watch and chain, which he was rather fond of showing in the town, and——eh?"

"It's a suspicious business," said Mallalieu. "You say Harborough saw Kitely take his money?"

"Couldn't fail," replied the bank-manager. "He was standing by him. The old man put it—notes and gold—in a pocket that he had inside his waistcoat."

Mallalieu lingered, as if in thought, rubbing his chin and staring at the carpet. "Well, that's a sort of additional clue," he remarked at last. "It looks very black against Harborough."

"We've the numbers of the notes that I handed to Kitely," observed the bank-manager. "They may be useful if there's any attempt to change any note, you know."

Mallalieu shook his head.

"Aye, just so," he answered. "But I should say there won't be—just yet. It's a queer business, isn't it—but, as I say, there's evidence against this fellow, and we must try to get him."

He went out then and crossed the street to the doctor's house—while he was about it, he wanted to know all he could. And with the doctor he stopped much longer than he had stopped at the bank, and when he left him he was puzzled. For the doctor said to him what he had said to Cotherstone and to Bent and to the rest of the group in the wood—that whoever had strangled Kitely had had experience in that sort of grim work before—or else he was a sailorman who had expert knowledge of tying knots. Now Mallalieu was by that time more certain than ever that Cotherstone was the murderer, and he felt sure that Cotherstone had no experience of that sort of thing.

"Done with a single twist and a turn!" he muttered to himself as he walked back to the police-station. "Aye—aye!—that seems to show knowledge. But it's not my business to follow that up just now—I know what my business is—nobody better."

The superintendent and the sergeant were giving orders to two sleepy-eyed policemen when Mallalieu rejoined them. He waited until the policemen had gone away to patrol the Shawl and then took the superintendent aside.

"I've heard a bit more incriminatory news against Harborough," he said. "He was in the bank this morning—or yesterday morning, as it now is—when Kitely drew his money. There may be naught in that—and there may be a lot. Anyway, he knew the old man had a goodish bit on him."

The superintendent nodded, but his manner was doubtful.

"Well, of course, that's evidence—considering things,"
he said, "but you know as well as I do, Mr. Mayor, that
Harborough's not a man that's ever been in want of
money. It's the belief of a good many folks in the town
that he has money of his own: he's always been a bit of a
mystery ever since I can remember. He could afford to
give that daughter of his a good education—good as a
young lady gets—and he spends plenty, and I never heard
of him owing aught. Of course, he's a queer lot—we know
he's a poacher and all that, but he's so skilful about it
that we've never been able to catch him. I can't think he's
the guilty party—and yet——"

"You can't get away from the facts," said Mallalieu.
"He'll have to be sought for. If he's made himself scarce—
if he doesn't come home——"

"Ah, that 'ud certainly be against him!" agreed the
superintendent. "Well, I'm doing all I can. We've got our
own men out, and there's three officers coming over from
Norcaster by motor—they're on the way now."

"Send for me if aught turns up," said Mallalieu.

He walked slowly home, his brain still busy with
possibilities and eventualities. And within five minutes of
his waking at his usual hour of six it was again busy—
and curious. For he and Cotherstone, both keen business
men who believed in constant supervision of their
workmen, were accustomed to meet at the yard at half-
past six every morning, summer or winter, and he was
wondering what his partner would say and do—and look
like.

Cotherstone was in the yard when Mallalieu reached
it. He was giving some orders to a carter, and he finished
what he was doing before coming up to Mallalieu. In the
half light of the morning he looked pretty much as
usual—but Mallalieu noticed a certain worn look under
his eyes and suppressed nervousness in his voice. He
himself remained silent and observant, and he let
Cotherstone speak first.

"Well?" said Cotherstone, coming close to him as they stood in a vacant space outside the office. "Well?"

"Well?" responded Mallalieu.

Cotherstone began to fidget with some account books and papers that he had brought from his house. He eyed his partner with furtive glances; Mallalieu eyed him with steady and watchful ones.

"I suppose you've heard all about it?" said Cotherstone, after an awkward silence.

"Aye!" replied Mallalieu, drily. "Aye, I've heard."

Cotherstone looked round. There was no one near him, but he dropped his voice to a whisper.

"So long as nobody but him knew," he muttered, giving Mallalieu another side glance, "so long as he hadn't said aught to anybody—and I don't think he had— we're—safe."

Mallalieu was still staring quietly at Cotherstone. And Cotherstone began to grow restless under that steady, questioning look.

"Oh?" observed Mallalieu, at last. "Aye? You think so? Ah!"

"Good God—don't you!" exclaimed Cotherstone, roused to a sudden anger. "Why——"

But just then a policeman came out of the High Street into the yard, caught sight of the two partners, and came over to them, touching his helmet.

"Can your Worship step across the way?" he asked. "They've brought Harborough down, and the Super wants a word with you."

8. RETAINED FOR THE DEFENCE

Instead of replying to the policeman by word or movement, Mallalieu glanced at Cotherstone. There was a curious suggestion in that glance which Cotherstone did not like. He was already angry; Mallalieu's inquiring look made him still angrier.

"Like to come?" asked Mallalieu, laconically.

"No!" answered Cotherstone, turning towards the office. "It's naught to me."

He disappeared within doors, and Mallalieu walked out of the yard into the High Street—to run against Bent and Brereton, who were hurrying in the direction of the police-station, in company with another constable.

"Ah!" said Mallalieu as they met. "So you've heard, too, I suppose? Heard that Harborough's been taken, I mean. Now, how was he taken?" he went on, turning to the policeman who had summoned him. "And when, and where?—let's be knowing about it."

"He wasn't taken, your Worship," replied the man. "Leastways, not in what you'd call the proper way. He came back to his house half an hour or so ago—when it was just getting nicely light—and two of our men that were there told him what was going on, and he appeared to come straight down with them. He says he knows naught, your Worship."

"That's what you'd expect," remarked Mallalieu, drily. "He'd be a fool if he said aught else."

He put his thumbs in the armholes of his waistcoat, and, followed by the others, strolled into the police-station as if he were dropping in on business of trifling importance. And there was nothing to be seen there which betokened that a drama of life and death was being constructed in that formal-looking place of neutral-

coloured walls, precise furniture, and atmosphere of
repression. Three or four men stood near the
superintendent's desk; a policeman was writing slowly
and laboriously on a big sheet of blue paper at a side-
table, a woman was coaxing a sluggish fire to burn.

"The whole thing's ridiculous!" said a man's scornful
voice. "It shouldn't take five seconds to see that."

Brereton instinctively picked out the speaker. That
was Harborough, of course—the tall man who stood
facing the others and looking at them as if he wondered
how they could be as foolish as he evidently considered
them to be. He looked at this man with great curiosity.
There was certainly something noticeable about him, he
decided. A wiry, alert, keen-eyed man, with good,
somewhat gipsy-like features, much tanned by the
weather, as if he were perpetually exposed to sun and
wind, rain and hail; sharp of movement, evidently of more
than ordinary intelligence, and, in spite of his rough
garments and fur cap, having an indefinable air of
gentility and breeding about him. Brereton had already
noticed the pitch and inflection of his voice; now, as
Harborough touched his cap to the Mayor, he noticed that
his hands, though coarsened and weather-browned, were
well-shaped and delicate. Something about him,
something in his attitude, the glance of his eye, seemed to
indicate that he was the social superior of the policemen,
uniformed or plain-clothed, who were watching him with
speculative and slightly puzzled looks.

"Well, and what's all this, now?" said Mallalieu
coming to a halt and looking round. "What's he got to say,
like?"

The superintendent looked at Harborough and
nodded. And Harborough took that nod at its true
meaning, and he spoke—readily.

"This!" he said, turning to the new-comers, and finally
addressing himself to Mallalieu. "And it's what I've
already said to the superintendent here. I know nothing
about what's happened to Kitely. I know no more of his

murder than you do—not so much, I should say—for I
know naught at all beyond what I've been told. I left my
house at eight o'clock last night—I've been away all
night—I got back at six o'clock this morning. As soon as I
heard what was afoot, I came straight here. I put it to
you, Mr. Mayor—if I'd killed this old man, do you think
I'd have come back? Is it likely?"

"You might ha' done, you know," answered Mallalieu.
"There's no accounting for what folks will do—in such
cases. But—what else? Say aught you like—it's all
informal, this."

"Very well," continued Harborough. "They tell me the
old man was strangled by a piece of cord that was
evidently cut off one of my coils. Now, is there any man in
his common senses would believe that if I did that job, I
should leave such a bit of clear evidence behind me? I'm
not a fool!"

"You might ha' been interrupted before you could take
that cord off his neck," suggested Mallalieu.

"Aye—but you'd have to reckon up the average
chances of that!" exclaimed Harborough, with a sharp
glance at the bystanders. "And the chances are in my
favour. No, sir!—whoever did this job, cut that length of
cord off my coil, which anybody could get at, and used it
to throw suspicion on me! That's the truth—and you'll
find it out some day, whatever happens now."

Mallalieu exchanged glances with the superintendent
and then faced Harborough squarely, with an air of
inviting confidence.

"Now, my lad!" he said, almost coaxingly. "There's a
very simple thing to do, and it'll clear this up as far as
you're concerned. Just answer a plain question. Where
ha' you been all night?"

A tense silence fell—broken by the crackling of the
wood in the grate, which the charwoman had at last
succeeded in stirring into a blaze, and by the rattling of
the fire-irons which she now arranged in the fender.
Everybody was watching the suspected man, and nobody

as keenly as Brereton. And Brereton saw that a deadlock was at hand. A strange look of obstinacy and hardness came into Harborough's eyes, and he shook his head.

"No!" he answered. "I shan't say! The truth'll come out in good time without that. It's not necessary for me to say. Where I was during the night is my business— nobody else's."

"You'll not tell?" asked Mallalieu.

"I shan't tell," replied Harborough.

"You're in danger, you know," said Mallalieu.

"In your opinion," responded Harborough, doggedly. "Not in mine! There's law in this country. You can arrest me, if you like—but you'll have your work set to prove that I killed yon old man. No, sir! But——" here he paused, and looking round him, laughed almost maliciously "—but I'll tell you what I'll do," he went on. "I'll tell you this, if it'll do you any good—if I liked to say the word, I could prove my innocence down to the ground! There!"

"And you won't say that word?" asked Mallalieu.

"I shan't! Why? Because it's not necessary. Why!" demanded Harborough, laughing with an expresssion of genuine contempt. "What is there against me? Naught! As I say, there's law in this country—there's such a thing as a jury. Do you believe that any jury would convict a man on what you've got? It's utter nonsense!"

The constable who had come down from the Shawl with Bent and Brereton had for some time been endeavouring to catch the eye of the superintendent. Succeeding in his attempts at last, he beckoned that official into a quiet corner of the room, and turning his back on the group near the fireplace, pulled something out of his pocket. The two men bent over it, and the constable began to talk in whispers.

Mallalieu meanwhile was eyeing Harborough in his stealthy, steady fashion. He looked as if he was reckoning him up.

"Well, my lad," he observed at last. "You're making a mistake. If you can't or won't tell what you've been doing with yourself between eight last night and six this morning, why, then——"

The superintendent came back, holding something in his hand. He, too, looked at Harborough.

"Will you hold up your left foot?—turn the sole up," he asked. "Just to see—something."

Harborough complied, readily, but with obvious scornful impatience. And when he had shown the sole of the left foot, the superintendent opened his hand and revealed a small crescent-shaped bit of bright steel.

"That's off the toe of your boot, Harborough," he said. "You know it is! And it's been picked up—just now, as it were—where this affair happened. You must have lost it there during the last few hours, because it's quite bright—not a speck of rust on it, you see. What do you say to that, now?"

"Naught!" retorted Harborough, defiantly. "It is mine, of course—I noticed it was working loose yesterday. And if it was picked up in that wood, what then? I passed through there last night on my way to—where I was going. God—you don't mean to say you'd set a man's life on bits o'things like that!"

Mallalieu beckoned the superintendent aside and talked with him. Almost at once he himself turned away and left the room, and the superintendent came back to the group by the fireplace.

"Well, there's no help for it, Harborough," he said. "We shall have to detain you—and I shall have to charge you, presently. It can't be helped—and I hope you'll be able to clear yourself."

"I expected nothing else," replied Harborough. "I'm not blaming you—nor anybody. Mr. Bent," he continued, turning to where Bent and Brereton stood a little apart. "I'd be obliged to you if you'd do something for me. Go and tell my daughter about this, if you please! You see, I came straight down here—I didn't go into my house when I got back. If you'd just step up and tell her—and bid her not be afraid—there's naught to be afraid of, as she'll find— as everybody'll find."

"Certainly," said Bent. "I'll go at once." He tapped Brereton on the arm, and led him out into the street. "Well?" he asked, when they were outside. "What do you think of that, now?"

"That man gives one all the suggestion of innocence," remarked Brereton, thoughtfully, "and from a merely superficial observation of him, I, personally, should say he is innocent. But then, you know, I've known the most hardened and crafty criminals assume an air of innocence, and keep it up, to the very end. However, we aren't concerned about that just now—the critical point here, for Harborough, at any rate, is the evidence against him."

"And what do you think of that?" asked Bent.

"There's enough to warrant his arrest," answered Brereton, "and he'll be committed on it, and he'll go for trial. All that's certain—unless he's a sensible man, and tells what he was doing with himself between eight and ten o'clock last night."

"Ah, and why doesn't he?" said Bent. "He must have some good reason. I wonder if his daughter can persuade him?"

"Isn't that his daughter coming towards us?" inquired Brereton.

Bent glanced along the road and saw Avice Harborough at a little distance, hastening in their direction and talking earnestly to a middle-aged man who was evidently listening with grave concern to what she said.

"Yes, that's she," he replied, "and that's Northrop with her—the man that Mallalieu was playing cards with last night. She's governess to Northrop's two younger children—I expect she's heard about her father, and has been to get Northrop to come down with her—he's a magistrate."

Avice listened with ill-concealed impatience while Bent delivered his message. He twice repeated Harborough's injunction that she was not to be afraid, and her impatience increased.

"I'm not afraid," she answered. "That is, afraid of nothing but my father's obstinacy! I know him. And I know that if he's said he won't tell anything about his whereabouts last night, he won't! And if you want to help him—as you seem to do—you must recognize that."

"Wouldn't he tell you?" suggested Brereton.

The girl shook her head.

"Once or twice a year," she answered, "he goes away for a night, like that, and I never know—never have known—where he goes. There's some mystery about it—I know there is. He won't tell—he'll let things go to the last, and even then he won't tell. You won't be able to help him that way—there's only one way you can help."

"What way?" asked Bent.

"Find the murderer!" exclaimed Avice with a quick flash of her eyes in Brereton's direction. "My father is as innocent as I am—find the man who did it and clear him that way. Don't wait for what these police people do— they'll waste time over my father. Do something! They're all on the wrong track—let somebody get on the right one!"

"She's right!" said Northrop, a shrewd-faced little man, who looked genuinely disturbed. "You know what police are, Mr. Bent—if they get hold of one notion they're deaf to all others. While they're concentrating on Harborough, you know, the real man'll be going free— laughing in his sleeve, very like."

"But—what are we to do?" asked Bent. "What are we to start on?"

"Find out about Kitely himself!" exclaimed Avice. "Who knows anything about him? He may have had enemies—he may have been tracked here. Find out if there was any motive!" She paused and looked half appealingly, half-searchingly at Brereton. "I heard you're a barrister—a clever one," she went on, hesitating a little. "Can't—can't you suggest anything?"

"There's something I'll suggest at once," responded Brereton impulsively. "Whatever else is done, your father's got to be defended. I'll defend him—to the best of my ability—if you'll let me—and at no cost to him."

"Well spoken, sir!" exclaimed Northrop. "That's the style!"

"But we must keep to legal etiquette," continued Brereton, smiling at the little man's enthusiasm. "You must go to a solicitor and tell him to instruct me—it's a mere form. Mr. Bent will take you to his solicitor, and he'll see me. Then I can appear in due form when they bring your father before the magistrates. Look here, Bent," he went on, wishing to stop any expression of gratitude from the girl, "you take Miss Harborough to your solicitor—if he isn't up, rouse him out. Tell him what I propose to do, and make an appointment with him for me. Now run along, both of you—I want to speak to this gentleman a minute."

He took Northrop's arm, turned him in the direction of the Shawl, walked him a few paces, and then asked him a direct question.

"Now, what do you know of this man Harborough?"

"He's a queer chap—a mystery man, sir," answered Northrop. "A sort of jack-of-all-trades. He's a better sort—you'd say, to hear him talk, he'd been a gentleman. You can see what his daughter is—he educated her well. He's means of some sort—apart from what he earns. Yes, there's some mystery about that man, sir—but I'll never believe he did this job. No, sir!"

"Then we must act on the daughter's suggestion and find out who did," observed Brereton. "There is as much mystery about that as about Harborough."

"All mystery, sir!" agreed Northrop. "It's odd—I came through them woods on the Shawl there about a quarter to ten last night: I'd been across to the other side to see a man of mine that's poorly in bed. Now, I never heard aught, never saw aught—but then, it's true I was hurrying—I'd made an appointment for a hand at whist with the Mayor at my house at ten o'clock, and I thought I was late. I never heard a sound—not so much as a dead twig snap! But then, it would ha' been before that—at some time."

"Yes, at some time," agreed Brereton. "Well,—I'll see you in court, no doubt."

He turned back, and followed Bent and Avice at a distance, watching them thoughtfully.

"At some time?" he mused. "Um! Well, I'm now conversant with the movements of two inhabitants of Highmarket at a critical period of last night. Mallalieu didn't go to cards with Northrop until ten o'clock, and at ten o'clock Cotherstone returned to his house after being absent—one hour."

9. ANTECEDENTS

During the interval which elapsed between these early morning proceedings and the bringing up of Harborough before the borough magistrates in a densely-packed court, Brereton made up his mind as to what he would do. He would act on Avice Harborough's suggestion, and, while watching the trend of affairs on behalf of the suspected man, would find out all he could about the murdered one. At that moment—so far as Brereton knew—there was only one person in Highmarket who was likely to know anything about Kitely: that person, of course, was the queer-looking housekeeper. He accordingly determined, even at that early stage of the proceedings, to have Miss Pett in the witness-box.

Harborough, who had been formally arrested and charged by the police after the conversation at the police-station, was not produced in court until eleven o'clock, by which time the whole town and neighbourhood were astir with excitement. Somewhat to Brereton's surprise, the prosecuting counsel, who had been hastily fetched from Norcaster and instructed on the way, went more fully into the case than was usual. Brereton had expected that the police would ask for an adjournment after the usual evidence of the superficial facts, and of the prisoner's arrest, had been offered; instead of that, the prosecution brought forward several witnesses, and amongst them the bank-manager, who said that when he cashed Kitely's draft for him the previous morning, in Harborough's presence, he gave Kitely the one half of the money in gold. The significance of this evidence immediately transpired: a constable succeeded the bank-manager and testified that after searching the prisoner after his arrest he found on him over twenty pounds in sovereigns and half-sovereigns, placed in a wash-leather bag.

Brereton immediately recognized the impression which this evidence made. He saw that it weighed with the half-dozen solid and slow-thinking men who sat on one side or the other of Mallalieu on the magisterial bench; he felt the atmosphere of suspicion which it engendered in the court. But he did nothing: he had already learned sufficient from Avice in a consultation with her and Bent's solicitor to know that it would be very easy to prove to a jury that it was no unusual thing for Harborough to carry twenty or thirty pounds in gold on him. Of all these witnesses Brereton asked scarcely anything—but he made it clear that when Harborough was met near his cottage at daybreak that morning by two constables who informed him of what had happened, he expressed great astonishment, jeered at the notion that he had had anything to do with the murder, and, without going on to his own door, offered voluntarily to walk straight to the police-station.

But when Miss Pett—who had discarded her red and yellow turban, and appeared in rusty black garments which accentuated the old-ivory tint of her remarkable countenance—had come into the witness-box and answered a few common-place questions as to the dead man's movements on the previous evening, Brereton prepared himself for the episode which he knew to be important. Amidst a deep silence—something suggesting to everybody that Mr. Bent's sharp-looking London friend was about to get at things—he put his first question to Miss Pett.

"How long have you known Mr. Kitely?"

"Ever since I engaged with him as his housekeeper," answered Miss Pett.

"How long since is that?" asked Brereton.

"Nine to ten years—nearly ten."

"You have been with him, as housekeeper, nearly ten years—continuously?"

"Never left him since I first came to him."

"Where did you first come to him—where did he live then?"

"In London."

"Yes—and where, in London?"

"83, Acacia Grove, Camberwell."

"You lived with Mr. Kitely at 83, Acacia Grove, Camberwell, from the time you became his housekeeper until now—nearly ten years in all. So we may take it that you knew Mr. Kitely very well indeed?"

"As well as anybody could know—him," replied Miss Pett, grimly. "He wasn't the sort that's easy to know."

"Still, you knew him for ten years. Now," continued Brereton, concentrating his gaze on Miss Pett's curious features, "who and what was Mr. Kitely?"

Miss Pett drummed her black-gloved fingers on the edge of the witness-box and shook her head.

"I don't know," she answered. "I never have known."

"But you must have some idea, some notion—after ten years' acquaintanceship! Come now. What did he do with himself in London? Had he no business?"

"He had business," said Miss Pett. "He was out most of the day at it. I don't know what it was."

"Never mentioned it to you?"

"Never in his life."

"Did you gain no idea of it? For instance, did it take him out at regular hours?"

"No, it didn't. Sometimes he'd go out very early— sometimes late—some days he never went out at all. And sometimes he'd be out at night—and away for days together. I never asked him anything, of course."

"Whatever it was, he retired from it eventually?"

"Yes—just before we came here."

"Do you know why Mr. Kitely came here?"

"Well," said Miss Pett, "he'd always said he wanted a nice little place in the country, and preferably in the North. He came up this way for a holiday some months since, and when he got back he said he'd found just the house and neighbourhood to suit him, so, of course, we removed here."

"And you have been here—how long?"

"Just over three months."

Brereton let a moment or two elapse before he asked his next question, which was accompanied by another searching inspection of the witness.

"Do you know anything about Mr. Kitely's relations?"

"No!" answered Miss Pett. "And for a simple reason. He always said he had none."

"He was never visited by anybody claiming to be a relation?"

"Not during the ten years I knew him."

"Do you think he had property—money—to leave to anybody?"

Miss Pett began to toy with the fur boa which depended from her thin neck.

"Well—yes, he said he had," she replied hesitatingly.

"Did you ever hear him say what would become of it at his death?"

Miss Pett looked round the court and smiled a little.

"Well," she answered, still more hesitatingly, "he—he always said that as he'd no relations of his own, he'd leave it to me."

Brereton leaned a little closer across the table towards the witness-box and dropped his voice.

"Do you know if Mr. Kitely ever made a will?" he asked.

"Yes," replied Miss Pett. "He did."

"When?"

"Just before we left London."

"Do you know the contents of that will?"

"No!" said Miss Pett. "I do not—so there!"

"Did you witness it?"

"No, I didn't."

"Do you know where it is?"

"Yes, I know that."

"Where is it?"

"My nephew has it," replied Miss Pett. "He's a solicitor, and he made it."

"What is your nephew's name and address?" asked Brereton.

"Mr. Christopher Pett, 23B Cursitor Street," answered Miss Pett, readily enough.

"Have you let him know of Mr. Kitely's death?"

"Yes. I sent him a telegram first thing this morning."

"Asking him to bring the will?"

"No, I did not!" exclaimed Miss Pett, indignantly. "I never mentioned the will. Mr. Kitely was very fond of my nephew—he considered him a very clever young man."

"We shall, no doubt, have the pleasure of seeing your nephew," remarked Brereton. "Well, now, I want to ask you a question or two about yourself. What had you been before you became housekeeper to Mr. Kitely?"

"Housekeeper to another gentleman!" replied Miss Pett, acidly.

"Who was he?"

"Well, if you want to know, he was a Major Stilman, a retired officer—though what that has——"

"Where did Major Stilman live?" asked Brereton.

"He lived at Kandahar Cottage, Woking," replied Miss Pett, who was now showing signs of rising anger. "But——"

"Answer my questions, if you please, and don't make remarks," said Brereton. "Is Major Stilman alive?"

"No, he isn't—he's dead this ten years," answered Miss Pett. "And if you're going to ask me any more questions about who and what I am, young man, I'll save you the trouble. I was with Major Stilman a many years, and before that I was store-keeper at one London hotel, and linen-keeper at another, and before that I lived at home with my father, who was a respectable farmer in Sussex. And what all this has to do with what we're here for, I should like——"

"Just give me the names of the two hotels you were at in London, will you?" asked Brereton.

"One was the *Royal Belvedere* in Bayswater, and the other the *Mervyn Crescent* in Kensington," replied Miss Pett. "Highly respectable, both of 'em."

"And you come originally from—where in Sussex?"

"Oakbarrow Farm, near Horsham. Do you want to know any——"

"I shan't trouble you much longer," said Brereton suavely. "But you might just tell me this—has Mr. Kitely ever had any visitors since he came to Highmarket?"

"Only one," answered Miss Pett. "And it was my nephew, who came up for a week-end to see him on business. Of course, I don't know what the business was. Mr. Kitely had property in London; house-property, and——"

"And your nephew, as his solicitor, no doubt came to see him about it," interrupted Brereton. "Thank you, Miss Pett—I don't want to trouble you any more."

He sat down as the housekeeper left the witness-box—confident that he had succeeded in introducing a new atmosphere into the case. Already there were whisperings going on in the crowded court; he felt that these country folk, always quick to form suspicions, were beginning to ask themselves if there was not something dark and sinister behind the mystery of Kitely's murder, and he was callous enough—from a purely professional standpoint—to care nothing if they began to form ideas about Miss Pett. For Brereton knew that nothing is so useful in the breaking-down of one prejudice as to set up another, and his great object just then was to divert primary prejudice away from his client. Nevertheless, nothing, he knew well, could at that stage prevent Harborough's ultimate committal—unless Harborough himself chose to prove the *alibi* of which he had boasted. But Harborough refused to do anything towards that, and when the case had been adjourned for a week, and the prisoner removed to a cell pending his removal to Norcaster gaol, a visit from Brereton and Avice in company failed to move him.

"It's no good, my girl; it's no good, sir," he said, when both had pleaded with him to speak. "I'm determined! I shall not say where I was last night."

"Tell me—in secret—and then leave me to make use of the knowledge, also in secret," urged Brereton.

"No, sir—once for all, no!" answered Harborough. "There's no necessity. I may be kept locked up for a bit, but the truth about this matter'll come out before ever I'm brought to trial—or ought to be. Leave me alone—I'm all right. All that bothers me now, my girl, is—you!"

"Then don't bother," said Avice. "I'm going to stay with Mrs. Northrop. They've insisted on it."

Brereton was going out of the cell, leaving father and daughter together, when he suddenly turned back.

"You're a man of sense, Harborough," he said. "Come, now—have you got anything to suggest as to how you can be helped?"

Harborough smiled and gave his counsel a knowing look.

"Aye, sir!" he answered. "The best suggestion you could get. If you want to find out who killed Kitely—go back! Go back, sir—go inch by inch, through Kitely's life!"

10. THE HOLE IN THE THATCH

Bent, taking his guest home to dinner after the police-court proceedings, showed a strong and encouraging curiosity. He, in common with all the rest of the townsfolk who had contrived to squeeze into the old court-house, had been immensely interested in Brereton's examination of Miss Pett. Now he wanted to know what it meant, what it signified, what was its true relation to the case?

"You don't mean to say that you suspect that queer old atomy of a woman!" he exclaimed incredulously as they sat down to Bent's bachelor table. "And yet—you really looked as if you did—and contrived to throw something very like it into your voice, too! Man, alive!—half the Highmarket wiseacres'll be sitting down to their roast mutton at this minute in the full belief that Miss Pett strangled her master!"

"Well, and why not?" asked Brereton, coolly. "Surely, if you face facts, there's just as much reason to suspect Miss Pett as there is to suspect Harborough. They're both as innocent as you are, in all probability. Granted there's some nasty evidence against Harborough, there's also the presumption—founded on words from her own lips—that Miss Pett expects to benefit by this old man's death. She's a strong and wiry woman, and you tell me Kitely was getting somewhat enfeebled—she might have killed him, you know. Murders, my dear fellow, are committed by the most unlikely people, and for curious reasons: they have been committed by quite respectable females—like Miss Pett—for nothing but a mere whim."

"Do you really suspect her?" demanded Bent. "That's what I want to know."

"That's what I shan't tell you," replied Brereton, with a good-humoured laugh. "All I shall tell you is that I believe this murder to be either an exceedingly simple affair, or a very intricate affair. Wait a little—wait, for instance, until Mr. Christopher Pett arrives with that will. Then we shall advance a considerable stage."

"I'm sorry for Avice Harborough, anyway," remarked Bent, "and it's utterly beyond me to imagine why her father can't say where he was last night. I suppose there'd be an end of the case if he'd prove where he was, eh?"

"He'd have to account for every minute between nine and ten o'clock," answered Brereton. "It would be no good, for instance, if we proved to a jury that from say ten o'clock until five o'clock next morning, Harborough was at—shall we say your county town, Norcaster. You may say it would take Harborough an hour to get from here to Norcaster, and an hour to return, and that would account for his whereabouts between nine and ten last night, and between five and six this morning. That wouldn't do— because, according to the evidence, Kitely left his house just before nine o'clock, and he may have been killed immediately. Supposing Harborough killed him at nine o'clock precisely, Harborough would even then be able to arrive in Norcaster by ten. What we want to know, in order to fully establish Harborough's innocence is—where was he, what was he doing, from the moment he left his cottage last night until say a quarter past nine, the latest moment at which, according to what the doctor said, the murder could have been committed?"

"Off on one of his poaching expeditions, I suppose," said Bent.

"No—that's not at all likely," answered Brereton. "There's some very strange mystery about that man, and I'll have to get at the truth of it—in spite of his determined reticence! Bent!—I'm going to see this thing right through! The Norcaster Assizes will be on next month, and of course Harborough will be brought up then. I shall stop in this neighbourhood and work out the case—it'll do me a lot of good in all sorts of ways—

experience—work—the interest in it—and the *kudos* I shall win if I get my man off—as I will! So I shall unashamedly ask you to give me house-room for that time."

"Of course," replied Bent. "The house is yours—only too glad, old chap. But what a queer case it is! I'd give something, you know, to know what you really think about it."

"I've not yet settled in my own mind what I do think about it," said Brereton. "But I'll suggest a few things to you which you can think over at your leisure. What motive could Harborough have had for killing Kitely? There's abundant testimony in the town—from his daughter, from neighbours, from tradesmen—that Harborough was never short of money—he's always had more money than most men in his position are supposed to have. Do you think it likely that he'd have killed Kitely for thirty pounds? Again—does anybody of sense believe that a man of Harborough's evident ability would have murdered his victim so clumsily as to leave a direct clue behind him? Now turn to another side. Is it not evident that if Miss Pett wanted to murder Kitely she'd excellent chances of not only doing so, but of directing suspicion to another person? She knew her master's habits—she knew the surroundings—she knew where Harborough kept that cord—she is the sort of person who could steal about as quietly as a cat. If—as may be established by the will which her nephew has, and of which, in spite of all she affirmed, or, rather, swore, she may have accurate knowledge—she benefits by Kitely's death, is there not motive there? Clearly, Miss Pett is to be suspected!"

"Do you mean to tell me that she'd kill old Kitely just to get possession of the bit he had to leave?" asked Bent incredulously. "Come, now,—that's a stiff proposition."

"Not to me," replied Brereton. "I've known of a case in which a young wife carefully murdered an old husband because she was so eager to get out of the dull life she led with him that she couldn't wait a year or two for his natural decease; I've heard of a case in which an elderly woman poisoned her twin-sister, so that she could inherit her share of an estate and go to live in style at Brighton. I don't want to do Miss Pett any injustice, but I say that there are grounds for suspecting her—and they may be widened."

"Then it comes to this," said Bent. "There are two people under suspicion: Harborough's suspected by the police—Miss Pett's suspected by you. And it may be, and probably is, the truth that both are entirely innocent. In that case, who's the guilty person?"

"Ah, who indeed?" assented Brereton, half carelessly. "That is a question. But my duty is to prove that my client is not guilty. And as you're going to attend to your business this afternoon, I'll do a little attending to mine by thinking things over."

When Bent had gone away to the town, Brereton lighted a cigar, stretched himself in an easy chair in front of a warm fire in his host's smoking-room, and tried to think clearly. He had said to Bent all that was in his mind about Harborough and about Miss Pett—but he had said nothing, had been determined to say nothing, about a curious thought, an unformed, vague suspicion which was there. It was that as yet formless suspicion which occupied all his mental powers now—he put Harborough and Miss Pett clean away from him.

And as he sat there, he asked himself first of all—why had this curious doubt about two apparently highly-respectable men of this little, out-of-the-world town come into his mind? He traced it back to its first source—Cotherstone. Brereton was a close observer of men; it was his natural instinct to observe, and he was always giving it a further training and development. He had felt certain as he sat at supper with him, the night before, that Cotherstone had something in his thoughts which was not of his guests, his daughter, or himself. His whole behaviour suggested pre-occupation, occasional absent-mindedness: once or twice he obviously did not hear the remarks which were addressed to him. He had certainly betrayed some curious sort of confusion when Kitely's name was mentioned. And he had manifested great astonishment, been much upset, when Garthwaite came in with the news of Kitely's death.

Now here came in what Brereton felt to be the all-important, the critical point of this, his first attempt to think things out. He was not at all sure that Cotherstone's astonishment on hearing Garthwaite's announcement was not feigned, was not a piece of pure acting. Why? He smiled cynically as he answered his own question. The answer was—*Because when Cotherstone, Garthwaite, Bent, and Brereton set out from Cotherstone's house to look at the dead man's body, Cotherstone led the way straight to it.*

How did Cotherstone know exactly where, in that half-mile of wooded hill-side, the murder had been committed of which he had only heard five minutes before? Yet, he led them all to within a few yards of the dead man, until he suddenly checked himself, thrust the lantern into Garthwaite's hands and said that of course he didn't know where the body was! Now might not that really mean, when fully analyzed, that even if Cotherstone did not kill Kitely himself during the full hour in which he was absent from his house he knew that Kitely had been killed, and where—and possibly by whom?

Anyway, here were certain facts—and they had to be reckoned with. Kitely was murdered about a quarter-past nine o'clock. Cotherstone was out of his house from ten minutes to nine o'clock until five minutes to ten. He was clearly excited when he returned: he was more excited when he went with the rest of them up the wood. Was it not probable that under the stress of that excitement he forgot his presence of mind, and mechanically went straight to the all-important spot?

So much for that. But there was something more. Mallalieu was Cotherstone's partner. Mallalieu went to

Northrop's house to play cards at ten o'clock. It might be well to find out, quietly, what Mallalieu was doing with himself up to ten o'clock. But the main thing was—what was Cotherstone doing during that hour of absence? And—had Cotherstone any reason—of his own, or shared with his partner—for wishing to get rid of Kitely?

Brereton sat thinking all these things over until he had finished his cigar; he then left Bent's house and strolled up into the woods of the Shawl. He wanted to have a quiet look round the scene of the murder. He had not been up there since the previous evening; it now occurred to him that it would be well to see how the place looked by daylight. There was no difficulty about finding the exact spot, even in those close coverts of fir and pine; a thin line of inquisitive sightseers was threading its way up the Shawl in front of him, each of its units agog to see the place where a fellow-being had been done to death.

But no one could get at the precise scene of the murder. The police had roped a portion of the coppice off from the rest, and two or three constables in uniform were acting as guards over this enclosed space, while a couple of men in plain clothes, whom Brereton by that time knew to be detectives from Norcaster, were inside it, evidently searching the ground with great care. Round and about the fenced-in portion stood townsfolk, young and old, talking, speculating, keenly alive to the goings-on, hoping that the searchers would find something just then, so that they themselves could carry some sensational news back to the town and their own comfortable tea-tables. Most of them had been in or outside the Court House that morning and recognized Brereton and made way for him as he advanced to the ropes. One of the detectives recognized him, too, and invited him to step inside.

"Found anything?" asked Brereton, who was secretly wondering why the police should be so foolish as to waste time in a search which was almost certain to be non-productive.

"No, sir—we've been chiefly making out for certain where the actual murder took place before the dead man was dragged behind that rock," answered the detective. "As far as we can reckon from the disturbance of these pine needles, the murderer must have sprung on Kitely from behind that clump of gorse—there where it's grown to such a height—and then dragged him here, away from that bit of a path. No—we've found nothing. But I suppose you've heard of the find at Harborough's cottage?"

"No!" exclaimed Brereton, startled out of his habitual composure. "What find?"

"Some of our people made a search there as soon as the police-court proceedings were over," replied the detective. "It was the first chance they'd had of doing anything systematically. They found the bank-notes which Kitely got at the Bank yesterday evening, and a quantity of letters and papers that we presume had been in that empty pocket-book. They were all hidden in a hole in the thatch of Harborough's shed."

"Where are they?" asked Brereton.

"Down at the police-station—the superintendent has them," answered the detective. "He'd show you them, sir, if you care to go down."

Brereton went off to the police-station at once and was shown into the superintendent's office without delay. That official immediately drew open a drawer of his desk and produced a packet folded in brown paper.

"I suppose this is what you want to see, Mr. Brereton," he said. "I guess you've heard about the discovery? Shoved away in a rat-hole in the thatch of Harborough's shed these were, sir—upon my honour, I don't know what to make of it! You'd have thought that a man of Harborough's sense and cleverness would never have put these things there, where they were certain to be found."

"I don't believe Harborough did put them there," said Brereton. "But what are they?"

The superintendent motioned his visitor to sit by him and then opened the papers out on his desk.

"Not so much," he answered. "Three five-pound notes—I've proved that they're those which poor Kitely got at the bank yesterday. A number of letters—chiefly about old books, antiquarian matters, and so forth—some scraps of newspaper cuttings, of the same nature. And this bit of a memorandum book, that fits that empty pocket-book we found, with pencil entries in it—naught of any importance. Look 'em over, if you like, Mr. Brereton. I make nothing out of 'em."

Brereton made nothing out either, at first glance. The papers were just what the superintendent described them to be, and he went rapidly through them without finding anything particularly worthy of notice. But to the little memorandum book he gave more attention, especially to the recent entries. And one of these, made within the last three months, struck him as soon as he looked at it, insignificant as it seemed to be. It was only of one line, and the one line was only of a few initials, an abbreviation or two, and a date: *M. & C. v. S. B. cir. 81.* And why this apparently innocent entry struck Brereton was because he was still thinking as an under-current to all this, of Mallalieu and Cotherstone—and M. and C. were certainly the initials of those not too common names.

11. CHRISTOPHER PETT

The two men sat staring silently at the paper-strewn desk for several moments; each occupied with his own thoughts. At last the superintendent began to put the several exhibits together, and he turned to Brereton with a gesture which suggested a certain amount of mental impatience.

"There's one thing in all this that I can't understand, sir," he said. "And it's this—it's very evident that whoever killed Kitely wanted the papers that Kitely carried in that pocket-book. Why did he take 'em out of the pocket-book and throw the pocket-book away? I don't know how that strikes you—but it licks me, altogether!"

"Yes," agreed Brereton, "it's puzzling—certainly. You'd think that the murderer would have carried off the pocket-book, there and then. That he took the papers from it, threw the pocket-book itself away, and then placed the papers—or some of them—where your people have just found them—in Harborough's shed—seems to me to argue something which is even more puzzling. I daresay you see what I mean?"

"Can't say that I do, sir," answered the superintendent. "I haven't had much experience in this sort of work, you know, Mr. Brereton—it's a good bit off our usual line. What do you mean, then?"

"Why," replied Brereton, laughing a little, "I mean this—it looks as if the murderer had taken his time about his proceedings!—after Kitely was killed. The pocket-book, as you know, was picked up close to the body. It was empty—as we all saw. Now what can we infer from that but that the murderer actually stopped by his victim to examine the papers? And in that case he must have had a light. He may have carried an electric torch. Let's try and reconstruct the affair. We'll suppose that the murderer, whoever he was, was so anxious to find some paper that he wanted, and that he believed Kitely to have on him, that he immediately examined the contents of the pocket-book. He turned on his electric torch and took all the papers out of the pocket-book, laying the pocket-book aside. He was looking through the papers when he heard a sound in the neighbouring coppices or bushes. He immediately turned off his light, made off with the papers, and left the empty case—possibly completely forgetting its existence for the moment. How does that strike you—as a theory?"

"Very good, sir," replied the superintendent. "Very good—but it is only a theory, you know, Mr. Brereton."

Brereton rose, with another laugh.

"Just so," he said. "But suppose you try to reduce it to practice? In this way—you no doubt have tradesmen in this town who deal in such things as electric torches. Find out—in absolute secrecy—if any of them have sold electric torches of late to any one in the town, and if so, to whom. For I'm certain of this—that pocket-book and its contents was examined on the spot, and that examination could only have been made with a light, and an electric torch would be the handiest means of providing that light. And so—so you see how even a little clue like that might help, eh?"

"I'll see to it," assented the superintendent. "Well, it's all very queer, sir, and I'm getting more than ever convinced that we've laid hands on the wrong man. And yet—what could, and what can we do?"

"Oh, nothing, at present," replied Brereton. "Let matters develop. They're only beginning."

He went away then, not to think about the last subject of conversation, but to take out his own pocket-book as soon as he was clear of the police-station, and to write down that entry which he had seen in Kitely's memoranda:—*M. & C. v. S. B. cir. 81.* And again he was struck by the fact that the initials were those of Mallalieu and Cotherstone, and again he wondered what they meant. They might have no reference whatever to the Mayor and his partner—but under the circumstances it was at any rate a curious coincidence, and he had an overwhelming intuition that something lay behind that entry. But—what?

That evening, as Bent and his guest were lighting their cigars after dinner, Bent's parlour-maid came into the smoking-room with a card. Bent glanced from it to Brereton with a look of surprise.

"Mr. Christopher Pett!" he exclaimed. "What on earth does he want me for? Bring Mr. Pett in here, anyway," he continued, turning to the parlour-maid. "Is he alone?—or is Miss Pett with him?"

"The police-superintendent's with him, sir," answered the girl. "They said—could they see you and Mr. Brereton for half an hour, on business?"

"Bring them both in, then," said Bent. He looked at Brereton again, with more interrogation. "Fresh stuff, eh?" he went on. "Mr. Christopher Pett's the old dragon's nephew, I suppose. But what can he want with—oh, well, I guess he wants you—I'm the audience."

Brereton made no reply. He was watching the door. And through it presently came a figure and face which he at once recognized as those of an undersized, common-looking, sly-faced little man whom he had often seen about the Law Courts in London, and had taken for a solicitor's clerk. He looked just as common and sly as ever as he sidled into the smoking-room, removing his silk hat with one hand and depositing a brief bag on the table with the other, and he favoured Brereton with a sickly grin of recognition after he had made a bow to the master of the house. That done he rubbed together two long and very thin white hands and smiled at Brereton once more.

"Good-evening, Mr. Brereton," he said in a thin, wheedling voice. "I've no doubt you've seen me before, sir?—I've seen you often—round about the Courts, Mr. Brereton—though I've never had the pleasure of putting business in your way—as yet, Mr. Brereton, as yet, sir! But——"

Brereton, to whom Bent had transferred Mr. Christopher Pett's card, glanced again at it, and from it to its owner.

"I see your address is that of Messrs. Popham & Pilboody in Cursitor Street, Mr. Pett," he observed frigidly. "Any connection with that well-known firm?"

Mr. Pett rubbed his hands, and taking the chair which Bent silently indicated, sat down and pulled his trousers up about a pair of bony knees. He smiled widely, showing a set of curiously shaped teeth.

"Mr. Popham, sir," he answered softly, "has always been my very good friend. I entered Mr. Popham's service, sir, at an early age. Mr. Popham, sir, acted very handsomely by me. He gave me my articles, sir. And when I was admitted—two years ago, Mr. Brereton— Messrs. Popham & Pilboody gave me—very generously— an office in their suite, so that I could have my name up, and do a bit on my own, sir. Oh yes!—I'm connected— intimately—with that famous firm, Mr. Brereton!"

There was an assurance about Mr. Pett, a cocksureness of demeanour, a cheerful confidence in himself, which made Brereton long to kick him; but he restrained his feelings and said coldly that he supposed Mr. Pett wished to speak to Mr. Bent and himself on business.

"Not on my own business, sir," replied Pett, laying his queer-looking white fingers on his brief bag. "On the business of my esteemed feminine relative, Miss Pett. I am informed, Mr. Brereton—no offence, sir, oh, none whatever!—that you put some—no doubt necessary— questions to Miss Pett at the court this morning which had the effect of prejudicing her in the eyes—or shall we say ears?—of those who were present. Miss Pett accordingly desires that I, as her legal representative, should lose no time in putting before you the true state of the case as regards her relations with Kitely, deceased, and I accordingly, sir, in the presence of our friend, the superintendent, whom I have already spoken to outside, desire to tell you what the truth is. Informally, you understand, Mr. Brereton, informally!"

"Just as you please," answered Brereton. "All this is, as you say, informal."

"Quite informal, sir," agreed Pett, who gained in cheerfulness with every word. "Oh, absolutely so. Between ourselves, of course. But it'll be all the pleasanter if you know. My aunt, Miss Pett, naturally does not wish, Mr. Brereton, that any person— hereabouts or elsewhere—should entertain such suspicions of her as you seemed—I speak, sir, from information furnished—to suggest, in your examination of her today. And so, sir, I wish to tell you this. I acted as legal adviser to the late Mr. Kitely. I made his will. I have that will in this bag. And—to put matters in a nutshell, Mr. Brereton—there is not a living soul in this world who knows the contents of that will but—your humble and obedient!"

"Do you propose to communicate the contents of the late Mr. Kitely's will to us?" asked Brereton, drily.

"I do, sir," replied Mr. Pett. "And for this reason. My relative—Miss Pett—does not know what Mr. Kitely's profession had been, nor what Mr. Kitely died possessed of. She does not know—anything! And she will not know until I read this will to her after I have communicated the gist of it to you. And I will do that in a few words. The late Mr. Kitely, sir, was an ex-member of the detective police force. By dint of economy and thrift he had got together a nice little property—house-property, in London—Brixton, to be exact. It is worth about one hundred and fifty pounds per annum. And—to cut matters short—he has left it absolutely to Miss Pett. I myself, Mr. Brereton, am sole executor. If you desire to see the will, sir, you, or Mr. Bent, or the superintendent, are at liberty to inspect it."

Brereton waved the proffered document aside and got up from his chair.

"No, thank you, Mr. Pett," he said. "I've no desire to see Mr. Kitely's will. I quite accept all that you say about it. You, as a lawyer, know very well that whatever I asked Miss Pett this morning was asked in the interests of my client. No—you can put the will away as far as I'm concerned. You've assured me that Miss Pett is as yet in ignorance of its contents, and—I take your word. I think, however, that Miss Pett won't be exactly surprised."

"Oh, I daresay my aunt has a pretty good idea, Mr. Brereton," agreed Pett, who having offered the will to both Bent and the superintendent, only to meet with a polite refusal from each, now put it back in his bag. "We all of us have some little idea which quarter the wind's in, you know, sir, in these cases. Of course, Kitely, deceased, had no relatives, Mr. Brereton: in fact, so far as Miss Pett and self are aware, beyond ourselves, he'd no friends."

"I was going to ask you a somewhat pertinent question, Mr. Pett," said Brereton. "Quite an informal one, you know. Do you think he had any enemies?"

Pett put his long white fingers together and inclined his head to one side. His slit of a mouth opened slightly, and his queer teeth showed themselves in a sly grin.

"Just so!" he said. "Of course, I take your meaning, Mr. Brereton. Naturally, you'd think that a man of his profession would make enemies. No doubt there must be a good many persons who'd have been glad—had he still been alive—to have had their knives into him. Oh, yes! But—unfortunately, I don't know of 'em, sir."

"Never heard him speak of anybody who was likely to cherish revenge, eh?" asked Brereton.

"Never, sir! Kitely, deceased," remarked Pett, meditatively, "was not given to talking of his professional achievements. I happen to know that he was concerned in some important cases in his time—but he rarely, if ever, mentioned them to me. In fact, I may say, gentlemen," he continued in a palpable burst of confidence, "I may say, between ourselves, that I'd had the honour of Mr. K.'s acquaintance for some time before ever I knew what his line of business had been! Fact!"

"A close man, eh?" asked Brereton.

"One of the very closest," replied Pett. "Yes, you may say that, sir."

"Not likely to let things out, I suppose?" continued Brereton.

"Not he! He was a regular old steel trap, Kitely was— shut tight!" said Pett.

"And—I suppose you've no theory, no idea of your own about his murder?" asked Brereton, who was watching the little man closely. "Have you formed any ideas or theories?"

Pett half-closed his eyes as he turned them on his questioner.

"Too early!" he replied, with a shake of his head. "Much too early. I shall—in due course. Meantime, there's another little commission I have to discharge, and I may as well do it at once. There are two or three trifling bequests in this will, gentlemen—one of 'em's to you, Mr. Bent. It wasn't in the original will—that was made before Kitely came to these parts. It's in a codicil—made when I came down here a few weeks ago, on the only visit I ever paid to the old gentleman. He desired, in case of his death, to leave you something—said you'd been very friendly to him."

"Very good of him, I'm sure," said Bent with a glance of surprise. "I'm rather astonished to hear of it, though."

"Oh, it's nothing much," remarked Pett, with a laugh as he drew from the brief bag what looked like an old quarto account book, fastened by a brass clasp. "It's a scrap-book that the old man kept—a sort of album in which he pasted up all sorts of odds and ends. He thought you'd find 'em interesting. And knowing of this bequest, sir, I thought I'd bring the book down. You might just give me a formal receipt for its delivery, Mr. Bent."

Bent took his curious legacy and led Mr. Pett away to a writing-desk to dictate a former of receipt. And as they turned away, the superintendent signed to Brereton to step into a corner of the room with him.

"You know what you said about that electric torch notion this afternoon, sir?" he whispered. "Well, after you left me, I just made an inquiry—absolutely secret, you know—myself. I went to Rellit, the ironmonger—I knew that if such things had ever come into the town, it 'ud be through him, for he's the only man that's at all up-to-date. And—I heard more than I expected to hear!"

"What?" asked Brereton.

"I think there may be something in what you said," answered the superintendent. "But, listen here—Rellit says he'd swear a solemn oath that nobody but himself ever sold an electric torch in Highmarket. And he's only sold to three persons—to the Vicar's son; to Mr. Mallalieu; and to Jack Harborough!"

12. PARENTAL ANXIETY

For a moment Brereton and the superintendent looked at each other in silence. Then Bent got up from his desk at the other side of the room, and he and the little solicitor came towards them.

"Keep that to yourself, then," muttered Brereton. "We'll talk of it later. It may be of importance."

"Well, there's this much to bear in mind," whispered the superintendent, drawing back a little with an eye on the others. "Nothing of that sort was found on your client! And he'd been out all night. That's worth considering—from his standpoint, Mr. Brereton."

Brereton nodded his assent and turned away with another warning glance. And presently Pett and the superintendent went off, and Bent dropped into his easy chair with a laugh.

"Queer sort of unexpected legacy!" he said. "I wonder if the old man really thought I should be interested in his scrap-book?"

"There may be a great deal that's interesting in it," remarked Brereton, with a glance at the book, which Bent had laid aside on top of a book-case. "Take care of it. Well, what did you think of Mr. Christopher Pett?"

"Cool hand, I should say," answered Bent. "But—what did you think of him?"

"Oh, I've met Mr. Christopher Pett's sort before," said Brereton, drily. "The Dodson & Fogg type of legal practitioner is by no means extinct. I should much like to know a good deal more about his various dealings with Kitely. We shall see and hear more about them, however—later on. For the present there are—other matters."

He changed the subject then—to something utterly apart from the murder and its mystery. For the one topic which filled his own mind was also the very one which he could not discuss with Bent. Had Cotherstone, had Mallalieu anything to do with Kitely's death? That question was beginning to engross all his attention: he thought more about it than about his schemes for a successful defence of Harborough, well knowing that his best way of proving Harborough's innocence lay in establishing another man's guilt.

"One would give a good deal," he said to himself, as he went to bed that night, "if one could get a moment's look into Cotherstone's mind—or into Mallalieu's either! For I'll swear that these two know something—possibly congratulating themselves that it will never be known to anybody else!"

If Brereton could have looked into the minds of either of the partners at this particular juncture he would have found much opportunity for thought and reflection, of a curious nature. For both were keeping a double watch—on the course of events on one hand; on each other, on the other hand. They watched the police-court proceedings against Harborough and saw, with infinite relief, that nothing transpired which seemed inimical to themselves. They watched the proceedings at the inquest held on Kitely; they, too, yielded nothing that could attract attention in the way they dreaded. When several days had gone by and the police investigations seemed to have settled down into a concentrated purpose against the suspected man, both Mallalieu and Cotherstone believed themselves safe from discovery—their joint secret appeared to be well buried with the old detective. But the secret was keenly and vividly alive in their own hearts, and when Mallalieu faced the truth he knew that he suspected Cotherstone, and when Cotherstone put things squarely to himself he knew that he suspected Mallalieu. And the two men got to eyeing each other furtively, and to addressing each other curtly, and when they happened to be alone there was a heavy atmosphere of mutual dislike and suspicion between them.

It was a strange psychological fact that though these men had been partners for a period covering the most important part of their lives, they had next to nothing in common. They were excellent partners in business matters; Mallalieu knew Cotherstone, and Cotherstone knew Mallalieu in all things relating to the making of money. But in taste, temperament, character, understanding, they were as far apart as the poles. This aloofness when tested further by the recent discomposing events manifested itself in a disinclination to confidence. Mallalieu, whatever he thought, knew very well that he would never say what he thought to Cotherstone; Cotherstone knew precisely the same thing with regard to Mallalieu. But this silence bred irritation, and as the days went by the irritation became more than Cotherstone could bear. He was a highly-strung, nervous man, quick to feel and to appreciate, and the averted looks and monosyllabic remarks and replies of a man into whose company he could not avoid being thrown began to sting him to something like madness. And one day, left alone in the office with Mallalieu when Stoner the clerk had gone to get his dinner, the irritation became unbearable, and he turned on his partner in a sudden white heat of ungovernable and impotent anger.

"Hang you!" he hissed between his set teeth. "I believe you think I did that job! And if you do, blast you, why don't you say so, and be done with it?"

Mallalieu, who was standing on the hearth, warming his broad back at the fire, thrust his hands deeply into his pockets and looked half-sneeringly at his partner out of his screwed-up eyes.

"I should advise you to keep yourself cool," he said with affected quietness. "There's more than me'll think a good deal if you chance to let yourself out like that."

"You do think it!" reiterated Cotherstone passionately. "Damn it, d'ye think I haven't noticed it? Always looking at me as if—as if——"

"Now then, keep yourself calm," interrupted Mallalieu. "I can look at you or at any other, in any way I like, can't I? There's no need to distress yourself—I shan't give aught away. If you took it in your head to settle matters—as they were settled—well, I shan't say a word. That is unless—you understand?"

"Understand what?" screamed Cotherstone.

"Unless I'm obliged to," answered Mallalieu. "I should have to make it clear that I'd naught to do with that particular matter, d'ye see? Every man for himself's a sound principle. But—I see no need. I don't believe there'll be any need. And it doesn't matter the value of that pen that's shaking so in your hand to me if an innocent man suffers—if he's innocent o' that, he's guilty o' something else. You're safe with me."

Cotherstone flung the pen on the floor and stamped on it. And Mallalieu laughed cynically and walked slowly across to the door.

"You're a fool, Cotherstone," he said. "Go on a bit more like that, and you'll let it all out to somebody 'at 'll not keep secrets as I can. Cool yourself, man, cool yourself!"

"Hang you!" shouted Cotherstone. "Mind I don't let something out about you! Where were you that night, I should like to know? Or, rather, I do know! You're no safer than I am! And if I told what I do know——"

Mallalieu, with his hand on the latch, turned and looked his partner in the face—without furtiveness, for once.

"And if you told aught that you do, or fancy you know," he said quietly, "there'd be ruin in your home, you soft fool! I thought you wanted things kept quiet for your lass's sake? Pshaw!—you're taking leave o' your senses!"

He walked out at that, and Cotherstone, shaking with anger, relapsed into a chair and cursed his fate. And after a time he recovered himself and began to think, and his thoughts turned instinctively to Lettie.

Mallalieu was right—of course, he was right! Anything that he, Cotherstone, could say or do in the way of bringing up the things that must be suppressed would ruin Lettie's chances. So, at any rate, it seemed to him. For Cotherstone's mind was essentially a worldly one, and it was beyond him to believe that an ambitious young man like Windle Bent would care to ally himself with the daughter of an ex-convict. Bent would have the best of excuses for breaking off all relations with the Cotherstone family if the unpleasant truth came out. No!—whatever else he did, he must keep his secret safe until Bent and Lettie were safely married. That once accomplished, Cotherstone cared little about the future: Bent could not go back on his wife. And so Cotherstone endeavoured to calm himself, so that he could scheme and plot, and before night came he paid a visit to his doctor, and when he went home that evening, he had his plans laid.

Bent was with Lettie when Cotherstone got home, and Cotherstone presently got the two of them into a little snuggery which he kept sacred to himself as a rule. He sat down in his easy chair, and signed to them to sit near him.

"I'm glad I found you together," he said. "There's something I want to say. There's no call for you to be frightened, Lettie—but what I've got to say is serious. And I'll put it straight—Bent'll understand. Now, you'd arranged to get married next spring—six months hence. I want you to change your minds, and to let it be as soon as you can."

He looked with a certain eager wistfulness at Lettie, expecting to see her start with surprise. But fond as he was of her, Cotherstone had so far failed to grasp the later developments of his daughter's character. Lettie Cotherstone was not the sort of young woman who allows herself to be surprised by anything. She was remarkably level-headed, cool of thought, well able to take care of herself in every way, and fully alive to the possibilities of her union with the rising young manufacturer. And instead of showing any astonishment, she quietly asked her father what he meant.

"I'll tell you," answered Cotherstone, greatly relieved to find that both seemed inclined to talk matters quietly over. "It's this—I've not been feeling as well as I ought to feel, lately. The fact is, Bent, I've done too much in my time. A man can work too hard, you know—and it tells on him in the end. So the doctor says, anyhow."

"The doctor!" exclaimed Lettie. "You haven't been to him?"

"Seen him this afternoon," replied Cotherstone. "Don't alarm yourself. But that's what he says—naught wrong, all sound, but—it's time I rested. Rest and change—complete change. And I've made up my mind—I'm going to retire from business. Why not? I'm a well-to-do man—better off than most folks 'ud think. I shall tell Mallalieu tomorrow. Yes—I'm resolved on it. And that done, I shall go and travel for a year or two—I've always wanted to go round the world. I'll go—that for a start, anyway. And the sooner the better, says the doctor. And——" here he looked searchingly at his listeners—"I'd like to see you settled before I go. What?"

Lettie's calm and judicial character came out in the first words she spoke. She had listened carefully to Cotherstone; now she turned to Bent.

"Windle," she said, as quietly as if she were asking the most casual of questions, "wouldn't it upset all your arrangements for next year? You see, father," she went on, turning to Cotherstone, "Windle had arranged everything. He was going to have the whole of the spring and summer away from business; we were going on the Continent for six months. And that would have to be entirely altered and——"

"We could alter it," interrupted Bent. He was watching Cotherstone closely, and fancying that he saw a strained and eager look in his face, he decided that

Cotherstone was keeping something back, and had not told them the full truth about his health.

"It's all a matter of arrangement. I could arrange to go away during the winter, Lettie."

"But I don't want to travel in winter," objected Lettie. "Besides—I've made all my arrangements about my gowns and things."

"That can be arranged, too," said Bent. "The dressmaker can work overtime."

"That'll mean that everything will be hurried—and spoiled," replied Lettie. "Besides, I've arranged everything with my bridesmaids. They can't be expected to——"

"We can do without bridesmaids," replied Bent, laying his hand on Lettie's arm. "If your father really feels that he's got to have the rest and the change he spoke of, and wants us to be married first, why, then——"

"But there's nothing to prevent you having a rest and a change now, father," said Lettie. "Why not? I don't like my arrangements to be altered—I had planned everything out so carefully. When we did fix on next spring, Windle, I had only just time as it was!"

"Pooh!" said Bent. "We could get married the day after tomorrow if we wanted! Bridesmaids—gowns—all that sort of tomfoolery, what does it matter?"

"It isn't tomfoolery," retorted Lettie. "If I am to be married I should like to be married properly."

She got up, with a heightened colour and a little toss of her head, and left the room, and the two men looked at each other.

"Talk to her, my lad," said Cotherstone at last. "Of course, girls think such a lot of—of all the accompaniments, eh?"

"Yes, yes—it'll be all right," replied Bent. He tapped Cotherstone's arm and gave him a searching look. "You're not keeping anything back—about your health, are you?" he asked.

Cotherstone glanced at the door and sank his voice to a whisper.

"It's my heart!" he answered. "Over-strained—much over-strained, the doctor says. Rest and change—imperative! But—not a word to Lettie, Bent. Talk her round—get it arranged. I shall feel safer—you understand?"

Bent was full of good nature, and though he understood to the full—it was a natural thing, this anxiety of a father for his only child. He promised to talk seriously to Lettie at once about an early wedding. And that night he told Brereton of what had happened, and asked him if he knew how special licences can be got, and Brereton informed him of all he knew on that point—and kept silence about one which to him was becoming deeply and seriously important.

13. THE ANONYMOUS LETTER

Within a week of that night Brereton was able to sum things up, to take stock, to put clearly before himself the position of affairs as they related to his mysterious client. They had by that time come to a clear issue: a straight course lay ahead with its ultimate stages veiled in obscurity. Harborough had again been brought up before the Highmarket magistrates, had stubbornly refused to give any definite information about his exact doings on the night of Kitely's murder, and had been duly committed for trial on the capital charge. On the same day the coroner, after holding an inquest extending over two sittings, had similarly committed him. There was now nothing to do but to wait until the case came on at Norcaster Assizes. Fortunately, the assizes were fixed for the middle of the ensuing month: Brereton accordingly had three weeks wherein to prepare his defence—or (which would be an eminently satisfactory equivalent) to definitely fix the guilt on some other person.

Christopher Pett, as legal adviser to the murdered man, had felt it his duty to remain in Highmarket until the police proceedings and the coroner's inquest were over. He had made himself conspicuous at both police-court and coroner's court, putting himself forward wherever he could, asking questions wherever opportunity offered. Brereton's dislike of him increased the more he saw of him; he specially resented Pett's familiarity. But Pett was one of those persons who know how to combine familiarity with politeness and even servility; to watch or hear him talk to any one whom he button-holed was to gain a notion of his veneration for them. He might have been worshipping Brereton when he buttoned-holed the young barrister after Harborough had been finally committed to take his trial.

"Ah, he's a lucky man, that, Mr. Brereton!" observed Pett, collaring Brereton in a corridor outside the crowded court. "Very fortunate man indeed, sir, to have you take so much interest in him. Fancy you—with all your opportunities in town, Mr. Brereton!—stopping down here, just to defend that fellow out of—what shall we call it?—pure and simple Quixotism! Quixotism!—I believe that's the correct term, Mr. Brereton. Oh, yes—for the man's as good as done for. Not a cat's chance! He'll swing, sir, will your client!"

"Your simile is not a good one, Mr. Pett," retorted Brereton. "Cats are said to have nine lives."

"Cat, rat, mouse, dog—no chance whatever, sir," said Pett, cheerfully. "I know what a country jury'll say. If I were a betting man, Mr. Brereton—which I ain't, being a regular church attendant—I'd lay you ten to one the jury'll never leave the box, sir!"

"No—I don't think they will—when the right man is put in the dock, Mr. Pett," replied Brereton.

Pett drew back and looked the young barrister in the face with an expression that was half quizzical and half serious.

"You don't mean to say that you really believe this fellow to be innocent, Mr. Brereton?" he exclaimed. "You!—with your knowledge of criminal proceedings! Oh, come now, Mr. Brereton—it's very kind of you, very Quixotic, as I call it, but——"

"You shall see," said Brereton and turned off. He had no mind to be more than civil to Pett, and he frowned when Pett, in his eagerness, laid a detaining hand on his gown. "I'm not going to discuss it, Mr. Pett," he added, a little warmly. "I've my own view of the case."

"But, but, Mr. Brereton—a moment!" urged Pett. "Just between ourselves as—well, not as lawyers but as—as one gentleman to another. *Do* you think it possible it was some other person? Do you now, really?"

"Didn't your estimable female relative, as you call her, say that I suggested she might be the guilty person?" demanded Brereton, maliciously. "Come, now, Mr. Pett! You don't know all that I know!"

Pett fell back, staring doubtfully at Brereton's curled lip, and wondering whether to take him seriously or not. And Brereton laughed and went off—to reflect, five minutes later, that this was no laughing matter for Harborough and his daughter, and to plunge again into the maze of thought out of which it was so difficult to drag anything that seemed likely to be helpful.

He interviewed Harborough again before he was taken back to Norcaster, and again he pressed him to speak, and again Harborough gave him a point-blank refusal.

"Not unless it comes to the very worst, sir," he said firmly, "and only then if I see there's no other way—and even then it would only be for my daughter's sake. But it won't come to that! There's three weeks yet—good—and if somebody can't find out the truth in three weeks——"

"Man alive!" exclaimed Brereton. "Your own common-sense ought to tell you that in cases like this three years isn't enough to get at the truth! What can I do in three weeks?"

"There's not only you, sir," replied Harborough. "There's the police—there's the detectives—there's——"

"The police and the detectives are all doing their best to fasten the crime on you!" retorted Brereton. "Of course they are! That's their way. When they've safely got one man, do you think they're going to look for another? If you won't tell me what you were doing, and where you were that night, well, I'll have to find out for myself."

Harborough gave his counsel a peculiar look which Brereton could not understand.

"Oh, well!" he said. "If *you* found it out——"

He broke off at that, and would say no more, and Brereton presently left him and walked thoughtfully homeward, reflecting on the prisoner's last words.

"He admits there is something to be found out," he mused. "And by that very admission he implies that it could be found out. Now—how? Egad!—I'd give something for even the least notion!"

Bent's parlour-maid, opening the door to Brereton, turned to a locked drawer in the old-fashioned clothes-press which stood in Bent's hall, and took from it a registered letter.

"For you, sir," she said, handing it to Brereton. "Came by the noon post, sir. The housekeeper signed for it."

Brereton took the letter into the smoking-room and looked at it with a sudden surmise that it might have something to do with the matter which was uppermost in his thoughts. He had had no expectation of any registered letter, no idea of anything that could cause any correspondent of his to send him any communication by registered post. There was no possibility of recognizing the handwriting of the sender, for there was no handwriting to recognize: the address was typewritten. And the postmark was London.

Brereton carefully cut open the flap of the envelope and drew out the enclosure—a square sheet of typewriting paper folded about a thin wad of Bank of England notes. He detached these at once and glanced quickly at them. There were six of them: all new and crisp—and each was for a hundred and fifty pounds.

Brereton laid this money aside and opened the letter. This, too, was typewritten: a mere glance at its termination showed that it was anonymous. He sat down at Bent's desk and carefully read it through.

There was no address: there was nothing beyond the postmark on the envelope to show where the letter came from; there was absolutely nothing in the contents to give any clue to the sender. But the wording was clear and plain.

"MR. GIFFORD BRERETON,—Having learnt from the newspapers that you are acting as counsel for John Harborough, charged with the murder of a man named

Kitely at Highmarket, I send you the enclosed £900 to be used in furthering Harborough's defence. You will use it precisely as you think fit. You are not to spare it nor any endeavour to prove Harborough's innocence—which is known to the sender. Whenever further funds are needed, all you need do is to insert an advertisement in the personal column of *The Times* newspaper in these words: *Highmarket Exchequer needs replenishing*, with your initials added. Allow me to suggest that you should at once offer a reward of £500 to whoever gives information which will lead to the capture and conviction of the real murderer or murderers. If this offer fails to bring information speedily, double it. I repeat that no pains must be spared in this matter, and that money to any amount is no object. The sender of this letter will keep well informed of the progress of events as narrated in the newspapers, to which you will please to afford all proper information."

Brereton read this extraordinary communication through three times; then he replaced letter and bank-notes in the envelope, put the envelope in an inner pocket, left the house, and walking across to the Northrop villa, asked to see Avice Harborough.

Avice came to him in Mrs. Northrop's drawing-room, and Brereton glancing keenly at her as she entered saw that she was looking worn and pale. He put the letter into her hands with a mere word.

"Your father has a powerful friend—somewhere," he said.

To his astonishment the girl showed no very great surprise. She started a little at the sight of the money; she flushed at one or two expressions in the letter. But she read the letter through without comment and handed it beck to him with a look of inquiry.

"You don't seem surprised!" said Brereton.

"There has always been so much mystery to me about my father that I'm not surprised," she replied. "No!—I'm just thankful! For this man—whoever he is—says that my father's innocence is known to him. And that's—just think what it means—to me!"

"Why doesn't he come forward and prove it, then?" demanded Brereton.

Avice shook her head.

"He—they—want it to be proved without that," she answered. "But—don't you think that if all else fails the man who wrote this would come forward? Oh, surely!"

Brereton stood silently looking at her for a full minute. From the first time of meeting with her he had felt strangely and strongly attracted to his client's daughter, and as he looked at her now he began to realize that he was perhaps more deeply interested in her than he knew.

"It's all the most extraordinary mystery—this about your father—that ever I came across!" he exclaimed suddenly. Then he looked still more closely at her. "You've been worrying!" he said impetuously. "Don't! I beg you not to. I'll move heaven and earth—because I, personally, am absolutely convinced of your father's innocence. And—here's powerful help."

"You'll do what's suggested here?" she asked.

"Certainly! It's a capital idea," he answered. "I'd have done it myself if I'd been a rich man—but I'm not. Cheer up, now!—we're getting on splendidly. Look here—ask Mrs. Northrop to let you come out with me. We'll go to the solicitor—together—and see about that reward at once."

As they presently walked down to the town Brereton gave Avice another of his critical looks of inspection.

"You're feeling better," he said in his somewhat brusque fashion. "Is it this bit of good news?"

"That—and the sense of doing something," she answered. "If I wasn't looking well when you came in just now, it was because this inaction is bad for me. I want to do something!—something to help. If I could only be stirring—moving about. You understand?"

"Quite!" responded Brereton. "And there is something you can do. I saw you on a bicycle the other day. Why not give up your teaching for a while, and scour the country round about, trying to get hold of some news about your father's movements that night? That he won't tell us anything himself is no reason why we shouldn't find out something for ourselves. He must have been somewhere—someone must have seen him! Why not begin some investigation?—you know the district. How does that strike you?"

"I should be only too thankful," she said. "And I'll do it. The Northrops are very kind—they'll understand, and they'll let me off. I'll begin at once—tomorrow. I'll hunt every village between the sea and the hills!"

"Good!" said Brereton. "Some work of that sort, and this reward—ah, we shall come out all right, you'll see."

"I don't know what we should have done if it hadn't been for you!" said Avice. "But—we shan't forget. My father is a strange man, Mr. Brereton, but he's not the sort of man he's believed to be by these Highmarket people—and he's grateful to you—as you'll see."

"But I must do something to merit his gratitude first, you know," replied Brereton. "Come!—I've done next to nothing as yet. But we'll make a fresh start with this reward—if your father's solicitor approves."

The solicitor did approve—strongly. And he opened his eyes to their widest extent when he read the anonymous letter and saw the bank-notes.

"Your father," he observed to Avice, "is the most mysterious man I ever heard of! The Kitely mystery, in my opinion, is nothing to the Harborough mystery. Do you really mean to tell me that you haven't an idea of what all this means?"

"Not an idea!" replied Avice. "Not the ghost of one."

"Well—we'll get these posters and handbills out, anyway, Mr. Brereton," said the solicitor. "Five hundred pounds is a good figure. Lord bless you!—some of these Highmarket folk would sell their mothers for half that! The whole population will be turned into amateur detectives. Now let's draft the exact wording, and then we'll see the printer."

Next day the bill-poster placarded Highmarket with the reward bills, and distributed them broadcast in shops and offices, and one of the first persons to lay hands on one was Mallalieu & Cotherstone's clerk, Herbert Stoner.

14. THE SHEET OF FIGURES

At that time Stoner had been in the employment of Mallalieu and Cotherstone for some five or six years. He was then twenty-seven years of age. He was a young man of some ability—sharp, alert, quick at figures, good at correspondence, punctual, willing: he could run the business in the absence of its owners. The two partners appreciated Stoner, and they had gradually increased his salary until it reached the sum of two pounds twelve shillings and sixpence per week. In their opinion a young single man ought to have done very well on that: Mallalieu and Cotherstone had both done very well on less when they were clerks in that long vanished past of which they did not care to think. But Stoner was a young man of tastes. He liked to dress well. He liked to play cards and billiards. He liked to take a drink or two at the Highmarket taverns of an evening, and to be able to give his favourite barmaids boxes of chocolate or pairs of gloves now and then—judiciously. And he found his salary not at all too great, and he was always on the look-out for a chance of increasing it.

Stoner emerged from Mallalieu & Cotherstone's office at his usual hour of half-past five on the afternoon of the day on which the reward bills were put out. It was his practice to drop in at the Grey Mare Inn every evening on his way to his supper, there to drink a half-pint of bitter ale and hear the news of the day from various cronies who were to be met with in the bar-parlour. As he crossed the street on this errand on this particular evening, Postick, the local bill-poster, came hurrying out of the printer's shop with a bundle of handbills under his arm, and as he sped past Stoner, thrust a couple of them into the clerk's hand.

"Here y'are, Mr. Stoner!" he said without stopping. "Something for you to set your wits to work on. Five hundred reward—for a bit o' brain work!"

Stoner, who thought Postick was chaffing him, was about to throw the handbills, still damp from the press, into the gutter which he was stepping over. But in the light of an adjacent lamp he caught sight of the word *Murder* in big staring capitals at the top of them. Beneath it he caught further sight of familiar names—and at that he folded up the bills, went into the Grey Mare, sat down in a quiet corner, and read carefully through the announcement. It was a very simple one, and plainly worded. Five hundred pounds would be paid by Mr. Tallington, solicitor, of Highmarket, to any person or persons who would afford information which would lead to the arrest and conviction of the murderer or murderers of the deceased Kitely.

No one was in the bar-parlour of the Grey Mare when Stoner first entered it, but by the time he had re-read the handbill, two or three men of the town had come in, and he saw that each carried a copy. One of them, a small tradesman whose shop was in the centre of the Market Square, leaned against the bar and read the terms of the reward aloud.

"And whose money might that be?" he asked, half-sneeringly. "Who's throwing brass round in that free-handed fashion? I should want to know if the money's safe before I wasted my time in trying to get it."

"Money'll be all right," observed one of the speaker's companions. "There's Lawyer Tallington's name at the foot o' that bill. He wouldn't put his name to no offer o' that sort if he hadn't the brass in hand."

"Whose money is it, then?" demanded the first speaker. "It's not a Government reward. They say that Kitely had no relatives, so it can't be them. And it can't be that old housekeeper of his, because they say she's satisfied enough that Jack Harborough's the man, and they've got him. Queer do altogether, I call it!"

"It's done in Harborough's interest," said a third man. "Either that, or there's something very deep in it. Somebody's not satisfied and somebody's going to have a flutter with his brass over it." He turned and glanced at Stoner, who had come to the bar for his customary half-pint of ale. "Your folks aught to do with this?" he asked. "Kitely was Mr. Cotherstone's tenant, of course."

Stoner laughed scornfully as he picked up his tankard.

"Yes, I don't think!" he sneered. "Catch either of my governors wasting five hundred pence, or five pence, in that way! Not likely!"

"Well, there's Tallington's name to back it," said one of the men. "We all know Tallington. What he says, he does. The money'll be there—if it's earned."

Then they all looked at each other silently, surmise and speculation in the eyes of each.

"Tell you what!" suddenly observed the little tradesman, as if struck with a clever idea. "It might be young Bent! Five hundred pound is naught to him. This here young London barrister that's defending Harborough is stopping with Bent—they're old schoolmates. Happen he's persuaded Bent to do the handsome: they say that this barrister chap's right down convinced that Harborough's innocent. It must be Bent's brass!"

"What's Popsie say?" asked one of the younger members of the party, winking at the barmaid, who, having supplied her customers' needs, was leaning over a copy of the handbill which somebody had laid on the bar. "Whose brass can it be, Popsie?"

The barmaid stood up, seized a glass and a cloth, and began to polish the glass with vigor.

"What's Popsie say?" she repeated. "Why, what she says is that you're a lot of donkeys for wasting your time in wondering whose brass it is. What does it matter whose brass it is, so long as it's safe? What you want to do is to try and earn it. You don't pick up five hundred pounds every day!"

"She's right!" said some man of the group. "But—how does anybody start on to them games?"

"There'll be plenty o' starters, for all that, my lads!" observed the little tradesman. "Never you fear! There'll be candidates."

Stoner drank off his ale and went away. Usually, being given to gossip, he stopped chatting with anybody he chanced to meet until it was close upon his supper-time. But the last remark sent him off. For Stoner meant to be a starter, and he had no desire that anybody should get away in front of him.

The lodging in which Stoner kept his bachelor state was a quiet and eminently respectable one. He had two small rooms, a parlour and a bedchamber, in the house of a widow with whom he had lodged ever since his first coming to Highmarket, nearly six years before. In the tiny parlour he kept a few books and a writing-desk, and on those evenings which he did not spend in playing cards or billiards, he did a little intellectual work in the way of improving his knowledge of French, commercial arithmetic, and business correspondence. And that night, his supper being eaten, and the door closed upon his landlady, he lighted his pipe, sat down to his desk, unlocked one of its drawers, and from an old file-box drew out some papers. One of these, a half-sheet of ruled foolscap, he laid in front of him, the rest he put back. And then, propping his chin on his folded hands, Stoner gave that half-sheet a long, speculative inspection.

If anybody had looked over Stoner's shoulder they would have seen him gazing at a mass of figures. The half-sheet of foolscap was covered with figures: the figuring extended to the reverse side. And—what a looker-on might not have known, but what Stoner knew very well—the figures were all of Cotherstone's making— clear, plain, well-formed figures. And amongst them, and on the margins of the half-sheet, and scrawled here and there, as if purposelessly and carelessly, was one word in Cotherstone's handwriting, repeated over and over again. That word was—*Wilchester.*

Stoner knew how that half-sheet of foolscap had come into his possession. It was a half-sheet which he had found on Cotherstone's desk when he went into the partners' private room to tidy things up on the morning after the murder of Kitely. It lay there, carelessly tossed aside amongst other papers of clearer meaning, and Stoner, after one glance at it, had carefully folded it, placed it in his pocket, taken it home, and locked it up, to be inspected at leisure.

He had had his reasons, of course, for this abstraction of a paper which rightfully belonged to Cotherstone. Those reasons were a little difficult to explain to himself in one way; easy enough to explain, in another. As regards the difficulty, Stoner had somehow or other got a vague idea, that evening of the murder, that something was wrong with Cotherstone. He had noticed, or thought he noticed, a queer look on old Kitely's face when the ex-detective left the private room—it was a look of quiet satisfaction, or triumph, or malice; any way, said Stoner, it was something. Then there was the fact of Cotherstone's curious abstraction when he, Stoner, entered and found his employer sitting in the darkness, long after Kitely had gone—Cotherstone had said he was asleep, but Stoner knew that to be a fib. Altogether, Stoner had gained a vague feeling, a curious intuition, that there was something queer, not unconnected with the visit of Cotherstone's new tenant, and when he heard, next morning, of what had befallen Kitely, all his suspicions were renewed.

So much for the difficult reasons which had made him appropriate the half-sheet of foolscap. But there was a reason which was not difficult. It lay in the presence of that word *Wilchester.* If not of the finest degree of intellect, Stoner was far from being a fool, and it had not taken him very long to explain to himself why

Cotherstone had scribbled the name of that far-off south-country town all over that sheet of paper, aimlessly, apparently without reason, amidst his figurings. *It was uppermost in his thoughts at the time*—and as he sat there, pen in hand, he had written it down, half-unconsciously, over and over again.... There it was—*Wilchester*—Wilchester—Wilchester.

The reiteration had a peculiar interest for Stoner. He had never heard Cotherstone nor Mallalieu mention Wilchester at any time since his first coming into their office. The firm had no dealings with any firm at Wilchester. Stoner, who dealt with all the Mallalieu & Cotherstone correspondence, knew that during his five and a half years' clerkship, he had never addressed a single letter to any one at Wilchester, never received a single letter bearing the Wilchester post-mark. Wilchester was four hundred miles away, far off in the south; ninety-nine out of every hundred persons in Highmarket had never heard the name of Wilchester. But Stoner had—quite apart from the history books, and the geography books, and map of England. Stoner himself was a Darlington man. He had a close friend, a bosom friend, at Darlington, named Myler—David Myler. Now David Myler was a commercial traveller—a smart fellow of Stoner's age. He was in the service of a Darlington firm of agricultural implement makers, and his particular round lay in the market-towns of the south and south-west of England. He spent a considerable part of the year in those districts, and Wilchester was one of his principal headquarters: Stoner had many a dozen letters of Myler's, which Myler had written to him from Wilchester. And only a year before all this, Myler had brought home a bride in the person of a Wilchester girl, the daughter of a Wilchester tradesman.

So the name of Wilchester was familiar enough to Stoner. And now he wanted to know what—what—what made it so familiar to Cotherstone that Cotherstone absent-mindedly scribbled it all over a half-sheet of foolscap paper?

But the figures? Had they any connexion with the word? This was the question which Stoner put to himself when he sat down that night in his parlour to seriously consider if he had any chance of winning that five hundred pounds reward. He looked at the figures again— more carefully. The truth was that until that evening he had never given much attention to those figures: it was the word Wilchester that had fascinated him. But now, summoning all his by no means small arithmetical knowledge to his aid, Stoner concentrated himself on an effort to discover what those figures meant. That they were a calculation of some sort he had always known— now he wanted to know of what.

The solution of the problem came to him all of a sudden—as the solution of arithmetical problems often does come. He saw the whole thing quite plainly and wondered that he had not seen it at a first glance. The figures represented nothing whatever but three plain and common sums—in compound arithmetic. Cotherstone, for some reason of his own, had taken the sum of two thousand pounds as a foundation, and had calculated (1st) what thirty years' interest on that sum at three and a half per cent. would come to; and (2nd) what thirty years' interest at five per cent. would come to; and (3rd) what the compound interest on two thousand pounds would come to—capital and compound interest—in the same period. The last reckoning—the compound interest one—had been crossed over and out with vigorous dashes of the pen, as if the calculator had been appalled on discovering what an original sum of two thousand pounds, left at compound interest for thirty years, would be transformed into in that time.

All this was so much Greek to Stoner. But he knew there was something in it—something behind those figures. They might refer to some Corporation financial business—Cotherstone being Borough Treasurer. But—

they might not. And why were they mixed up with Wilchester?

For once in a way, Stoner took no walk abroad that night. Usually, even when he stopped in of an evening, he had a brief stroll to the Grey Mare and back last thing before going to bed. But on this occasion he forgot all about the Grey Mare, and Popsie the barmaid did not come into his mind for even a second. He sat at home, his feet on the fender, his eyes fixed on the dying coals in the grate. He thought—thought so hard that he forgot that his pipe had gone out. The fire had gone out, too, when he finally rose and retired. And he went on thinking for a long time after his head had sought his pillow.

"Well, it's Saturday tomorrow, anyway!" he mused at last. "Which is lucky."

Next day—being Saturday and half-holiday—Stoner attired himself in his best garments, and, in the middle of the afternoon, took train for Darlington.

15. ONE THING LEADS TO ANOTHER

Although Stoner hailed from Darlington, he had no folk of his own left there—they were all dead and gone. Accordingly he put himself up at a cheap hotel, and when he had taken what its proprietors called a meat tea, he strolled out and made for that part of the town in which his friend Myler had set up housekeeping in a small establishment wherein there was just room for a couple of people to turn round. Its accommodation, indeed, was severely taxed just then, for Myler's father and mother-in-law had come to visit him and their daughter, and when Stoner walked in on the scene and added a fifth the tiny parlour was filled to its full extent.

"Who'd ha' thought of seeing you, Stoner!" exclaimed Myler joyously, when he had welcomed his old chum, and had introduced him to the family circle. "And what brings you here, anyway? Business?"

"Just a bit of business," answered Stoner. "Nothing much, though—only a call to make, later on. I'm stopping the night, though."

"Wish we could ha' put you up here, old sport!" said Myler, ruefully. "But we don't live in a castle, yet. All full here!—unless you'd like a shakedown on the kitchen table, or in the wood-shed. Or you can try the bath, if you like."

Amidst the laughter which succeeded this pleasantry, Stoner said that he wouldn't trouble the domestic peace so far—he'd already booked his room. And while Myler—who, commercial-traveller like, cultivated a reputation for wit—indulged in further jokes, Stoner stealthily inspected the father-in-law. What a fortunate coincidence! he said to himself; what a lucky stroke! There he was, wanting badly to find out something about

Wilchester—and here, elbow to elbow with him, was a Wilchester man! And an elderly Wilchester man, too—one who doubtless remembered all about Wilchester for many a long year. That was another piece of luck, for Stoner was quite certain that if Cotherstone had ever had any connexion with Wilchester it must have been a long, long time ago: he knew, from information acquired, that Cotherstone had been a fixture in Highmarket for thirty years.

He glanced at Myler's father-in-law again as Myler, remarking that when old friends meet, the flowing bowl must flow, produced a bottle of whisky from a brand-new chiffonier, and entreated his bride to fetch what he poetically described as the crystal goblets and the sparkling stream. The father-in-law was a little apple-faced old gentleman with bright eyes and a ready smile, who evidently considered his son-in-law a born wit, and was ready to laugh at all his sallies. A man of good memory, that, decided Stoner, and wondered how he could diplomaticaly lead Mr. Pursey to talk about the town he came from. But Mr. Pursey was shortly to talk about Wilchester to some purpose—and with no drawing-out from Stoner or anybody.

"Well," remarked Myler, having supplied his guests with spirituous refreshment, and taken a pull at his own glass. "I'm glad to see you, Stoner, and so's the missis, and here's hoping you'll come again as often as the frog went to the water. You've been having high old times in that back-of-beyond town of yours, haven't you? Battles, murders, sudden deaths!—who'd ha' thought a slow old hill-country town like Highmarket could have produced so much excitement! What's happened to that chap they collared?—I haven't had time to look at the papers this last day or two—been too busy."

"Committed for trial," answered Stoner. "He'll come up at Norcaster Assizes next month."

"Do they think he did it?" asked Myler. "Is it a sure thing?"

Before Stoner could reply Mr. Pursey entered the arena. His face displayed the pleased expression of the man who has special information.

"It's an odd thing, now, David," he said in a high, piping voice, "a very odd thing, that this should happen when I come up into these parts—almost as foreign to me as the Fiji Islands might be. Yes, sir," he went on, turning to Stoner, "it's very odd! I knew that man Kitely."

Stoner could have jumped from his seat, but he restrained himself, and contrived to show no more than a polite interest.

"Oh, indeed, sir?" he said. "The poor man that was murdered? You knew him?"

"I remember him very well indeed," assented Mr. Pursey. "Yes, although I only met him once, I've a very complete recollection of the man. I spent a very pleasant evening with him and one or two more of his profession— better sort of police and detectives, you know—at a friend's of mine, who was one of our Wilchester police officials—oh, it's—yes—it must be thirty years since. They'd come from London, of course, on some criminal business. Deary me!—the tales them fellows could tell!"

"Thirty years is a long time, sir," observed Stoner politely.

"Aye, but I remember it quite well," said Mr. Pursey, with a confident nod. "I know it was thirty years ago, 'cause it was the Wilchester Assizes at which the Mallows & Chidforth case was tried. Yes—thirty years. Eighteen hundred and eighty-one was the year. Mallows & Chidforth—aye!"

"Famous case that, sir?" asked Stoner. He was almost bursting with excitement by that time, and he took a big gulp of whisky and water to calm himself. "Something special, sir? Murder, eh?"

"No—fraud, embezzlement, defalcation—I forget what the proper legal term 'ud be," replied Mr. Pursey. "But it was a bad case—a real bad 'un. We'd a working men's building society in Wilchester in those days—it's there now for that matter, but under another name—and there were two better-class young workmen, smart fellows, that acted one as secretary and t'other as treasurer to it. They'd full control, those two had, and they were trusted, aye, as if they'd been the Bank of England! And all of a sudden, something came out, and it was found that these two, Mallows, treasurer, Chidforth, secretary, had made away with two thousand pounds of the society's money. Two thousand pounds!"

"Two thousand pounds?" exclaimed Stoner, whose thoughts went like lightning to the half-sheet of foolscap. "You don't say!"

"Yes—well, it might ha' been a pound or two more or less," said the old man, "but two thousand was what they called it. And of course Mallows and Chidforth were prosecuted—and they got two years. Oh, yes, we remember that case very well indeed in Wilchester, don't we, Maria?"

"And good reason!" agreed Mrs. Pursey warmly. "There were a lot of poor people nearly ruined by them bad young men."

"There were!" affirmed Mr. Pursey. "Yes—oh, yes! Aye—I've often wondered what became of 'em—Mallows and Chidforth, I mean. For from the time they got out of prison they've never been heard of in our parts. Not a word!—they disappeared completely. Some say, of course, that they had that money safely planted, and went to it. I don't know. But—off they went."

"Pooh!" said Myler. "That's an easy one. Went off to some colony or other, of course. Common occurrence, father-in-law. Bert, old sport, what say if we rise on our pins and have a hundred at billiards at the Stag and Hunter—good table there."

Stoner followed his friend out of the little house, and once outside took him by the arm.

"Confound the billards, Dave, old man!" he said, almost trembling with suppressed excitement. "Look here!—d'you know a real quiet corner in the Stag where

we can have an hour's serious consultation. You do?—
then come on, and I'll tell you the most wonderful story
you ever heard since your ears were opened!"

Myler, immediately impressed, led the way into a
small and vacant parlour in the rear of a neighbouring
hostelry, ordered refreshments, bade the girl who brought
them to leave him and his friend alone, and took the
liberty of locking the door on their privacy. And that done
he showed himself such a perfect listener that he never
opened his lips until Stoner had set forth everything
before him in detail. Now and then he nodded, now and
then his sharp eyes dilated, now and then he clapped his
hands. And in the end he smote Stoner on the shoulder.

"Stoner, old sport!" he exclaimed. "It's a sure thing!
Gad, I never heard a clearer. That five hundred is
yours—aye, as dead certain as that my nose is mine!
It's—it's—what they call inductive reasoning. The initials
M. and C.—Mallows and Chidforth—Mallalieu and
Cotherstone—the two thousand pounds—the fact that
Kitely was at Wilchester Assizes in 1881—that he became
Cotherstone's tenant thirty years after—oh, I see it all,
and so will a judge and jury! Stoner, one, or both of 'em
killed that old chap to silence him!"

"That's my notion," assented Stoner, who was highly
pleased with himself, and by that time convinced that his
own powers, rather than a combination of lucky
circumstances, had brought the desired result about. "Of
course, I've worked it out to that. And the thing now is—
what's the best line to take? What would you suggest,
Dave?"

Myler brought all his business acumen to bear on the
problem presented to him.

"What sort of chap is this Tallington?" he asked at
last, pointing to the name at the foot of the reward
handbill.

"Most respectable solicitor in Highmarket," answered
Stoner, promptly.

"Word good?" asked Myler.

"Good as—gold," affirmed Stoner.

"Then if it was me," said Myler, "I should make a summary of what I knew, on paper—carefully—and I should get a private interview with this Tallington and tell him—all. Man!—you're safe of that five hundred! For there's no doubt, Stoner, on the evidence, no doubt whatever!"

Stoner sat silently reflecting things for a while. Then he gave his friend a sly, somewhat nervous look. Although he and Myler had been bosom friends since they were breeched, Stoner was not quite certain as to what Myler would say to what he, Stoner, was just then thinking of.

"Look here," he said suddenly. "There's this about it. It's all jolly well, but a fellow's got to think for himself, Dave, old man. Now it doesn't matter a twopenny cuss to me about old Kitely—I don't care if he was scragged twice over—I've no doubt he deserved it. But it'll matter a lot to M. & C. if they're found out. I can touch that five hundred easy as winking—but—you take my meaning?—I daresay M. & C. 'ud run to five thousand if I kept my tongue still. What?"

But Stoner knew at once that Myler disapproved. The commercial traveller's homely face grew grave, and he shook his head with an unmistakable gesture.

"No, Stoner," he said. "None o' that! Play straight, my lad! No hush-money transactions. Keep to the law, Stoner, keep to the law! Besides, there's others than you can find all this out. What you want to do is to get in first. See Tallington as soon as you get back."

"I daresay you're right," admitted Stoner. "But—I know M. & C, and I know they'd give—aye, half of what they're worth—and that's a lot!—to have this kept dark."

That thought was with him whenever he woke in the night, and as he strolled round Darlington next morning, it was still with him when, after an early dinner, he set off homeward by an early afternoon train which carried him to High Gill junction; whence he had to walk five miles across the moors and hills to Highmarket. And he was still pondering it weightily when, in one of the loneliest parts of the solitudes which he was crossing, he turning the corner of a little pine wood, and came face to face with Mallalieu.

16. THE LONELY MOOR

During the three hours which had elapsed since his departure from Darlington, Stoner had been thinking things over. He had seen his friend Myler again that morning; they had had a drink or two together at the station refreshment room before Stoner's train left, and Myler had once more urged upon Stoner to use his fortunately acquired knowledge in the proper way. No doubt, said Myler, he could get Mallalieu and Cotherstone to square him; no doubt they would cheerfully pay thousands where the reward only came to hundreds—but, when everything was considered, was it worth while? No!—a thousand times, no, said Myler. The mere fact that Stoner had found out all this was a dead sure proof that somebody else might find it out. The police had a habit, said Myler, of working like moles—underground. How did Stoner know that some of the Norcaster and London detectives weren't on the job already? They knew by that time that old Kitely was an ex-detective; they'd be sure to hark back on his past doings, in the effort to trace some connexion between one or other of them and his murder. Far away as it was, that old Wilchester affair would certainly come up again. And when it came up— ah, well, observed Myler, with force and earnestness, it would be a bad job for Stoner if it were found out that he'd accepted hush-money from his masters. In fact— Myler gave it as his decided opinion, though, as he explained, he wasn't a lawyer—he didn't know but what Stoner, in that case, would be drawn in as an accessory after the fact.

"Keep to the law, Bert, old man!" counselled Myler, as they parted. "You'll be all right then. Stick to my advice— see Tallington at once—this very afternoon!—and put in for the five hundred. You'll be safe as houses in doing that—but there'd be an awful risk about t'other, Bert. Be wise!—you'll get no better counsel."

Stoner knew that his sagacious friend was right, and he was prepared to abide by his counsel—as long as Myler was at his elbow. But when he had got away from him, his mind began to wobble. Five hundred pounds!— what was it in comparison with what he might get by a little skilful playing of his cards? He knew Mallalieu and he knew Cotherstone—knew much more about both of them than they had any idea of. He knew that they were rich men—very rich men. They had been making money for years, and of late certain highly successful and profitable contracts had increased their wealth in a surprising fashion. Everything had gone right with them—every contract they had taken up had turned out a gold mine. Five thousand pounds would be nothing to them singly—much less jointly. In Stoner's opinion, he had only to ask in order to have. He firmly believed that they would pay—pay at once, in good cash. And if they did—well, he would take good care that no evil chances came to him! If he laid hands on five thousand pounds, he would be out of Highmarket within five hours, and half-way across the Atlantic within five days. No—Dave Myler was a good sort—one of the best—but he was a bit straight-laced, and old-fashioned—especially since he had taken a wife—and after all, every man has a right to do his best for himself. And so, when Stoner came face to face with Mallalieu, on the lonely moor between High Gill and Highmarket, his mind was already made up to blackmail.

The place in which they met was an appropriate one— for Stoner's purpose. He had crossed the high ground between the railway and the little moorland town by no definite track, but had come in a bee-line across ling and bracken and heather. All around stretched miles upon miles of solitude—nothing but the undulating moors, broken up by great masses of limestone rock and occasional clumps and coverts of fir and pine; nothing but the blue line of the hills in the west; nothing but the grey northern skies overhead; nothing but the cry of the curlew and the bleating of the mountain sheep. It was in the midst of this that he met his senior employer—at the corner of a thin spinney which ran along the edge of a disused quarry. Mallalieu, as Stoner well knew, was a great man for walking on these moors, and he always walked alone. He took these walks to keep his flesh down; here he came, swinging his heavy oak walking-stick, intent on his own thoughts, and he and Stoner, neither hearing the other's footfall on the soft turf, almost ran into each other. Stoner, taken aback, flushed with the sudden surprise.

But Mallalieu, busied with his own reflections, had no thought of Stoner in his mind, and consequently showed no surprise at meeting him. He made a point of cultivating friendly relations with all who worked for him, and he grinned pleasantly at his clerk.

"Hullo!" he exclaimed cordially. "Taking your walks alone, eh? Now I should ha' thought a young fellow like you would ha' been taking one o' Miss Featherby's little milliners out for a dander, like—down the river-side, what?"

Stoner smiled—not as Mallalieu smiled. He was in no mood for persiflage; if he smiled it was because he thought that things were coming his way, that the game was being played into his hands. And suddenly he made up his mind.

"Something better to do than that, Mr. Mallalieu," he answered pertly. "I don't waste my time on dress-makers' apprentices. Something better to think of than that, sir."

"Oh!" said Mallalieu. "Ah! I thought you looked pretty deep in reflection. What might it be about, like?"

Something within Stoner was urging him on to go straight to the point. No fencing, said this inward monitor, no circumlocution—get to it, straight out. And Stoner thrust his hand into his pocket, and pulled out a copy of the reward bill. He opened it before his employer, watching Mallalieu's face.

"That!" he said. "Just that, Mr. Mallalieu."

Mallalieu glanced at the handbill, started a little, and looked half-sharply, half-angrily, at his clerk.

"What about it?" he growled. His temper, as Stoner well knew, was quickly roused, and it showed signs of awakening now. "What're you showing me that bit o' paper for? Mind your manners, young man!"

"No offence meant," retorted Stoner, coolly. He looked round him, noticed some convenient railings, old and worn, which fenced in the quarry, and stepping back to them, calmly leaned against the top one, put his hands in his pockets and looked at Mallalieu with a glance which was intended to show that he felt himself top dog in any encounter that might come. "I want a word or two with you, Mr. Mallalieu," he said.

Mallalieu, who was plainly amazed by this strange conduct, glared at Stoner.

"You want a word—or two—with—me?" he exclaimed. "For why, pray?—and why here?"

"Here's a convenient spot," said Stoner, with a nasty laugh. "We're all alone. Not a soul near us. You wouldn't like anybody to overhear what I've got to say."

Mallalieu stared at the clerk during a full minute's silence. He had a trick of silently staring people out of countenance. But he found that Stoner was not to be stared down, and eventually he spoke.

"I'll tell you what it is, my lad!" he said. "I don't know whether you've been drinking, or if you've some bee in your bonnet, but I don't allow nobody, and especially a man as I pay wages to, to speak in them tones to me! What d'ye mean by it?"

"I'll tell you what I mean, Mr. Mallalieu," replied Stoner, still regarding his man fixedly, and nerving himself for the contest. "I mean this—I know who killed Kitely!"

Mallalieu felt himself start again; he felt his face flush warm. But he managed to show a fairly controlled front, and he made shift to sneer.

"Oh, indeed," he said, twisting his mouth in derision. "Do you now? Deary me!—it's wonderful how clever some young folks is! So you know who killed Kitely, do you, my lad? Ah! And who did kill Kitely, now? Let's be knowing! Or happen you'd rather keep such a grand secret to yourself—till you can make something out of it?"

"I can make something out of it now," retorted Stoner, who was sharp enough to see through Mallalieu's affectation of scorn. "Just you realize the importance of what I'm saying. I tell you once again—I know who killed Kitely!"

"And who did kill him, then?" demanded Mallalieu. "Psha!—you know naught about it!"

Stoner laughed, looked round, and then leaned his head forward.

"Don't I?" he said, with a sneer that exceeded his employer's in significance and meaning. "But you're wrong—I do! Kitely was murdered by either you or Cotherstone! How's that, Mr. Mallalieu?"

Mallalieu again regarded his clerk in silence. He knew by that time that this fellow was in possession of some information, and his characteristic inclination was to fence with him. And he made a great effort to pull himself together, so as to deal better with whatever might be in store.

"Either me or Mr. Cotherstone!" he repeated sarcastically. "Oh! Now which on us would you be inclined to fix it on, Mr. Stoner? Eh?"

"May have been one, may have been the other, may have been both, for aught I know," retorted Stoner. "But you're both guilty, any way! It's no use, Mr. Mallalieu—I know you killed him. And—I know why!"

Again there was silence, and again a duel of staring eyes. And at its end Mallalieu laughed again, still affecting sneering and incredulous sentiments.

"Aye?—and why did one or t'other or both—have it which way you will—murder this here old gentleman?" he demanded. "Why, Mr. Sharp-nose?"

"I'll tell you—and then you'll know what I know," answered Stoner. "Because the old gentleman was an ex-detective, who was present when you and Cotherstone, under your proper names of Mallows and Chidforth, were tried for fraud at Wilchester Assizes, thirty years ago, and sentenced to two years! That's why, Mr. Mallalieu. The old chap knew it, and he let you know that he knew it, and you killed him to silence him. You didn't want it to get out that the Mayor and Borough Treasurer of Highmarket, so respected, so much thought of, are—a couple of old gaol-birds!"

Mallalieu's hot temper, held very well in check until then, flamed up as Stoner spat out the last contemptuous epithet. He had stood with his right hand behind him, grasping his heavy oaken stick—now, as his rage suddenly boiled, he swung hand and stick round in a savage blow at his tormentor, and the crook of the stick fell crashing against Stoner's temples. So quick was the blow, so sudden the assault, that the clerk had time to do no more than throw up an arm. And as he threw it up, and as the heavy blow fell, the old, rotten railing against which Stoner had leant so nonchalantly, gave way, and he fell back through it, and across the brow of the quarry—and without a sound. Mallalieu heard the crash of his stick on his victim's temples; he heard the rending and crackling of the railings—but he heard neither cry, nor sigh, nor groan from Stoner. Stoner fell backward and disappeared—and then (it seemed an age in coming) Mallalieu's frightened senses were aware of a dull thud somewhere far down in the depths into which he had fallen. Then came silence—deep, heavy silence—broken at last by the cry of a curlew flying across the lonely moor.

Mallalieu was seized with a trembling fit. He began to shake. His heavy frame trembled as if under the effects of a bad ague; the hand which had struck the blow shook so violently that the stick dropped from it. And Mallalieu looked down at the stick, and in a sudden overwhelming rage kicked it away from him over the brink of the quarry. He lifted his fist and shook it—and just as suddenly dropped it. The trembling passed, and he broke out into a cold sweat of fear.

"God ha' mercy!" he muttered. "If—if he's killed? He shouldn't ha' plagued me—he shouldn't ha' dared me! It was more than flesh and blood could stand, and—Lord ha' mercy, what's to be done?"

The autumn twilight was creeping over the moor. The sun had set behind the far-off western hills just before Mallalieu and Stoner had met, and while they talked dusk had come on. The moorlands were now growing dark and vague, and it seemed to Mallalieu that as the light failed the silence increased. He looked round him, fearful lest any of the shepherds of the district had come up to take a Sunday glance at their flocks. And once he thought he saw a figure at a little distance away along the edge of the trees, and he strained and strained his eyes in its direction—and concluded it was nothing. Presently he strained his eyes in another way—he crept cautiously to the edge of the quarry, and looked over the broken railing, and far down on the limestone rocks beneath he saw Stoner, lying on his back, motionless.

Long experience of the moorlands and their nooks and crannies enabled Mallalieu to make his way down to the bottom of the quarry by a descent through a brake of gorse and bramble. He crept along by the undergrowth to where the body lay, and fearfully laid a hand on the still figure. One touch was sufficient—he stood up trembling and shaking more than ever.

"He's dead—dead!" he muttered. "Must ha' broken his neck—it's a good fifty feet down here. Was ever aught so unfortunate! And—whatever shall I say and do about it?"

Inspiration came to him quickly—as quickly as the darkness came into that place of death. He made an effort, and regained his composure, and presently was able to think and to decide. He would say and do nothing—nothing whatever. No one had witnessed the meeting between Stoner and himself. No one had seen the blow. No one had seen Stoner's fall. Far better to say nothing, do nothing—far best to go away and let things take their course. Stoner's body would be found, next day, the day after, some day—and when it was found, people would say that Stoner had been sitting on those rotten railings, and they had given way, and he had fallen—and whatever marks there were on him would be attributed to the fall down the sharp edges of the old quarry.

So Mallalieu presently went away by another route, and made his way back to Highmarket in the darkness of the evening, hiding himself behind hedges and walls until he reached his own house. And it was not until he lay safe in bed that night that he remembered the loss of his stick.

17. THE MEDICAL OPINION

The recollection of that stick plunged Mallalieu into another of his ague-like fits of shaking and trembling. There was little sleep for him after that: he spent most of the night in thinking, anticipating, and scheming. That stick would almost certainly be found, and it would be found near Stoner's body. A casual passer-by would not recognize it, a moorland shepherd would not recognize it. But the Highmarket police, to whom it would be handed, would know it at once to be the Mayor's: it was one which Mallalieu carried almost every day—a plain, very stout oak staff. And the police would want to know how it came to be in that quarry. Curse it!—was ever anything so unfortunate!—however could he have so far lost his head as to forget it? He was half tempted to rise in the middle of the night and set out for the moors, to find it. But the night was dark, and solitary as the moors and the quarry where he dared not risk the taking of a lantern. And so he racked his brains in the effort to think of some means of explaining the presence of the stick. He hit on a notion at last—remembering suddenly that Stoner had carried neither stick nor umbrella. If the stick were found he would say that he had left it at the office on the Saturday, and that the clerk must have borrowed it. There was nothing unlikely in that: it was a good reason, it would explain why it came to be found near the body. Naturally, the police would believe the word of the Mayor: it would be a queer thing if they didn't, in Mallalieu's opinion. And therewith he tried to go to sleep, and made a miserable failure of it.

As he lay tossing and groaning in his comfortable bed that night, Mallalieu thought over many things. How had Stoner acquired his information? Did anybody else know what Stoner knew? After much reflection he decided that nobody but Stoner did know. Further reckoning up of matters gave him a theory as to how Stoner had got to know. He saw it all—according to his own idea. Stoner had overheard the conversation between old Kitely and Cotherstone in the private office, of course! That was it— he wondered he had never thought of it before. Between the partners' private room and the outer office in which Stoner sat, there was a little window in the wall; it had been specially made so that papers could be passed from one room to the other. And, of course, on that afternoon it had probably been a little way open, as it often was, and Stoner had heard what passed between Cotherstone and his tenant. Being a deep chap, Stoner had kept the secret to himself until the reward was offered. Of course, his idea was blackmail—Mallalieu had no doubt about that. No—all things considered, he did not believe that Stoner had shared his knowledge—Stoner would be too well convinced of its value to share it with anybody. That conclusion comforted Mallalieu—once more he tried to sleep.

But his sleep was a poor thing that night, and he felt tired and worn when, as usual, he went early to the yard. He was there before Cotherstone; when Cotherstone came, no more than a curt nod was exchanged between them. They had never spoken to each other except on business since the angry scene of a few days before, and now Mallalieu, after a glance at some letters which had come in the previous evening, went off down the yard. He stayed there an hour: when he re-entered the office he looked with an affectation of surprise at the clerk's empty desk.

"Stoner not come?" he demanded curtly.

Cotherstone, who was turning over the leaves of an account book, replied just as curtly.

"Not yet!"

Mallalieu fidgeted about for a while, arranging some papers he had brought in from the yard. Suddenly he uttered an exclamation of impatience, and going to the door, called to a lad who was passing.

"Here, you!" he said. "You know where Mr. Stoner lodges?—Mrs. Battley's. Run round there, and see why he hasn't come to his work. It's an hour and a half past his time. Happen he's poorly—run now, sharp!"

He went off down the yard again when he had despatched this message; he came back to the office ten minutes later, just as the messenger returned.

"Well?" he demanded, with a side-glance to assure himself that Cotherstone was at hand. "Where is he, like?"

"Please, sir, Mrs. Battley, she says as how Mr. Stoner went away on Saturday afternoon, sir," answered the lad, "and he hasn't been home since. She thinks he went to Darlington, sir, on a visit."

Mallalieu turned into the office, growling.

"Must ha' missed his train," he muttered as he put more papers on Stoner's desk. "Here—happen you'll attend to these things—they want booking up."

Cotherstone made no reply, and Mallalieu presently left him and went home to get his breakfast. And as he walked up the road to his house he wondered why Stoner had gone to Darlington. Was it possible that he had communicated what he knew to any of his friends? If so—

—

"Confound the suspense and the uncertainty!" growled Mallalieu. "It 'ud wear the life out of a man. I've a good mind to throw the whole thing up and clear out! I could do it easy enough wi' my means. A clear track—and no more o' this infernal anxiety."

He reflected, as he made a poor show of eating his breakfast, on the ease with which he could get away from Highmarket and from England. Being a particularly astute man of business, Mallalieu had taken good care that all his eggs were not in one basket. He had many baskets—his Highmarket basket was by no means the principal one. Indeed all that Mallalieu possessed in

Highmarket was his share of the business and his private house. As he had made his money he had invested it in easily convertible, gilt-edged securities, which would be realized at an hour's notice in London or New York, Paris or Vienna. It would be the easiest thing in the world for him, as Mayor of Highmarket, to leave the town on Corporation business, and within a few hours to be where nobody could find him; within a few more, to be out of the country. Lately, he had often thought of going right away, to enjoy himself for the rest of his life. He had made one complete disappearance already; why not make another? Before he went townwards again that morning, he was beginning to give serious attention to the idea.

Meanwhile, however, there was the business of the day to attend to, and Stoner's absence threw additional work on the two partners. Then at twelve o'clock, Mallalieu had to go over to the Town Hall to preside at a meeting of the General Purposes Committee. That was just over, and he was thinking of going home to his lunch when the superintendent of police came into the committee-room and drew him aside.

"I've bad news for you, Mr. Mayor," he announced in a whisper. "Your clerk—he hasn't been at work this morning, I suppose?"

"Well?" demanded Mallalieu, nerving himself for what he felt to be coming. "What about it?"

"He's met with a bad accident," replied the superintendent. "In fact, sir, he's dead! A couple of men found his body an hour or so ago in Hobwick Quarry, up on the moor, and it's been brought down to the mortuary. You'd better come round, Mr. Mayor—Mr. Cotherstone's there, now."

Mallalieu followed without a word. But once outside the Town Hall he turned to his companion.

"Have you made aught out of it?" he asked. "He's been away, so his landlady says, since Saturday afternoon: I sent round to inquire for him when he didn't turn up this morning. What do you know, like?"

"It looks as if it had been an accident," answered the superintendent. "These men that found him noticed some broken railings at top of the quarry. They looked down and saw a body. So they made their way down and found—Stoner. It would seem as if he'd leaned or sat on the railings and they'd given way beneath him, and of course he'd pitched headlong into the quarry. It's fifty feet deep, Mr. Mayor! That's all one can think of. But Dr. Rockcliffe's with him now."

Mallalieu made a mighty effort to appear calm, as, with a grave and concerned face, he followed his guide into the place where the doctor, an official or two, and Cotherstone were grouped about the dead man. He gave one glance at his partner and Cotherstone gave one swift look at him—and there was something in Cotherstone's look which communicated a sudden sense of uneasy fear to Mallalieu: it was a look of curious intelligence, almost a sort of signal. And Mallalieu experienced a vague feeling of dread as he turned to the doctor.

"A bad job—a bad job!" he muttered, shaking his head and glancing sideways at the body. "D'ye make aught out of it, doctor? Can you say how it came about?"

Dr. Rockcliffe pursed up his lips and his face became inscrutable. He kept silence for a moment—when he spoke his voice was unusually stern.

"The lad's neck is broken, and his spine's fractured," he said in a low voice. "Either of those injuries was enough to cause death. But—look at that!"

He pointed to a contusion which showed itself with unmistakable plainness on the dead man's left temple, and again he screwed up his lips as if in disgust at some deed present only to the imagination.

"That's a blow!" he said, more sternly than before. "A blow from some blunt instrument! It was a savage blow, too, dealt with tremendous force. It may—may, I say— have killed this poor fellow on the spot—he may have been dead before ever he fell down that quarry."

It was only by an enormous effort of will that Mallalieu prevented himself from yielding to one of his shaking fits.

"But—but mightn't he ha' got that with striking his head against them rocks as he fell?" he suggested. "It's a rocky place, that, and the rocks project, like, so——"

"No!" said the doctor, doggedly. "That's no injury from any rock or stone or projection. It's the result of a particularly fierce blow dealt with great force by some blunt instrument—a life preserver, a club, a heavy stick. It's no use arguing it. That's a certainty!"

Cotherstone, who had kept quietly in the background, ventured a suggestion.

"Any signs of his having been robbed?" he asked.

"No, sir," replied the superintendent promptly. "I've everything that was on him. Not much, either. Watch and chain, half a sovereign, some loose silver and copper, his pipe and tobacco, a pocket-book with a letter or two and such-like in it—that's all. There'd been no robbery."

"I suppose you took a look round?" asked Cotherstone. "See anything that suggested a struggle? Or footprints? Or aught of that sort?"

The superintendent shook his head.

"Naught!" he answered. "I looked carefully at the ground round those broken railings. But it's the sort of ground that wouldn't show footprints, you know—covered with that short, wiry mountain grass that shows nothing."

"And nothing was found?" asked Mallalieu. "No weapons, eh?"

For the life of him he could not resist asking that—his anxiety about the stick was overmastering him. And when the superintendent and the two policemen who had been with him up to Hobwick Quarry had answered that they had found nothing at all, he had hard work to repress a sigh of relief. He presently went away hoping that the oak stick had fallen into a crevice of the rocks or amongst the brambles which grew out of them; there was a lot of tangle-wood about that spot, and it was quite possible that the stick, kicked violently away, had fallen where it would never be discovered. And—there was yet a chance for him to make that possible discovery impossible. Now that the body had been found, he himself could visit the spot with safety, on the pretext of curiosity. He could look round; if he found the stick he could drop it into a safe fissure of the rocks, or make away with it. It was a good notion—and instead of going home to lunch Mallalieu turned into a private room of the Highmarket Arms, ate a sandwich and drank a glass of ale, and hurried off, alone, to the moors.

The news of this second mysterious death flew round Highmarket and the neighbourhood like wild-fire. Brereton heard of it during the afternoon, and having some business in the town in connexion with Harborough's defence, he looked in at the police-station and found the superintendent in an unusually grave and glum mood.

"This sort of thing's getting beyond me, Mr. Brereton," he said in a whisper. "Whether it is that I'm not used to such things—thank God! we've had little experience of violence in this place in my time!—or what it is, but I've got it into my head that this poor young fellow's death's connected in some way with Kitely's affair! I have indeed, sir!—it's been bothering me all the afternoon. For all the doctors—there's been several of 'em in during the last two hours—are absolutely agreed that Stoner was felled, sir—felled by a savage blow, and they say he may ha' been dead before ever he fell over that quarry edge. Mr. Brereton—I misdoubt it's another murder!"

"Have you anything to go on?" asked Brereton. "Had anybody any motive? Was there any love affair—jealousy, you know—anything of that sort?"

"No, I'm sure there wasn't," replied the superintendent. "The whole town and county's ringing with the news, and I should ha' heard something by now. And it wasn't robbery—not that he'd much on him, poor fellow! There's all he had," he went on, opening a drawer. "You can look at 'em, if you like."

He left the room just then, and Brereton, disregarding the cheap watch and chain and the pigskin purse with its light load, opened Stoner's pocket-book. There was not much in that, either—a letter or two, some receipted bills, a couple of much creased copies of the reward bill, some cuttings from newspapers. He turned from these to the pocket-book itself, and on the last written page he found an entry which made him start. For there again were the initials!

"—*M. & C.—fraud—bldg. soc.—Wilchester Assizes— 81—£2000—money never recovered—2 yrs.—K. pres.*"

Not much—but Brereton hastily copied that entry. And he had just written the last word when the superintendent came back into the room with a man who was in railway uniform.

"Come in here," the superintendent was saying. "You can tell me what it is before this gentleman. Some news from High Gill junction, Mr. Brereton," he went on, "something about Stoner. Well, my lad, what is it?"

"The station-master sent me over on his bicycle," replied the visitor. "We heard over there this afternoon about Stoner's body being found, and that you were thinking he must have fallen over into the quarry in the darkness. And we know over yonder that that's not likely."

"Aye?" said the superintendent. "Well, as a matter of fact, my lad, we weren't thinking that, but no doubt that rumour's got out. Now why do you railway folks know it isn't likely?"

"That's what I've come to tell," answered the man, a sharp, intelligent-looking fellow. "I'm ticket-collector over there, as you know, sir. Now, young Stoner came to the junction on Saturday afternoon and booked for Darlington, and of course went to Darlington. He came back yesterday afternoon—Sunday—by the train that gets to our junction at 3.3. I took his ticket. Instead of going out of the station by the ordinary way, he got over the fence on the down line side, saying to me that he'd take a straight cut across the moor to Highmarket. I saw him going Highmarket way for some distance. And he'd be at Hobwick Quarry by 4.30 at the latest—long before darkness."

"Just about sunset, as a matter of fact," remarked the superintendent. "The sun sets about 4.18."

"So he couldn't have fallen over in the darkness," continued the ticket-collector. "If all had gone well with him, he'd have been down in Highmarket here by dusk."

"I'm obliged to you," said the superintendent. "It's worth knowing, of course. Came from Darlington, eh? Was he alone?"

"Quite alone, sir."

"You didn't see anybody else going that way across the moors, did you? Didn't notice anybody following him?"

"No," replied the ticket-collector with decision. "Me and one of my mates watched him a long way, and I'll swear there was no one near him till he was out of sight. We didn't watch him on purpose, neither. When the down-train had gone, me and my mate sat down to smoke our pipes, and from where we were we could see right across the moors in this direction. We saw Stoner—now and then, you understand—right away to Chat Bank."

"You didn't notice any suspicious characters come to your station that afternoon or evening?" asked the superintendent.

The ticket-collector replied that nothing of that sort had been seen, and he presently went away. And Brereton, after an unimportant word or two, went away too, certain by that time that the death of Stoner had some sinister connexion with the murder of Kitely.

18. THE SCRAP BOOK

Brereton went back to his friend's house more puzzled than ever by the similarity of the entries in Kitely's memoranda and in Stoner's pocket-book. Bent had gone over to Norcaster that afternoon, on business, and was not to be home until late in the evening: Brereton accordingly dined alone and had ample time to reflect and to think. The reflecting and the thinking largely took the form of speculating—on the fact that certain terms and figures which had been set down by Kitely had also been set down by Stoner. There were the initials—M. & C. There was a date—if it was a date—81. What in Kitely's memorandum the initials S. B. might mean, it was useless to guess at. His memorandum, indeed, was as cryptic as an Egyptian hieroglyph. But Stoner's memorandum was fuller, more explicit. The M. & C. of the Kitely entry had been expanded to Mallows and Chidforth. The entry "fraud" and the other entries "Wilchester Assizes" and the supplementary words, clearly implied that two men named Mallows and Chidforth were prosecuted at Wilchester Assizes in the year 1881 for fraud, that a sum of £2,000 was involved, which was never recovered, that Mallows and Chidforth, whoever they were, were convicted and were sentenced to two years' imprisonment. So much for Stoner's memorandum. But did it refer to the same event to which Kitely made reference in his memorandum? It seemed highly probable that it did. It seemed highly probable, too, that the M. & C. of Kitely's entry were the Mallows & Chidforth of Stoner's. And now the problem narrowed to one most serious and crucial point—were the Mallows and Chidforth of these references the Mallalieu and Cotherstone of Highmarket.

Speculating on this possibility, Brereton after his solitary dinner went into Bent's smoking-room, and throwing himself into a chair before the fire, lighted his pipe and proceeded to think things out. It was abundantly clear to him by that time that Kitely and Stoner had been in possession of a secret: it seemed certain that both had been murdered by some person who desired to silence them. There was no possible doubt as to Kitely's murder: from what Brereton had heard that afternoon there seemed to be just as little doubt that Stoner had also been murdered. He had heard what the local medical men had to say—one and all agreed that though the clerk had received injuries in his fall which would produce almost instantaneous death he had received a mortal blow before he fell. Who struck that blow? Everything seemed to point to the fact that the man who struck it was the man who strangled Kitely—a man of great muscular power.

Glancing around the room as he sat in a big easy chair, his hands behind his head, Brereton's eyes fell suddenly on Kitely's legacy to Windle Bent. The queer-looking old volume which, because of its black calf binding and brass clasp, might easily have been taken for a prayer-book, lay just where Bent had set it down on his desk when Christopher Pett formally handed it over—so far as Brereton knew Bent up to now had never even opened it. And it was with no particular motive that Brereton now reached out and picked it up, and unsnapping the clasp began idly to turn over the leaves on which the old detective had pasted cuttings from newspapers and made entries in his crabbed handwriting. Brereton believed that he was idly handling what Pett had jocosely described the book to be—a mere scrap-book. It never entered his head that he held in his hands almost the whole solution of the mystery which was puzzling him.

No man knows how inspiration comes to him, and Brereton never knew how it was that suddenly, in the flash of an eye, in the swiftness of thought, he knew that he had found what he wanted. Suggestion might have had something to do with it. Kitely had written the word *Scrap-book* on the first blank page. Afterwards, at the tops of pages, he had filled in dates in big figures—for reference—1875—1879—1887—and so on. And Brereton suddenly saw, and understood, and realized. The cryptic entry in Kitely's pocket-book became plain as the plainest print. *M. & C. v. S. B. cir. 81:*—Brereton could amplify that now. Kitely, like all men who dabble in antiquarian pursuits, knew a bit of Latin, and naturally made an occasional airing of his knowledge. The full entry, of course, meant M. &. C. *vide* (=see) Scrap-Book *circa* (=about) 1881.

With a sharp exclamation of delight, Brereton turned over the pages of that queer record of crime and detection until he came to one over which the figure 1881 stood out boldly. A turn or two more of pages, and he had found what he wanted. There it was—a long cutting from what was evidently a local newspaper—a cutting which extended over two or three leaves of the book—and at the end a memorandum in Kitely's handwriting, evidently made some years before. The editor of that local newspaper had considered the case which Kitely had so carefully scissored from his columns worthy of four headlines in big capitals:—

THE BUILDING SOCIETY DEFALCATIONS MALLOWS AND CHIDFORTH AT THE WILCHESTER ASSIZES VERDICT AND SENTENCE

Brereton settled down to a careful reading of the report. There was really nothing very remarkable about it—nothing exciting nor sensational. It was indeed no more than a humdrum narrative of a vulgar crime. But it was necessary that he should know all about it, and be able to summarize it, and so he read it over with unusual care. It was a very plain story—there were no complications. It appeared from the evidence adduced that for some time previous to 1881 there had been in existence in Wilchester a building society, the members of which were chiefly of the small tradesman and better-class working-man order. Its chief officials for a year or two had been John Mallows and Mark Chidforth, who were respectively treasurer and secretary. Mallows was foreman to a builder in the town; Chidforth was clerk to the same employer. Both were young men. They were evidently regarded as smart fellows. Up to the time of the revelations they had borne the very best of characters. Each had lived in Wilchester since childhood; each had continued his education at night schools and institute classes after the usual elementary school days were over; each was credited with an ambitious desire to rise in the world. Each, as a young man, was attached to religious organizations—Mallows was a sidesman at one of the churches, Chidforth was a Sunday-school teacher at one of the chapels. Both had been fully and firmly trusted, and it appeared from the evidence that they had had what practically amounted to unsupervised control of the building society's funds. And—the really important point—there was no doubt whatever that they had helped themselves to some two thousand pounds of their fellow-members' money.

All this was clear enough: it took little time for Brereton to acquaint himself with these facts. What was not so clear was the whereabouts or disposal of the money. From the evidence there appeared to be two conflicting notions current in Wilchester at the time. Some people apparently believed confidently that the two culprits had lost the money in secret speculation and in gambling: other people were just as certain that they had quietly put the money away in some safe quarter. The prisoners themselves absolutely refused to give the least scrap of information: ever since their arrest they had maintained a stolid silence and a defiant demeanour. More than once during the progress of the trial they had opportunities of making clean breasts of their misdoings and refused to take them. Found guilty, they were put back until next day for sentence—that, of course, was to give them another chance of saying what they had done with the money. But they had kept up their silence to the end, and they had been sentenced to two years' imprisonment, with hard labour, and so had disappeared from public view, with their secret—if there really was a secret—intact.

So much for the newspaper cutting from the *Wilchester Sentinel*. But there was more to read. The cutting came to an end on the top half of a page in the scrap-book; underneath it on the blank half of the page Kitely had made an entry, dated three years after the trial.

"Wilchester: June 28, 1884. *Re* above. Came down here on business today and had a talk with police about M. & C. and the money. M. & C. never been heard of since their release. Were released at same time, and seen in the town an hour or two later, after which they disappeared—a man who spoke to M. says that M. told him they were going to emigrate. They are believed to have gone to Argentine. Both had relatives in Wilchester, but either they don't know anything of M. & C.'s subsequent doings, or they keep silence. No further trace of money, and opinion still divided as to what they really did with it: many people in W. firmly convinced that they had it safely planted, and have gone to it."

To Brereton the whole affair was now as plain as a pikestaff. The old detective, accidentally settling down at Highmarket, had recognized Mallalieu and Cotherstone, the prosperous tradesmen of that little, out-of-the-way town, as the Mallows and Chidforth whom he had seen in the dock at Wilchester, and he had revealed his knowledge to one or the other or both. That was certain. But there were many things that were far from certain. What had happened when Kitely revealed himself as a man who had been a witness of their conviction in those far-off days? How had he revealed himself? Had he endeavoured to blackmail them? It was possible.

But there was still more to think over. How had the dead clerk, Stoner, got his knowledge of this great event in the life of his employers? Had he got it from Kitely? That was not likely. Yet Stoner had written down in his pocket-book an entry which was no more and no less than a *précis* of the absolute facts. Somehow, somewhere, Stoner had made himself fully acquainted with Mallalieu and Cotherstone's secret. Did Stoner's death arise out of a knowledge of that secret? On the face of things there could be little doubt that it did. Who, then, struck the blow which killed Stoner, or, if it did not actually kill him, caused his death by bringing about the fall which broke his neck? Was it Mallalieu?—or was it Cotherstone?

That one or other, or both, were guilty of Kitely's murder, and possibly of Stoner's, Brereton was by that time absolutely certain. And realizing that certainty, he felt himself placed in a predicament which could not fail to be painful. It was his duty, as counsel for an innocent man, to press to the full his inquiries into the conduct of men whom he believed to be guilty. In this he was faced with an unpleasant situation. He cared nothing about Mallalieu. If Mallalieu was a guilty man, let Mallalieu pay the richly-deserved consequences of his misdeeds. Brereton, without being indifferent or vindictive or callous, knew that it would not give him one extra heart-throb if he heard Mallalieu found guilty and sentenced to the gallows. But Cotherstone was the father of the girl to whom Windle Bent was shortly to be married—and Bent and Brereton had been close friends ever since they first went to school together.

It was a sad situation, an unpleasant thing to face. He had come on a visit to Bent, he had prolonged that visit in order to defend a man whom he firmly believed to be as innocent as a child—and now he was to bring disgrace and shame on a family with whom his host and friend was soon to be allied by the closest of ties. But—better that than that an innocent man should suffer! And walking up and down Bent's smoking-room, and thinking the whole thing through and through, he half made up his mind to tell Bent all about it when he returned.

Brereton presently put on hat and coat and left the house. It was then half-past seven; a sharp, frosty November evening, with an almost full moon rising in a clear, star-sprinkled sky. The sudden change from the warmth of the house to the frost-laden atmosphere of the hillside quickened his mental faculties; he lighted his pipe, and resolved to take a brisk walk along the road which led out of Highmarket and to occupy himself with another review of the situation. A walk in the country by day or night and in solitude had always had attractions for Brereton and he set out on this with zest. But he had not gone a hundred yards in the direction of the moors when Avice Harborough came out of the gate of Northrop's garden and met him.

"I was coming to see you," she said quietly. "I have heard something that I thought you ought to hear, too—at once."

"Yes?" responded Brereton.

Avice drew an envelope from her muff and gave it to him.

"A boy brought that to me half an hour ago," she said. "It is from an old woman, Mrs. Hamthwaite, who lives in a very lonely place on the moors up above Hobwick Quarry. Can you read it in this light?"

"I will," answered Brereton, drawing a scrap of paper from the envelope. "Here," he went on, giving it back to Avice, "you hold it, and I'll strike a match—the moonlight's scarcely strong enough. Now," he continued, taking a box of vestas from his pocket and striking one, "steady—'If Miss Harborough will come up to see Susan Hamthwaite I will tell you something that you might like to know.' Ah!" he exclaimed, throwing away the match. "Now, how far is it to this old woman's cottage?"

"Two miles," replied Avice.

"Can you go there now?" he asked.

"I thought of doing so," she answered.

"Come along, then," said Brereton. "We'll go together. If she objects to my presence I'll leave you with her and wait about for you. Of course, she wants to tell you something relating to your father."

"You think so?" said Avice. "I only hope it is!"

"Certain to be," he replied. "What else could it be?"

"There are so many strange things to tell about, just now," she remarked. "Besides, if old Mrs. Hamthwaite knows anything, why hasn't she let me know until tonight?"

"Oh, there's no accounting for that!" said Brereton. "Old women have their own way of doing things. By the by," he continued, as they turned out of the road and began to climb a path which led to the first ridge of the moors outside the town, "I haven't seen you today—you've heard of this Stoner affair?"

"Mr. Northrop told me this afternoon," she replied. "What do you think about it?"

Brereton walked on a little way without replying. He was asking a serious question of himself. Should he tell all he knew to Avice Harborough?

19. A TALL MAN IN GREY CLOTHES

That question remained unanswered, and Brereton remained silent, until he and Avice had reached the top of the path and had come out on the edge of the wide stretch of moorland above the little town. He paused for a moment and looked back on the roofs and gables of Highmarket, shining and glittering in the moonlight; the girl paused too, wondering at his silence. And with a curious abruptness he suddenly turned, laid a hand on her arm, and gave it a firm, quick pressure.

"Look here!" he said. "I'm going to trust you. I'm going to say to you what I haven't said to a soul in that town!—not even to Tallington, who's a man of the law, nor to Bent, who's my old friend. I want to say something to somebody whom I can trust. I can trust you!"

"Thank you," she answered quietly. "I—I think I understand. And you'll understand, too, won't you, when I say—you can!"

"That's all right," he said, cheerfully. "Of course! Now we understand each other. Come on, then—you know the way—act as guide, and I'll tell you as we go along."

Avice turned off into what appeared to be no more than a sheep-track across the heather. Within a few minutes they were not only quite alone, but out of sight of any human habitation. It seemed to Brereton that they were suddenly shut into a world of their own, as utterly apart from the little world they had just left as one star is from another. But even as he thought this he saw, far away across the rising and falling of the heather-clad undulations, the moving lights of a train that was speeding southward along the coast-line from Norcaster, and presently the long scream of a whistle from its engine came on the light breeze that blew inland from the hidden sea, and the sight and sound recalled him to the stern realities of life.

"Listen, then, carefully," he began. "And bear in mind that I'm putting what I believe to be safety of other men in your hands. It's this way...."

Avice Harborough listened in absolute silence as Brereton told her his carefully arranged story. They walked slowly across the moor as he told it; now dipping into a valley, now rising above the ridge of a low hill; sometimes pausing altogether as he impressed some particular point upon her. In the moonlight he could see that she was listening eagerly and intently, but she never interrupted him and never asked a question. And at last, just as they came in sight of a light that burned in the window of a little moorland cottage, snugly planted in a hollow beneath the ridge which they were then traversing, he brought his story to an end and turned inquiringly to her.

"There!" he said. "That's all. Now try to consider it without prejudice—if you can. How does it appear to you?"

Instead of replying directly the girl walked on in silence for a moment or two, and suddenly turned to Brereton with an impulsive movement.

"You've given me your confidence and I'll give you mine!" she exclaimed. "Perhaps I ought to have given it before—to you or to Mr. Tallington—but—I didn't like. I've wondered about Mallalieu! Wondered if—if he did kill that old man. And wondered if he tried to put the blame on my father out of revenge!"

"Revenge!" exclaimed Brereton. "What do you mean?"

"My father offended him—not so very long ago, either," she answered. "Last year—I'll tell you it all, plainly—Mr. Mallalieu began coming to our cottage at times. First he came to see my father about killing the rats which had got into his out-buildings. Then he made

excuses—he used to come, any way—at night. He began
to come when my father was out, as he often was. He
would sit down and smoke and talk. I didn't like it—I
don't like him. Then he used to meet me in the wood in
the Shawl, as I came home from the Northrops'. I
complained to my father about it and one night my father
came in and found him here. My father, Mr. Brereton, is
a very queer man and a very plain-spoken man. He told
Mr. Mallalieu that neither of us desired his company and
told him to go away. And Mr. Mallalieu lost his temper
and said angry things."

"And your father?" said Brereton. "Did he lose his
temper, too?"

"No!" replied Avice. "He has a temper—but he kept it
that night. He never spoke to Mr. Mallalieu in return. He
let him say his say—until he'd got across the threshold,
and then he just shut the door on him. But—I know how
angry Mr. Mallalieu was."

Brereton stood silently considering matters for a
moment. Then he pointed to the light in the window
beneath them, and moved towards it.

"I'm glad you told me that," he said. "It may account
for something that's puzzled me a great deal—I must
think it out. But at present—is that the old woman's
lamp?"

Avice led the way down to the hollow by a narrow
path which took them into a little stone-walled enclosure
where a single Scotch fir-tree stood sentinel over a typical
moorland homestead of the smaller sort—a one-storied
house of rough stone, the roof of which was secured from
storm and tempest by great boulders slung on stout
ropes, and having built on to it an equally rough shelter
for some small stock of cows and sheep. Out of a sheer
habit of reflection on things newly seen, Brereton could
not avoid wondering what life was like, lived in this
solitude, and in such a perfect hermitage—but his
speculations were cut short by the opening of the door set
deep within the whitewashed porch. An old woman, much

bent by age, looked out upon him and Avice, holding a small lamp so that its light fell on their faces.

"Come your ways in, joy!" she said hospitably. "I was expecting you'd come up tonight: I knew you'd want to have a word with me as soon as you could. Come in and sit you down by the fire—it's coldish o' nights, to be sure, and there's frost in the air.

"This gentleman may come in, too, mayn't he, Mrs. Hamthwaite?" asked Avice as she and Brereton stepped within the porch. "He's the lawyer-gentleman who's defending my father—you won't mind speaking before him, will you?"

"Neither before him, nor behind him, nor yet to him," answered Mrs. Hamthwaite with a chuckle. "I've talked to lawyers afore today, many's the time! Come your ways in, sir—sit you down."

She carefully closed the door on her guests and motioned them to seats by a bright fire of turf, and then setting the lamp on the table, seated herself in a corner of her long-settle and folding her hands in her apron took a long look at her visitors through a pair of unusually large spectacles. And Brereton, genuinely interested, took an equally long look at her; and saw a woman who was obviously very old but whose face was eager, intelligent, and even vivacious. As this queer old face turned from one to the other, its wrinkles smoothed out into a smile.

"You'll be wondering what I've got to tell, love," said Mrs. Hamthwaite, turning to Avice. "And no doubt you want to know why I haven't sent for you before now. But you see, since that affair happened down your way, I been away. Aye, I been to see my daughter—as lives up the coast. And I didn't come home till today. And I'm no hand at writing letters. However here we are, and better late than never and no doubt this lawyer gentleman'll be glad to hear what I can tell him and you."

"Very glad indeed!" responded Brereton. "What is it?"

The old woman turned to a box which stood in a recess in the ingle-nook at her elbow and took from it a folded newspaper.

"Me and my daughter and her husband read this here account o' the case against Harborough as it was put before the magistrates," she said. "We studied it. Now you want to know where Harborough was on the night that old fellow was done away with. That's it, master, what?"

"That is it," answered Brereton, pressing his arm against Avice, who sat close at his side. "Yes, indeed! And you——"

"I can tell you where Harborough was between nine o'clock and ten o'clock that night," replied Mrs. Hamthwaite, with a smile that was not devoid of cunning. "I know, if nobody else knows!"

"Where, then?" demanded Brereton.

The old woman leaned forward across the hearth.

"Up here on the moor!" she whispered. "Not five minutes' walk from here. At a bit of a place—Miss there'll know it—called Good Folks' Lift. A little rise i' the ground where the fairies used to dance, you know, master."

"You saw him?" asked Brereton.

"I saw him," chuckled Mrs. Hamthwaite. "And if I don't know him, why then, his own daughter doesn't!"

"You'd better tell us all about it," said Brereton.

Mrs. Hamthwaite gave him a sharp look. "I've given evidence to law folks before today," she said. "You'll want to know what I could tell before a judge, like?"

"Of course," replied Brereton.

"Well, then——" she continued. "You see, master, since my old man died, I've lived all alone up here. I've a bit to live on—not over much, but enough. All the same, if I can save a bit by getting a hare or a rabbit, or a bird or two now and then, off the moor—well, I do! We all of us does that, as lives on the moor: some folks calls it poaching, but we call it taking our own. Now then, on that night we're talking about, I went along to Good Folks' Lift to look at some snares I'd set early that day.

There's a good deal of bush and scrub about that place—I was amongst the bushes when I heard steps, and I looked out and saw a tall man in grey clothes coming close by. How did I know he were in grey clothes? Why, 'cause he stopped close by me to light his pipe! But he'd his back to me, so I didn't see his full face, only a side of it. He were a man with a thin, greyish beard. Well, he walks past there, not far—and then I heard other steps. Then I heard your father's voice, miss—and I see the two of 'em meet. They stood, whispering together, for a minute or so—then they came back past me, and they went off across the moor towards Hexendale. And soon they were out of sight, and when I'd finished what I was after I came my ways home. That's all, master—but if yon old man was killed down in Highmarket Shawl Wood between nine and ten o'clock that night, then Jack Harborough didn't kill him, for Jack was up here at soon after nine, and him and the tall man went away in the opposite direction!"

"You're sure about the time?" asked Brereton anxiously.

"Certain, master! It was ten minutes to nine when I went out—nearly ten when I come back. My clock's always right—I set it by the almanack and the sunrise and sunset every day—and you can't do better," asserted Mrs. Hamthwaite.

"You're equally sure about the second man being Harborough?" insisted Brereton. "You couldn't be mistaken?"

"Mistaken? No!—master, I know Harborough's voice, and his figure, aye, and his step as well as I know my own fireside," declared Mrs. Hamthwaite. "Of course I know it were Harborough—no doubt on't!"

"How are you sure that this was the evening of the murder?" asked Brereton. "Can you prove that it was?"

"Easy!" said Mrs. Hamthwaite. "The very next morning I went away to see my daughter up the coast. I heard of the old man's murder at High Gill Junction. But

I didn't hear then that Harborough was suspected—didn't hear that till later on, when we read it in the newspapers."

"And the other man—the tall man in grey clothes, who has a slightly grey beard—you didn't know him?"

Mrs. Hamthwaite made a face which seemed to suggest uncertainty.

"Well, I'll tell you," she answered. "I believe him to be a man that I have seen about this here neighbourhood two or three times during this last eighteen months or so. If you really want to know, I'm a good deal about them moors o' nights; old as I am, I'm very active, and I go about a goodish bit—why not? And I have seen a man about now and then—months between, as a rule—that I couldn't account for—and I believe it's this fellow that was with Harborough."

"And you say they went away in the direction of Hexendale?" said Brereton. "Where is Hexendale?"

The old woman pointed westward.

"Inland," she answered. "Over yonder. Miss there knows Hexendale well enough."

"Hexendale is a valley—with a village of the same name in it—that lies about five miles away on the other side of the moors," said Avice. "There's another line of railway there—this man Mrs. Hamthwaite speaks of could come and go by that."

"Well," remarked Brereton presently, "we're very much obliged to you, ma'am, and I'm sure you won't have any objection to telling all this again at the proper time and place, eh?"

"Eh, bless you, no!" answered Mrs. Hamthwaite. "I'll tell it wherever you like, master—before Lawyer Tallington, or the magistrates, or the crowner, or anybody! But I'll tell you what, if you'll take a bit of advice from an old woman—you're a sharp-looking young man, and I'll tell you what I should do if I were in your place—now then!"

"Well, what?" asked Brereton good-humouredly.

Mrs. Hamthwaite clapped him on the shoulder as she opened the door for her visitors.

"Find that tall man in the grey clothes!" she said. "Get hold of him! He's the chap you want!"

Brereton went silently away, meditating on the old woman's last words.

"But where are we to find him?" he suddenly exclaimed. "Who is he?"

"I don't think that puzzles me," remarked Avice. "He's the man who sent the nine hundred pounds."

Brereton smote his stick on the heather at their feet.

"By George!—I never thought of that!" he exclaimed. "I shouldn't wonder!—I shouldn't wonder at all. Hooray!—we're getting nearer and nearer to something."

But he knew that still another step was at hand—an unpleasant, painful step—when, on getting back to Bent's, an hour later, Bent told him that Lettie had been cajoled into fixing the day of the wedding, and that the ceremony was to take place with the utmost privacy that day week.

20. AT BAY

It was only by an immense effort of will that Brereton prevented an exclamation and a start of surprise. But of late he had been perpetually on the look-out for all sorts of unforeseen happenings and he managed to do no more than show a little natural astonishment.

"What, so soon!" he said. "Dear me, old chap!—I didn't think of its being this side of Christmas."

"Cotherstone's set on it," answered Bent. "He seems to be turning into a regular hypochondriac. I hope nothing is really seriously wrong with him. But anyway—this day week. And you'll play your part of best man, of course."

"Oh, of course!" agreed Brereton. "And then—are you going away?"

"Yes, but not for as long as we'd meant," said Bent. "We'll run down to the Riviera for a few weeks—I've made all my arrangements today. Well, any fresh news about this last bad business? This Stoner affair, of course, has upset Cotherstone dreadfully. When is all this mystery coming to an end, Brereton? There is one thing dead certain—Harborough isn't guilty in this case. That is, if Stoner really was killed by the blow they talk of."

But Brereton refused to discuss matters that night. He pleaded fatigue, he had been at it all day long, he said, and his brain was confused and tired and needed rest. And presently he went off to his room—and when he got there he let out a groan of dismay. For one thing was imperative—Bent's marriage must not take place while there was the least chance of a terrible charge being suddenly let loose on Cotherstone.

He rose in the morning with his mind made up on the matter. There was but one course to adopt—and it must be adopted immediately. Cotherstone must be spoken to—Cotherstone must be told of what some people at any rate knew about him and his antecedents. Let him have a chance to explain himself. After all, he might have some explanation. But—and here Brereton's determination became fixed and stern—it must be insisted upon that he should tell Bent everything.

Bent always went out very early in the morning, to give an eye to his business, and he usually breakfasted at his office. That was one of the mornings on which he did not come back to the house, and Brereton accordingly breakfasted alone, and had not seen his host when he, too, set out for the town. He had already decided what to do—he would tell everything to Tallington. Tallington was a middle-aged man of a great reputation for common-sense and for probity; as a native of the town, and a dweller in it all his life, he knew Cotherstone well, and he would give sound advice as to what methods should be followed in dealing with him. And so to Tallington Brereton, arriving just after the solicitor had finished reading his morning's letters, poured out the whole story which he had learned from the ex-detective's scrap-book and from the memorandum made by Stoner in his pocket-book.

Tallington listened with absorbed attention, his face growing graver and graver as Brereton marshalled the facts and laid stress on one point of evidence after another. He was a good listener—a steady, watchful listener—Brereton saw that he was not only taking in every fact and noting every point, but was also weighing up the mass of testimony. And when the story came to its end he spoke with decision, spoke, too, just as Brereton expected he would, making no comment, offering no opinion, but going straight to the really critical thing.

"There are only two things to be done," said Tallington. "They're the only things that can be done. We

must send for Bent, and tell him. Then we must get
Cotherstone here, and tell him. No other course—none!"

"Bent first?" asked Brereton.

"Certainly! Bent first, by all means. It's due to him.
Besides," said Tallington, with a grim smile, "it would be
decidedly unpleasant for Cotherstone to compel him to
tell Bent, or for us to tell Bent in Cotherstone's presence.
And—we'd better get to work at once, Brereton!
Otherwise—this will get out in another way."

"You mean—through the police?" said Brereton.

"Surely!" replied Tallington. "This can't be kept in a
corner. For anything we know somebody may be at work,
raking it all up, just now. Do you suppose that
unfortunate lad Stoner kept his knowledge to himself? I
don't! No—at once! Come, Bent's office is only a minute
away—I'll send one of my clerks for him. Painful, very—
but necessary."

The first thing that Bent's eyes encountered when he
entered Tallington's private room ten minutes later was
the black-bound, brass-clasped scrap-book, which
Brereton had carried down with him and had set on the
solicitor's desk. He started at the sight of it, and turned
quickly from one man to the other.

"What's that doing here?" he asked, "is—have you
made some discovery? Why am I wanted?"

Once more Brereton had to go through the story. But
his new listener did not receive it in the calm and
phlegmatic fashion in which it had been received by the
practised ear of the man of law. Bent was at first utterly
incredulous; then indignant: he interrupted; he asked
questions which he evidently believed to be difficult to
answer; he was fighting—and both his companions,
sympathizing keenly with him, knew why. But they never
relaxed their attitude, and in the end Bent looked from
one to the other with a cast-down countenance in which
doubt was beginning to change into certainty.

"You're convinced of—all this?" he demanded
suddenly. "Both of you? It's your conviction?"

"It's mine," answered Tallington quietly.

"I'd give a good deal for your sake, Bent, if it were not mine," said Brereton. "But—it is mine. I'm—sure!"

Bent jumped from his chair.

"Which of them is it, then?" he exclaimed. "Gad!—you don't mean to say that Cotherstone is—a murderer! Good heavens!—think of what that would mean to—to——"

Tallington got up and laid a hand on Bent's arm.

"We won't say or think anything until we hear what Cotherstone has to say," he said. "I'll step along the street and fetch him, myself. I know he'll be alone just now, because I saw Mallalieu go into the Town Hall ten minutes ago—there's an important committee meeting there this morning over which he has to preside. Pull yourself together, Bent—Cotherstone may have some explanation of everything."

Mallalieu & Cotherstone's office was only a few yards away along the street; Tallington was back from it with Cotherstone in five minutes. And Brereton, looking closely at Cotherstone as he entered and saw who awaited him, was certain that Cotherstone was ready for anything. A sudden gleam of understanding came into his sharp eyes; it was as if he said to himself that here was a moment, a situation, a crisis, which he had anticipated, and—he was prepared. It was an outwardly calm and cool Cotherstone, who, with a quick glance at all three men and at the closed door, took the chair which Tallington handed to him, and turned on the solicitor with a single word.

"Well?"

"As I told you in coming along," said Tallington, "we want to speak to you privately about some information which has been placed in our hands—that is, of course, in Mr. Brereton's and in mine. We have thought it well to already acquaint Mr. Bent with it. All this is between ourselves, Mr. Cotherstone—so treat us as candidly as we'll treat you. I can put everything to you in a few words. They're painful. Are you and your partner, Mr.

Mallalieu, the same persons as the Chidforth and Mallows who were prosecuted for fraud at Wilchester Assizes in 1881 and sentenced to two years' imprisonment?"

Cotherstone neither started nor flinched. There was no sign of weakness nor of hesitation about him now. Instead, he seemed to have suddenly recovered all the sharpness and vigour with which two at any rate of the three men who were so intently watching him had always associated with him. He sat erect and watchful in his chair, and his voice became clear and strong.

"Before I answer that question, Mr. Tallington," he said, "I'll ask one of Mr. Bent here. It's this—is my daughter going to suffer from aught that may or may not be raked up against her father? Let me know that!—if you want any words from me."

Bent flushed angrily.

"You ought to know what my answer is!" he exclaimed. "It's no!"

"That'll do!" said Cotherstone. "I know you—you're a man of your word." He turned to Tallington. "Now I'll reply to you," he went on. "My answer's in one word, too. Yes!"

Tallington opened Kitely's scrap-book at the account of the trial at Wilchester, placed it before Cotherstone, and indicated certain lines with the point of a pencil.

"You're the Chidforth mentioned there?" he asked quietly. "And your partner's the Mallows?"

"That's so," replied Cotherstone, so imperturbably that all three looked at him in astonishment "That's quite so, Mr. Tallington."

"And this is an accurate report of what happened?" asked Tallington, trailing the pencil over the newspaper. "That is, as far as you can see at a glance?"

"Oh, I daresay it is," said Cotherstone, airily. "That was the best paper in the town—I daresay it's all right. Looks so, anyway."

"You know that Kitely was present at that trial?" suggested Tallington, who, like Brereton, was beginning to be mystified by Cotherstone's coolness.

"Well," answered Cotherstone, with a shake of his head, "I know now. But I never did know until that afternoon of the day on which the old man was murdered. If you're wanting the truth, he came into our office that afternoon to pay his rent to me, and he told me then. And—if you want more truth—he tried to blackmail me. He was to come next day—at four o'clock—to hear what me and Mallalieu 'ud offer him for hush-money."

"Then you told Mallalieu?" asked Tallington.

"Of course I told him!" replied Cotherstone. "Told him as soon as Kitely had gone. It was a facer for both of us— to be recognized, and to have all that thrown up against us, after thirty years' honest work!"

The three listeners looked silently at each other. A moment of suspence passed. Then Tallington put the question which all three were burning with eagerness to have answered.

"Mr. Cotherstone!—do you know who killed Kitely?"

"No!" answered Cotherstone. "But I know who I think killed him!"

"Who, then?" demanded Tallington.

"The man who killed Bert Stoner," said Cotherstone firmly. "And for the same reason."

"And this man is——"

Tallington left the question unfinished. For Cotherstone's alert face took a new and determined expression, and he raised himself a little in his chair and brought his lifted hand down heavily on the desk at his side.

"Mallalieu!" he exclaimed. "Mallalieu! I believe he killed Kitely. I suspicioned it from the first, and I came certain of it on Sunday night. Why? *Because I saw Mallalieu fell Stoner!*"

There was a dead silence in the room for a long, painful minute. Tallington broke it at last by repeating Cotherstone's last words.

"You saw Mallalieu fell Stoner? Yourself?"

"With these eyes! Look here!" exclaimed Cotherstone, again bringing his hand down heavily on the desk. "I went up there by Hobwick Quarry on Sunday afternoon—to do a bit of thinking. As I got to that spinney at the edge of the quarry, I saw Mallalieu and our clerk. They were fratching—quarrelling—I could hear 'em as well as see 'em. And I slipped behind a big bush and waited and watched. I could see and hear, even at thirty yards off, that Stoner was maddening Mallalieu, though of course I couldn't distinguish precise words. And all of a sudden Mallalieu's temper went, and he lets out with that heavy oak stick of his and fetches the lad a crack right over his forehead—and with Stoner starting suddenly back the old railings gave way and—down he went. That's what I saw—and I saw Mallalieu kick that stick into the quarry in a passion, and—I've got it!"

"You've got it?" said Tallington.

"I've got it!" repeated Cotherstone. "I watched Mallalieu—after this was over. Once I thought he saw me—but he evidently decided he was alone. I could see he was taking on rarely. He went down to the quarry as it got dusk—he was there some time. Then at last he went away on the opposite side. And I went down when he'd got clear away and I went straight to where the stick was. And as I say, I've got it."

Tallington looked at Brereton, and Brereton spoke for the first time.

"Mr. Cotherstone must see that all this should be told to the police," he said.

"Wait a bit," replied Cotherstone. "I've not done telling my tales here yet. Now that I am talking, I will talk! Bent!" he continued, turning to his future son-in-law. "What I'm going to say now is for your benefit. But these lawyers shall hear. This old Wilchester business has been raked up—how, I don't know. Now then, you shall all know the truth about that! I did two years—for what? For being Mallalieu's catspaw!"

Tallington suddenly began to drum his fingers on the blotting-pad which lay in front of him. From this point he watched Cotherstone with an appearance of speculative interest which was not lost on Brereton.

"Ah!" he remarked quietly. "You were Mallalieu's—or Mallows'—catspaw? That is—he was the really guilty party in the Wilchester affair, of Which that's an account?"

"Doesn't it say here that he was treasurer?" retorted Cotherstone, laying his hand on the open scrap-book. "He was—he'd full control of the money. He drew me into things—drew me into 'em in such a clever way that when the smash came I couldn't help myself. I had to go through with it. And I never knew until—until the two years was over—that Mallalieu had that money safely put away."

"But—you got to know, eventually," remarked Tallington. "And—I suppose—you agreed to make use of it?"

Cotherstone smote the table again.

"Yes!" he said with some heat. "And don't you get any false ideas, Mr. Tallington. Bent!—I've paid that money back—I, myself. Each penny of it—two thousand pound, with four per cent. interest for thirty years! I've done it— Mallalieu knows naught about it. And here's the receipt. So now then!"

"When did you pay it, Mr. Cotherstone?" asked Tallington, as Bent unwillingly took the paper which Cotherstone drew from a pocket-book and handed to him. "Some time ago, or lately?"

"If you want to know," retorted Cotherstone, "it was the very day after old Kitely was killed. I sent it through a friend of mine who still lives in Wilchester. I wanted to be done with it—I didn't want to have it brought up against me that anybody lost aught through my fault. And so—I paid."

"But—I'm only suggesting—you could have paid a long time before that, couldn't you?" said Tallington. "The longer you waited, the more you had to pay. Two thousand pounds, with thirty years' interest, at four per cent.—why, that's four thousand four hundred pounds altogether!"

"That's what he paid," said Bent. "Here's the receipt.

"Mr. Cotherstone is telling us—privately— everything," remarked Tallington, glancing at the receipt and passing it on to Brereton. "I wish he'd tell us— privately, as I say—why he paid that money the day after Kitely's murder. Why, Mr. Cotherstone?"

Cotherstone, ready enough to answer and to speak until then, flushed angrily and shook his head. But he was about to speak when a gentle tap came at Tallington's door, and before the solicitor could make any response, the door was opened from without, and the police-superintendent walked in, accompanied by two men whom Brereton recognized as detectives from Norcaster.

"Sorry to interrupt, Mr. Tallington," said the superintendent, "but I heard Mr. Cotherstone was here. Mr. Cotherstone!—I shall have to ask you to step across with me to the office. Will you come over now?—it'll be best."

"Not until I know what I'm wanted for," answered Cotherstone determinedly. "What is it?"

The superintendent sighed and shook his head.

"Very well—it's not my fault, then," he answered. "The fact is we want both you and Mr. Mallalieu for this Stoner affair. That's the plain truth! The warrants were issued an hour ago—and we've got Mr. Mallalieu already. Come on, Mr. Cotherstone!—there's no help for it."

21. THE INTERRUPTED FLIGHT

Twenty-four hours after he had seen Stoner fall headlong into Hobwick Quarry, Mallalieu made up his mind for flight. And as soon as he had come to that moment of definite decision, he proceeded to arrange for his disappearance with all the craft and subtlety of which he was a past master. He would go, once and for all, and since he was to go he would go in such a fashion that nobody should be able to trace him.

After munching his sandwich and drinking his ale at the Highmarket Arms, Mallalieu had gone away to Hobwick Quarry and taken a careful look round. Just as he had expected, he found a policeman or two and a few gaping townsfolk there. He made no concealment of his own curiosity; he had come up, he said, to see what there was to be seen at the place where his clerk had come to this sad end. He made one of the policemen take him up to the broken railings at the brink of the quarry; together they made a careful examination of the ground.

"No signs of any footprints hereabouts, the superintendent says," remarked Mallalieu as they looked around. "You haven't seen aught of that sort!"

"No, your Worship—we looked for that when we first came up," answered the policeman. "You see this grass is that short and wiry that it's too full of spring to show marks. No, there's naught, anywhere about—we've looked a goodish way on both sides."

Mallalieu went close to the edge of the quarry and looked down. His sharp, ferrety eyes were searching everywhere for his stick. A little to the right of his position the side of the quarry shelved less abruptly than at the place where Stoner had fallen; on the gradual slope there, a great mass of bramble and gorse, broom and bracken, clustered: he gazed hard at it, thinking that the stick might have lodged in its meshes. It would be an easy thing to see that stick in daylight; it was a brightish yellow colour and would be easily distinguished against the prevalent greens and browns around there. But he saw nothing of it, and his brain, working around the event of the night before, began to have confused notions of the ringing of the stick on the lime-stone slabs at the bottom of the quarry.

"Aye!" he said musingly, with a final look round. "A nasty place to fall over, and a bad job—a bad job! Them rails," he continued, pointing to the broken fencing, "why, they're rotten all through! If a man put his weight on them, they'd be sure to give way. The poor young fellow must ha' sat down to rest himself a bit, on the top one, and of course, smash they went."

"That's what I should ha' said, your Worship," agreed the policeman, "but some of 'em that were up here seemed to think he'd been forced through 'em, or thrown against 'em, violent, as it might be. They think he was struck down—from the marks of a blow that they found."

"Aye, just so," said Mallalieu, "but he could get many blows on him as he fell down them rocks. Look for yourself!—there's not only rough edges of stone down there, but snags and roots of old trees that he'd strike against in falling. Accident, my lad!—that's what it's been—sheer and pure accident."

The policeman neither agreed with nor contradicted the Mayor, and presently they went down to the bottom of the quarry again, where Mallalieu, under pretence of thoroughly seeing into everything, walked about all over the place. He did not find the stick, and he was quite sure that nobody else had found it. Finally he went away, convinced that it lay in some nook or cranny of the shelving slope on to which he had kicked it in his sudden passion of rage. There, in all probability, it would remain for ever, for it would never occur to the police that whoever wielded whatever weapon it was that struck the blow would not carry the weapon away with him. No—on the point of the stick Mallalieu began to feel easy and confident.

He grew still easier and more confident about the whole thing during the course of the afternoon. He went about the town; he was in and out of the Town Hall; he kept calling in at the police-station; he became certain towards evening that no suspicion attached to himself—as yet. But—only as yet. He knew something would come out. The big question with him as he went home in the evening was—was he safe until the afternoon of the next day? While he ate and drank in his lonely dining-room, he decided that he was; by the time he had got through his after-dinner cigar he had further decided that when the next night came he would be safely away from Highmarket.

But there were things to do that night. He spent an hour with a Bradshaw and a map. While he reckoned up trains and glanced at distances and situations his mind was busy with other schemes, for he had all his life been a man who could think of more than one thing at once. And at the end of the hour he had decided on a plan of action.

Mallalieu had two chief objects in immediate view. He wanted to go away openly from Highmarket without exciting suspicion: that was one. He wanted to make it known that he had gone to some definite place, on some definite mission; that was the other. And in reckoning up his chances he saw how fortune was favouring him. At that very time the Highmarket Town Council was very much concerned and busied about a new water-supply. There was a project afoot for joining with another town, some miles off, in establishing a new system and making a new reservoir on the adjacent hills, and on the very next morning Mallalieu himself was to preside over a specially-summoned committee which was to debate

certain matters relating to this scheme. He saw how he
could make use of that appointment. He would profess
that he was not exactly pleased with some of the
provisions of the proposed amalgamation, and would
state his intention, in open meeting, of going over in
person to the other town that very evening to see its
authorities on the points whereon he was not satisfied.
Nobody would see anything suspicious in his going away
on Corporation business. An excellent plan for his
purpose—for in order to reach the other town it would be
necessary to pass through Norcaster, where he would
have to change stations. And Norcaster was a very big
city, and a thickly-populated one, and it had some obscure
parts with which Mallalieu was well-acquainted—and in
Norcaster he could enter on the first important stage of
his flight.

And so, being determined, Mallalieu made his final
preparations. They were all connected with money. If he
felt a pang at the thought of leaving his Highmarket
property behind him, it was assuaged by the reflection
that, after all, that property only represented the price of
his personal safety—perhaps (though he did not like to
think of that) of his life. Besides, events might turn out so
luckily that the enjoyment of it might be restored to
him—it was possible. Whether that possibility ever came
off or not, he literally dared not regard it just then. To put
himself in safety was the one, the vital consideration. And
his Highmarket property and his share in the business
only represented a part of Mallalieu's wealth. He could
afford to do without all that he left behind him; it was a
lot to leave, he sighed regretfully, but he would still be a
very wealthy man if he never touched a pennyworth of it
again.

From the moment in which Mallalieu had discovered
that Kitely knew the secret of the Wilchester affair he
had prepared for eventualities, and Kitely's death had
made no difference to his plans. If one man could find all
that out, he argued, half a dozen other men might find it

out. The murder of the ex-detective, indeed, had strengthened his resolve to be prepared. He foresaw that suspicion might fall on Cotherstone; deeper reflection showed him that if Cotherstone became an object of suspicion he himself would not escape. And so he had prepared himself. He had got together his valuable securities; they were all neatly bestowed in a stout envelope which fitted into the inner pocket of a waistcoat which he once had specially made to his own design: a cleverly arranged garment, in which a man could carry a lot of wealth—in paper. There in that pocket it all was— Government stock, railway stock, scrip, shares, all easily convertible, anywhere in the world where men bought and sold the best of gilt-edged securities. And in another pocket Mallalieu had a wad of bank-notes which he had secured during the previous week from a London bank at which he kept an account, and in yet another, a cunningly arranged one, lined out with wash-leather, and secured by a strong flap, belted and buckled, he carried gold.

Mallalieu kept that waistcoat and its precious contents under his pillow that night. And next morning he attired himself with particular care, and in the hip pocket of his trousers he placed a revolver which he had recently purchased, and for the first time for a fortnight he ate his usual hearty breakfast. After which he got into his most serviceable overcoat and went away townwards ... and if anybody had been watching him they would have seen that Mallalieu never once turned his head to take a look at the house which he had built, and might be leaving for ever.

Everything that Mallalieu did that morning was done with method. He was in and about his office and his yard for an hour or two, attending to business in his customary fashion. He saw Cotherstone, and did not speak to him except on absolutely necessary matters. No word was said by either in relation to Stoner's death. But about ten o'clock Mallalieu went across to the police-station and into the superintendent's office, and convinced himself that nothing further had come to light, and no new information had been given. The coroner's officer was with the police, and Mallalieu discussed with him and them some arrangements about the inquest. With every moment the certainty that he was safe increased—and at eleven o'clock he went into the Town Hall to his committee meeting.

Had Mallalieu chanced to look back at the door of the police-station as he entered the ancient door of the Town Hall he would have seen three men drive up there in a motor-car which had come from Norcaster—one of the men being Myler, and the other two Norcaster detectives. But Mallalieu did not look back. He went up to the committee-room and became absorbed in the business of the meeting. His fellow committee-men said afterwards that they never remembered the Mayor being in such fettle for business. He explained his objections to the scheme they Were considering; he pointed out this and urged that—finally, he said that he was so little satisfied with the project that he would go and see the Mayor of the sister town that very evening, and discuss the matter with him to the last detail.

Mallalieu stepped out of the committee-room to find the superintendent awaiting him in the corridor. The superintendent was pale and trembling, and his eyes met Mallalieu's with a strange, deprecating expression. Before he could speak, two strangers emerged from a doorway and came close up. And a sudden sickening sense of danger came over Mallalieu, and his tongue failed him.

"Mr. Mayor!" faltered the superintendent. "I—I can't help it! These are officers from Norcaster, sir—there's a warrant for your arrest. It's—it's the Stoner affair!"

22. THE HAND IN THE DARKNESS

The Highmarket clocks were striking noon when Mallalieu was arrested. For three hours he remained under lock and key, in a room in the Town Hall—most of the time alone. His lunch was brought to him; every consideration was shown him. The police wanted to send for his solicitor from Norcaster; Mallalieu bade them mind their own business. He turned a deaf ear to the superintendent's entreaties to him to see some friend; let him mind his own business too, said Mallalieu. He himself would do nothing until he saw the need to do something. Let him hear what could be brought against him—time enough to speak and act then. He ate his lunch, he smoked a cigar; he walked out of the room with defiant eye and head erect when they came to fetch him before a specially summoned bench of his fellow-magistrates. And it was not until he stepped into the dock, in full view of a crowded court, and amidst quivering excitement, that he and Cotherstone met.

The news of the partners' arrest had flown through the little town like wildfire. There was no need to keep it secret; no reason why it should be kept secret. It was necessary to bring the accused men before the magistrates as quickly as possible, and the days of private inquiries were long over. Before the Highmarket folk had well swallowed their dinners, every street in the town, every shop, office, bar-parlour, public-house, private house rang with the news—Mallalieu and Cotherstone, the Mayor and the Borough Treasurer, had been arrested for the murder of their clerk, and would be put before the magistrates at three o'clock. The Kitely affair faded into insignificance—except amongst the cute and knowing few, who immediately began to ask if the

Hobwick Quarry murder had anything to do with the murder on the Shawl.

If Mallalieu and Cotherstone could have looked out of the windows of the court in the Town Hall, they would have seen the Market Square packed with a restless and seething crowd of townsfolk, all clamouring for whatever news could permeate from the packed chamber into which so few had been able to fight a way. But the prisoners seemed strangely indifferent to their surroundings. Those who watched them closely—as Brereton and Tallington did—noticed that neither took any notice of the other. Cotherstone had been placed in the dock first. When Mallalieu was brought there, a moment later, the two exchanged one swift glance and no more—Cotherstone immediately moved off to the far corner on the left hand, Mallalieu remained in the opposite one, and placing his hands in the pockets of his overcoat, he squared his shoulders and straitened his big frame and took a calm and apparently contemptuous look round about him.

Brereton, sitting at a corner of the solicitor's table, and having nothing to do but play the part of spectator, watched these two men carefully and with absorbed interest from first to last. He was soon aware of the vastly different feelings with which they themselves watched the proceedings. Cotherstone was eager and restless; he could not keep still; he moved his position; he glanced about him; he looked as if he were on the verge of bursting into indignant or explanatory speech every now and then—though, as a matter of fact, he restrained whatever instinct he had in that direction. But Mallalieu never moved, never changed his attitude. His expression of disdainful, contemptuous watchfulness never left him—after the first moments and the formalities were over, he kept his eyes on the witness-box and on the people who entered it. Brereton, since his first meeting with Mallalieu, had often said to himself that the Mayor of Highmarket had the slyest eyes of any man he had even seen—but he was forced to admit now that, however sly Mallalieu's eyes were, they could, on occasion, be extraordinarily steady.

The truth was that Mallalieu was playing a part. He had outlined it, unconsciously, when he said to the superintendent that it would be time enough for him to do something when he knew what could be brought against him. And now all his attention was given to the two or three witnesses whom the prosecution thought it necessary to call. He wanted to know who they were. He curbed his impatience while the formal evidence of arrest was given, but his ears pricked a little when he heard one of the police witnesses speak of the warrant having been issued on information received. "What information? Received from whom? He half-turned as a sharp official voice called the name of the first important witness.

"David Myler!"

Mallalieu stared at David Myler as if he would tear whatever secret he had out of him with a searching glance. Who was David Myler? No Highmarket man— that was certain. Who was he, then?—what did he know?—was he some detective who had been privately working up this case? A cool, quiet, determined-looking young fellow, anyway. Confound him! But—what had he to do with this?

Those questions were speedily answered for Mallalieu. He kept his immovable attitude, his immobile expression, while Myler told the story of Stoner's visit to Darlington, and of the revelation which had resulted. And nothing proved his extraordinary command over his temper and his feelings better than the fact that as Myler narrated one damning thing after another, he never showed the least concern or uneasiness.

But deep within himself Mallalieu was feeling a lot. He knew now that he had been mistaken in thinking that Stoner had kept his knowledge to himself. He also knew what line the prosecution was taking. It was seeking to show that Stoner was murdered by Cotherstone and himself, or by one or other, separately or in collusion, in order that he might be silenced. But he knew more than that. Long practice and much natural inclination had taught Mallalieu the art of thinking ahead, and he could foresee as well as any man of his acquaintance. He foresaw the trend of events in this affair. This was only a preliminary. The prosecution was charging him and Cotherstone with the murder of Stoner today: it would be charging them with the murder of Kitely tomorrow.

Myler's evidence caused a profound sensation in court—but there was even more sensation and more excitement when Myler's father-in-law followed him in the witness-box. It was literally in a breathless silence that the old man told the story of the crime of thirty years ago; it was a wonderfully dramatic moment when he declared that in spite of the long time that had elapsed he recognized the Mallalieu and Cotherstone of Highmarket as the Mallows and Chidforth whom he had known at Wilchester.

Even then Mallalieu had not flinched. Cotherstone flushed, grew restless, hung his head a little, looked as if he would like to explain. But Mallalieu continued to stare fixedly across the court. He cared nothing that the revelation had been made at last. Now that it had been made, in full publicity, he did not care a brass farthing if every man and woman in Highmarket knew that he was an ex-gaol-bird. That was far away in the dead past— what he cared about was the present and the future. And his sharp wits told him that if the evidence of Myler and of old Pursey was all that the prosecution could bring against him, he was safe. That there had been a secret, that Stoner had come into possession of it, that Stoner was about to make profit of it, was no proof that he and Cotherstone, or either of them, had murdered Stoner. No—if that was all....

But in another moment Mallalieu knew that it was not all. Up to that moment he had firmly believed that he had got away from Hobwick Quarry unobserved. Here he was wrong. He had now to learn that a young man from Norcaster had come over to Highmarket that Sunday afternoon to visit his sweetheart; that this couple had gone up the moors; that they were on the opposite side of Hobwick Quarry when he went down into it after Stoner's fall; that they had seen him move about and finally go away; what was more, they had seen Cotherstone descend into the quarry and recover the stick; Cotherstone had passed near them as they stood hidden in the bushes; they had seen the stick in his hand.

When Mallalieu heard all this and saw his stick produced and identified, he ceased to take any further interest in that stage of the proceedings. He knew the worst now, and he began to think of his plans and schemes. And suddenly, all the evidence for that time being over, and the magistrates and the officials being in the thick of some whispered consultations about the adjournment, Mallalieu spoke for the first time.

"I shall have my answer about all this business at the right time and place," he said loudly. "My partner can do what he likes. All I have to say now is that I ask for bail. You can fix it at any amount you like. You all know me."

The magistrates and the officials looked across the well of the court in astonishment, and the chairman, a mild old gentleman who was obviously much distressed by the revelation, shook his head deprecatingly.

"Impossible!" he remonstrated. "Quite impossible! We haven't the power——"

"You're wrong!" retorted Mallalieu, masterful and insistent as ever. "You have the power! D'ye think I've been a justice of the peace for twelve years without knowing what law is? You've the power to admit to bail in all charges of felony, at your discretion. So now then!"

The magistrates looked at their clerk, and the clerk smiled.

"Mr. Mallalieu's theory is correct," he said quietly. "But no magistrate is obliged to admit to bail in felonies and misdemeanours, and in practice bail is never allowed in cases where—as in this case—the charge is one of murder. Such procedure is unheard of."

"Make a precedent, then!" sneered Mallalieu. "Here!— you can have twenty thousand pounds security, if you like."

But this offer received no answer, and in five minutes more Mallalieu heard the case adjourned for a week and himself and Cotherstone committed to Norcaster Gaol in the meantime. Without a look at his fellow-prisoner he turned out of the dock and was escorted back to the private room in the Town Hall from which he had been brought.

"Hang 'em for a lot of fools!" he burst out to the superintendent, who had accompanied him. "Do they think I'm going to run away? Likely thing—on a trumped-up charge like this. Here!—how soon shall you be wanting to start for yon place?"

The superintendent, who had cherished considerable respect for Mallalieu in the past, and was much upset and very downcast about this sudden change in the Mayor's fortunes, looked at his prisoner and shook his head.

"There's a couple of cars ordered to be ready in half an hour, Mr. Mallalieu," he answered. "One for you, and one for Mr. Cotherstone."

"With armed escorts in both, I suppose!" sneered Mallalieu. "Well, look here—you've time to get me a cup of tea. Slip out and get one o' your men to nip across to the Arms for it—good, strong tea, and a slice or two of bread-and-butter. I can do with it."

He flung half a crown on the table, and the superintendent, suspecting nothing, and willing to oblige a man who had always been friendly and genial towards himself, went out of the room, with no further precautions than the turning of the key in the lock when he had once got outside the door. It never entered his head that the prisoner would try to escape, never crossed his mind that Mallalieu had any chance of escaping. He went away along the corridor to find one of his men who could be dispatched to the Highmarket Arms.

But the instant Mallalieu was left alone he started into action. He had not been Mayor of Highmarket for two years, a member of its Corporation for nearly twenty, without knowing all the ins-and-outs of that old Town Hall. And as soon as the superintendent had left him he drew from his pocket a key, went across the room to a door which stood in a corner behind a curtain, unlocked it, opened it gently, looked out, passed into a lobby without, relocked the door behind him, and in another instant was stealing quietly down a private staircase that led to an entrance into the quaint old garden at the back of the premises. One further moment of suspense and of looking round, and he was safely in that garden and behind the thick shrubs which ran along one of its high walls. Yet another and he was out of the garden, and in an old-fashioned orchard which ran, thick with trees, to the very edge of the coppices at the foot of the Shawl. Once in that orchard, screened by its close-branched, low-spreading boughs, leafless though they were at that period of the year, he paused to get his breath, and to chuckle over the success of his scheme. What a mercy, what blessing, he thought, that they had not searched him on his arrest!—that they had delayed that interesting ceremony until his committal! The omission, he knew, had been winked at—purposely—and it had left him with his precious waistcoat, his revolver, and the key that had opened his prison door.

Dusk had fallen over Highmarket before the hearing came to an end, and it was now dark. Mallalieu knew that he had little time to lose—but he also knew that his pursuers would have hard work to catch him. He had laid his plans while the last two witnesses were in the box: his detailed knowledge of the town and its immediate neighbourhood stood in good stead. Moreover, the geographical situation of the Town Hall was a great help. He had nothing to do but steal out of the orchard into the coppices, make his way cautiously through them into the deeper wood which fringed the Shawl, pass through that to the ridge at the top, and gain the moors. Once on those moors he would strike by devious way for Norcaster—he knew a safe place in the Lower Town there where he could be hidden for a month, three months, six months, without fear of discovery, and from whence he could get away by ship.

All was quiet as he passed through a gap in the orchard hedge and stole into the coppices. He kept stealthily but swiftly along through the pine and fir until he came to the wood which covered the higher part of the Shawl. The trees were much thicker there, the brakes and bushes were thicker, and the darkness was greater. He was obliged to move at a slower pace—and suddenly he heard men's voices on the lower slopes beneath him. He paused catching his breath and listening. And then, just as suddenly as he had heard the voices, he felt a hand, firm, steady, sinewy, fasten on his wrist and stay there.

23. COMFORTABLE CAPTIVITY

The tightening of that sinewy grip on Mallalieu's wrist so startled him that it was only by a great effort that he restrained himself from crying out and from breaking into one of his fits of trembling. This sudden arrest was all the more disturbing to his mental composure because, for the moment, he could not see to whom the hand belonged. But as he twisted round he became aware of a tall, thin shape at his elbow; the next instant a whisper stole to his ear.

"H'sh! Be careful!—there's men down there on the path!—they're very like after you," said the voice. "Wait here a minute!"

"Who are you?" demanded Mallalieu hoarsely. He was endeavouring to free his wrist, but the steel-like fingers clung. "Let go my hand!" he said. "D'ye hear?—let it go!"

"Wait!" said the voice. "It's for your own good. It's me—Miss Pett. I saw you—against that patch of light between the trees there—I knew your big figure. You've got away, of course. Well, you'll not get much further if you don't trust to me. Wait till we hear which way them fellows go."

Mallalieu resigned himself. As his eyes grew more accustomed to the gloom of the wood, he made out that Miss Pett was standing just within an opening in the trees; presently, as the voices beneath them became fainter, she drew him into it.

"This way!" she whispered. "Come close behind me—the house is close by."

"No!" protested Mallalieu angrily. "None of your houses! Here, I want to be on the moors. What do you want—to keep your tongue still?"

Miss Pett paused and edged her thin figure close to Mallalieu's bulky one.

"It'll not be a question of my tongue if you once go out o' this wood," she said. "They'll search those moors first thing. Don't be a fool!—it'll be known all over the town by now! Come with me and I'll put you where all the police in the county can't find you. But of course, do as you like—only, I'm warning you. You haven't a cat's chance if you set foot on that moor. Lord bless you, man!—don't they know that there's only two places you could make for—Norcaster and Hexendale? Is there any way to either of 'em except across the moors? Come on, now—be sensible."

"Go on, then!" growled Mallalieu. Wholly suspicious by nature, he was wondering why this she-dragon, as he had so often called her, should be at all desirous of sheltering him. Already he suspected her of some design, some trick—and in the darkness he clapped his hand on the hip-pocket in which he had placed his revolver. That was safe enough—and again he thanked his stars that the police had not searched him. But however well he might be armed, he was for the time being in Miss Pett's power—he knew very well that if he tried to slip away Miss Pett had only to utter one shrill cry to attract attention. And so, much as he desired the freedom of the moors, he allowed himself to be taken captive by this gaoler who promised eventual liberty.

Miss Pett waited in the thickness of the trees until the voices at the foot of the Shawl became faint and far off; she herself knew well enough that they were not the voices of men who were searching for Mallalieu, but of country folk who had been into the town and were now returning home by the lower path in the wood. But it suited her purposes to create a spirit of impending danger in the Mayor, and so she kept him there, her hand still on his arm, until the last sound died away. And while she thus held him, Mallalieu, who had often observed Miss Pett in her peregrinations through the Market Place, and

had been accustomed to speaking of her as a thread-
paper, or as Mother Skin-and-Bones, because of her
phenomenal thinness, wondered how it was that a woman
of such extraordinary attenuation should possess such
powerful fingers—her grip on his wrist was like that of a
vice. And somehow, in a fashion for which he could not
account, especially in the disturbed and anxious state of
his mind, he became aware that here in this strange
woman was some mental force which was superior to and
was already dominating his own, and for a moment he
was tempted to shake the steel-like fingers off and make
a dash for the moorlands.

But Miss Pett presently moved forward, holding
Mallalieu as a nurse might hold an unwilling child. She
led him cautiously through the trees, which there became
thicker, she piloted him carefully down a path, and into a
shrubbery—she drew him through a gap in a hedgerow,
and Mallalieu knew then that they were in the kitchen
garden at the rear of old Kitely's cottage. Quietly and
stealthily, moving herself as if her feet were shod with
velvet, Miss Pett made her way with her captive to the
door; Mallalieu heard the rasping of a key in a lock, the
lifting of a latch; then he was gently but firmly pushed
into darkness. Behind him the door closed—a bolt was
shot home.

"This way!" whispered Miss Pett. She drew him after
her along what he felt to be a passage, twisted him to the
left through another doorway, and then, for the first time
since she had assumed charge of him, released his wrist.
"Wait!" she said. "We'll have a light presently."

Mallalieu stood where she had placed him, impatient
of everything, but feeling powerless to move. He heard
Miss Pett move about; he heard the drawing to and
barring of shutters, the swish of curtains being pulled
together; then the spurt and glare of a match—in its
feeble flame he saw Miss Pett's queer countenance,
framed in an odd-shaped, old-fashioned poke bonnet,

bending towards a lamp. In the gradually increasing light of that lamp Mallalieu looked anxiously around him.

He was in a little room which was half-parlour, half bed-room. There was a camp bed in one corner; there was an ancient knee-hole writing desk under the window across which the big curtains had been drawn; there were a couple of easy-chairs on either side of the hearth. There were books and papers on a shelf; there were pictures and cartoons on the walls. Mallalieu took a hasty glance at those unusual ornaments and hated them: they were pictures of famous judges in their robes, and of great criminal counsel in their wigs—and over the chimney-piece, framed in black wood, was an old broad-sheet, printed in big, queer-shaped letters: Mallalieu's hasty glance caught the staring headline—*Dying Speech and Confession of the Famous Murderer*....

"This was Kitely's snug," remarked Miss Pett calmly, as she turned up the lamp to the full. "He slept in that bed, studied at that desk, and smoked his pipe in that chair. He called it his sanctum-something-or-other—I don't know no Latin. But it's a nice room, and it's comfortable, or will be when I put a fire in that grate, and it'll do very well for you until you can move. Sit you down—would you like a drop of good whisky, now?"

Mallalieu sat down and stared his hardest at Miss Pett. He felt himself becoming more confused and puzzled than ever.

"Look here, missis!" he said suddenly. "Let's get a clear idea about things. You say you can keep me safe here until I can get away. How do you know I shall be safe?"

"Because I'll take good care that you are," answered Miss Pett. "There's nobody can get into this house without my permission, and before I let anybody in, no matter with what warrants or such-like they carried, I'd see that you were out of it before they crossed the threshold. I'm no fool, I can tell you, Mr. Mallalieu, and if you trust me——"

"I've no choice, so it seems," remarked Mallalieu, grimly. "You've got me! And now, how much are you reckoning to get out of me—what?"

"No performance, no pay!" said Miss Pett. "Wait till I've managed things for you. I know how to get you safely away from here—leave it to me, and I'll have you put down in any part of Norcaster you like, without anybody knowing. And if you like to make me a little present then——"

"You're certain?" demanded Mallalieu, still suspicious, but glad to welcome even a ray of hope. "You know what you're talking about?"

"I never talk idle stuff," retorted Miss Pett. "I'm telling you what I know."

"All right, then," said Mallalieu. "You do your part, and I'll do mine when it comes to it—you'll not find me ungenerous, missis. And I will have that drop of whisky you talked about."

Miss Pett went away, leaving Mallalieu to stare about him and to meditate on this curious change in his fortunes. Well, after all, it was better to be safe and snug under this queer old woman's charge than to be locked up in Norcaster Gaol, or to be hunted about on the bleak moors and possibly to go without food or drink. And his thoughts began to assume a more cheerful complexion when Miss Pett presently brought him a stiff glass of undeniably good liquor, and proceeded to light a fire in his prison: he even melted so much as to offer her some thanks.

"I'm sure I'm much obliged to you, missis," he said, with an attempt at graciousness. "I'll not forget you when it comes to settling up. But I should feel a good deal easier in my mind if I knew two things. First of all—you know, of course, I've got away from yon lot down yonder, else I shouldn't ha' been where you found me. But— they'll raise the hue-and-cry, missis! Now supposing they come here?"

Miss Pett lifted her queer face from the hearth, where she had been blowing the sticks into a blaze.

"There's such a thing as chance," she observed. "To start with, how much chance is there that they'd ever think of coming here? Next to none! They'd never suspect me of harbouring you. There is a chance that when they look through these woods—as they will—they'll ask if I've seen aught of you—well, you can leave the answer to me."

"They might want to search," suggested Mallalieu.

"Not likely!" answered Miss Pett, with a shake of the poke bonnet. "But even if they did, I'd take good care they didn't find you!"

"Well—and what about getting me away?" asked Mallalieu. "How's that to be done?"

"I'll tell you that tomorrow," replied Miss Pett. "You make yourself easy—I'll see you're all right. And now I'll go and cook you a nice chop, for no doubt you'll do with something after all the stuff you had to hear in the court."

"You were there, then?" asked Mallalieu. "Lot o' stuff and nonsense! A sensible woman like you——"

"A sensible woman like me only believes what she can prove," answered Miss Pett.

She went away and shut the door, and Mallalieu, left to himself, took another heartening pull at his glass and proceeded to re-inspect his quarters. The fire was blazing up: the room was warm and comfortable; certainly he was fortunate. But he assured himself that the window was properly shuttered, barred, and fully covered by the thick curtain, and he stood by it for a moment listening intently for any sound of movement without. No sound came, not even the wail of a somewhat strong wind which he knew to be sweeping through the pine trees, and he came to the conclusion that the old stone walls were almost sound-proof and that if he and Miss Pett conversed in ordinary tones no eavesdroppers outside the cottage could hear them. And presently he caught a sound within the cottage—the sound of the sizzling of chops on a gridiron, and with it came the pleasant and grateful smell of cooking meat, and Mallalieu decided that he was hungry.

To a man fixed as Mallalieu was at that time the evening which followed was by no means unpleasant. Miss Pett served him as nice a little supper as his own housekeeper would have given him; later on she favoured him with her company. They talked of anything but the events of the day, and Mallalieu began to think that the queer-looking woman was a remarkably shrewd and intelligent person. There was but one drawback to his captivity—Miss Pett would not let him smoke. Cigars, she said, might be smelt outside the cottage, and nobody would credit her with the consumption of such gentleman-like luxuries.

"And if I were you," she said, at the end of an interesting conversation which had covered a variety of subjects, "I should try to get a good night's rest. I'll mix you a good glass of toddy such as the late Kitely always let me mix for his nightcap, and then I'll leave you. The bed's aired, there's plenty of clothing on it, all's safe, and you can sleep as if you were a baby in a cradle, for I always sleep like a dog, with one ear and an eye open, and I'll take good care naught disturbs you, so there!"

Mallalieu drank the steaming glass of spirits and water which Miss Pett presently brought him, and took her advice about going to bed. Without ever knowing anything about it he fell into such a slumber as he had never known in his life before. It was indeed so sound that he never heard Miss Pett steal into his room, was not aware that she carefully withdrew the precious waistcoat which, through a convenient hole in the wall, she had watched him deposit under the rest of his garments on the chair at his side, never knew that she carried it away into the living-room on the other side of the cottage. For the strong flavour of the lemon and the sweetness of the sugar which Miss Pett had put into the hot toddy had utterly obscured the very slight taste of something else which she had put in—something which was much stronger than the generous dose of whisky, and was calculated to plunge Mallalieu into a stupor from which not even an earthquake could have roused him.

Miss Pett examined the waistcoat at her leisure. Her thin fingers went through every pocket and every paper, through the bank-notes, the scrip, the shares, the securities. She put everything back in its place, after a careful reckoning and estimation of the whole. And Mallalieu was as deeply plunged in his slumbers as ever when she went back into his room with her shaded light and her catlike tread, and she replaced the garment exactly where she found it, and went out and shut the door as lightly as a butterfly folds its wings.

It was then eleven o'clock at night, and Miss Pett, instead of retiring to her bed, sat down by the living-room fire and waited. The poke bonnet had been replaced by the gay turban, and under its gold and scarlet her strange, skeleton-like face gleamed like old ivory as she sat there with the firelight playing on it. And so immobile was she, sitting with her sinewy skin-and-bone arms lying folded over her silk apron, that she might have been taken for an image rather than for a living woman.

But as the hands of the clock on the mantelpiece neared midnight, Miss Pett suddenly moved. Her sharp ears caught a scratching sound on the shutter outside the window. And noiselessly she moved down the passage, and noiselessly unbarred the front door, and just as noiselessly closed it again behind the man who slipped in—Christopher, her nephew.

24. STRICT BUSINESS LINES

Mr. Christopher Pett, warned by the uplifted finger of his aunt, tip-toed into the living-room, and setting down his small travelling bag on the table proceeded to divest himself of a thick overcoat, a warm muffler, woollen gloves, and a silk hat. And Miss Pett, having closed the outer and inner doors, came in and glanced inquiringly at him.

"Which way did you come, this time?" she inquired.

"High Gill," replied Christopher. "Got an afternoon express that stopped there. Jolly cold it was crossing those moors of yours, too, I can tell you!—I can do with a drop of something. I say—is there anything afoot about here?—anything going on?"

"Why?" asked Miss Pett, producing the whisky and the lemons. "And how do you mean?"

Christopher pulled an easy chair to the fire and stretched his hands to the blaze.

"Up there, on the moor," he answered. "There's fellows going about with lights—lanterns, I should say. I didn't see 'em close at hand—there were several of 'em crossing about—like fire-flies—as if the chaps who carried 'em were searching for something."

Miss Pett set the decanter and the materials for toddy on the table at her nephew's side, and took a covered plate from the cupboard in the corner.

"Them's potted meat sandwiches," she said. "Very toothsome you'll find 'em—I didn't prepare much, for I knew you'd get your dinner on the train. Yes, well, there is something afoot—they are searching. Not for something, though, but for somebody. Mallalieu!"

Christopher, his mouth full of sandwiches, and his hand laid on the decanter, lifted a face full of new and alert interest.

"The Mayor!" he exclaimed.

"Quite so," assented Miss Pett. "Anthony Mallalieu, Esquire, Mayor of Highmarket. They want him, does the police—bad!"

Christopher still remained transfixed. The decanter was already tilted in his hand, but he tilted it no further; the sandwich hung bulging in his cheek.

"Good Lord!" he said. "Not for——" he paused, nodding his head towards the front of the cottage where the wood lay "—not for—that? They ain't suspicioning *him*?"

"No, but for killing his clerk, who'd found something out," replied Miss Pett. "The clerk was killed Sunday; they took up Mallalieu and his partner today, and tried 'em, and Mallalieu slipped the police somehow, after the case was adjourned, and escaped. And—he's here!"

Christopher had begun to pour the whisky into his glass. In his astonishment he rattled the decanter against the rim.

"What!" he exclaimed. "Here? In this cottage?"

"In there," answered Miss Pett. "In Kitely's room. Safe and sound. There's no danger. He'll not wake. I mixed him a glass of toddy before he went to bed, and neither earthquakes nor fire-alarms 'ull wake him before nine o'clock tomorrow morning."

"Whew!" said Christopher. "Um! it's a dangerous game—it's harbouring, you know. However, they'd suspect that he'd come here. Whatever made him come here?"

"I made him come here," replied Miss Pett. "I caught him in the wood outside there, as I was coming back from the Town Hall, so I made him come in. It'll pay very well, Chris."

Mr. Pett, who was lifting his glass to his lips, arrested it in mid-air, winked over its rim at his aunt, and smiled knowingly.

"You're a good hand at business, I must say, old lady!" he remarked admiringly. "Of course, of course, if you're doing a bit of business out of it——"

"That'll come tomorrow," said Miss Pett, seating herself at the table and glancing at her nephew's bag. "We'll do our own business tonight. Well, how have you come on?"

Christopher munched and drank for a minute or two. Then he nodded, with much satisfaction in his manner.

"Very well," he answered. "I got what I consider a very good price. Sold the whole lot to another Brixton property-owner, got paid, and have brought you the money. All of it—ain't even taken my costs, my expenses, and my commission out of it—yet."

"How much did you sell for?" asked Miss Pett.

Christopher pulled his bag to his side and took a bundle of red-taped documents from it.

"You ought to think yourself jolly lucky," he said, wagging his head admonitorily at his aunt. "I see a lot of the state of the property market, and I can assure you I did uncommonly well for you. I shouldn't have got what I did if it had been sold by auction. But the man I sold to was a bit keen, 'cause he's already got adjacent property, and he gave rather more than he would ha' done in other circumstances. I got," he continued, consulting the topmost of his papers, "I got, in round figures, three thousand four hundred—to be exact, three thousand four hundred, seventeen, five, eleven."

"Where's the money?" demanded Miss Pett.

"It's here," answered Christopher, tapping his breast. "In my pocket-book. Notes, big and little—so that we can settle up."

Miss Pett stretched out her hand.

"Hand it over!" she said.

Christopher gave his aunt a sidelong glance.

"Hadn't we better reckon up my costs and commission first?" he suggested. "Here's an account of the costs—the commission, of course, was to be settled between you and me."

"We'll settle all that when you've handed the money over," said Miss Pett. "I haven't counted it yet."

There was a certain unwillingness in Christopher Pett's manner as he slowly produced a stout pocket-book and took from it a thick wad of bank-notes. He pushed this across to his aunt, with a tiny heap of silver and copper.

"Well, I'm trusting to you, you know," he said a little doubtfully. "Don't forget that I've done well for you."

Miss Pett made no answer. She had taken a pair of spectacles from her pocket, and with these perched on the bridge of her sharp nose she proceeded to count the notes, while her nephew alternately sipped at his toddy and stroked his chin, meanwhile eyeing his relative's proceedings with somewhat rueful looks.

"Three thousand, four hundred and seventeen pounds, five shillings and elevenpence," and Miss Pett calmly. "And them costs, now, and the expenses—how much do they come to, Chris?"

"Sixty-one, two, nine," answered Christopher, passing one of his papers across the table with alacrity. "You'll find it quite right—I did it as cheap as possible for you."

Miss Pett set her elbow on her heap of bank-notes while she examined the statement. That done, she looked over the tops of her spectacles at the expectant Christopher.

"Well, about that commission," she said. "Of course, you know, Chris, you oughtn't to charge me what you'd charge other folks. You ought to do it very reasonable indeed for me. What were you thinking of, now?"

"I got the top price," remarked Christopher reflectively. "I got you quite four hundred more than the market price. How would—how would five per cent. be, now?"

Miss Pett threw up the gay turban with a toss of surprise.

"Five per cent!" she ejaculated. "Christopher Pett!—whatever are you talking about? Why, that 'ud be a hundred and seventy pound! Eh, dear!—nothing of the sort—it 'ud be as good as robbery. I'm astonished at you."

"Well, how much, then?" growled Christopher. "Hang it all!—don't be close with your own nephew."

"I'll give you a hundred pounds—to include the costs," said Miss Pett firmly. "Not a penny more—but," she added, bending forward and nodding her head towards that half of the cottage wherein Mallalieu slumbered so heavily, "I'll give you something to boot—an opportunity of feathering your nest out of—him!"

Christopher's face, which had clouded heavily, lightened somewhat at this, and he too glanced at the door.

"Will it be worth it?" he asked doubtfully. "What is there to be got out of him if he's flying from justice? He'll carry naught—and he can't get at anything that he has, either."

Miss Pett gave vent to a queer, dry chuckle; the sound of her laughter always made her nephew think of the clicking of machinery that badly wanted oiling.

"He's heaps o' money on him!" she whispered. "After he dropped off tonight I went through his pockets. We've only got to keep a tight hold on him to get as much as ever we like! So—put your hundred in your pocket, and we'll see about the other affair tomorrow."

"Oh, well, of course, in that case!" said Christopher. He picked up the banknote which his aunt pushed towards him and slipped it into his purse. "We shall have to play on his fears a bit, you know," he remarked.

"I think we shall be equal to it—between us," answered Miss Pett drily. "Them big, flabby men's easy frightened."

Mallalieu was certainly frightened when he woke suddenly next morning to find Miss Pett standing at the side of his bed. He glared at her for one instant of wild alarm and started up on his pillows. Miss Pett laid one of her claw-like hands on his shoulder.

"Don't alarm yourself, mister," she said. "All's safe, and here's something that'll do you good—a cup of nice hot coffee—real Mocha, to which the late Kitely was partial—with a drop o'rum in it. Drink it—and you shall have your breakfast in half an hour. It's past nine o'clock."

"I must have slept very sound," said Mallalieu, following his gaoler's orders. "You say all's safe? Naught heard or seen?"

"All's safe, all's serene," replied Miss Pett. "And you're in luck's way, for there's my nephew Christopher arrived from London, to help me about settling my affairs and removing my effects from this place, and he's a lawyer and'll give you good advice."

Mallalieu growled a little. He had seen Mr. Christopher Pett and he was inclined to be doubtful of him.

"Is he to be trusted?" he muttered. "I expect he'll have to be squared, too!"

"Not beyond reason," replied Miss Pett. "We're not unreasonable people, our family. He's a very sensible young man, is Christopher. The late Kitely had a very strong opinion of his abilities."

Mallalieu had no doubt of Mr. Christopher Pett's abilities in a certain direction after he had exchanged a few questions and answers with that young gentleman. For Christopher was shrewd, sharp, practical and judicial.

"It's a very dangerous and—you'll excuse plain speaking under the circumstances, sir—very foolish thing that you've done, Mr. Mallalieu," he said, as he and the prisoner sat closeted together in the still shuttered and curtained parlour-bedroom. "The mere fact of your making your escape, sir, is what some would consider a proof of guilt—it is indeed! And of course my aunt—and myself, in my small way—we're running great risks, Mr. Mallalieu—we really are—great risks!"

"Now then, you'll not lose by me," said Mallalieu. "I'm not a man of straw."

"All very well, sir," replied Christopher, "but even if you were a millionaire and recompensed us on what I may term a princely scale—not that we shall expect it, Mr. Mallalieu—the risks would be extraordinary—ahem! I mean will be extraordinary. For you see, Mr. Mallalieu, there's two or three things that's dead certain. To start with, sir, it's absolutely impossible for you to get away from here by yourself—you can't do it!"

"Why not?" growled Mallalieu. "I can get away at nightfall."

"No, sir," affirmed Christopher stoutly. "I saw the condition of the moors last night. Patrolled, Mr. Mallalieu, patrolled! By men with lights. That patrolling, sir, will go on for many a night. Make up your mind, Mr. Mallalieu, that if you set foot out of this house, you'll see the inside of Norcaster Gaol before two hours is over!"

"What do you advise, then?" demanded Mallalieu. "Here!—I'm fairly in for it, so I'll tell you what my notion was. If I can once get to a certain part of Norcaster, I'm safe. I can get away to the Continent from there."

"Then, sir," replied Christopher, "the thing is to devise a plan by which you can be conveyed to Norcaster without suspicion. That'll have to be arranged between me and my aunt—hence our risks on your behalf."

"Your aunt said she'd a plan," remarked Mallalieu.

"Not quite matured, sir," said Christopher. "It needs a little reflection and trimming, as it were. Now what I advise, Mr. Mallalieu, is this—you keep snug here, with my aunt as sentinel—she assures me that even if the police—don't be frightened, sir!—did come here, she could hide you quite safely before ever she opened the door to them. As for me, I'll go, casual-like, into the town, and do a bit of quiet looking and listening. I shall be able to find out how the land lies, sir—and when I return I'll report to you, and the three of us will put our heads together."

Leaving the captive in charge of Miss Pett, Christopher, having brushed his silk hat and his overcoat and fitted on a pair of black kid gloves, strolled solemnly into Highmarket. He was known to a few people there, and he took good care to let those of his acquaintance who met him hear that he had come down to arrange his aunt's affairs, and to help in the removal of the household goods bequeathed to her by the deceased Kitely. In proof of this he called in at the furniture remover's, to get an estimate of the cost of removal to Norcaster Docks— thence, said Christopher, the furniture could be taken by sea to London, where Miss Pett intended to reside in future. At the furniture remover's, and in such other shops as he visited, and in the bar-parlour of the Highmarket Arms, where he stayed an hour or so, gossiping with the loungers, and sipping a glass or two of dry sherry, Christopher picked up a great deal of information. And at noon he returned to the cottage, having learned that the police and everybody in Highmarket firmly believed that Mallalieu had got clear and clean away the night before, and was already far beyond pursuit. The police theory was that there had been collusion, and that immediately on his escape he had been whirled off by some person to whose identity there was as yet no clue.

But Christopher Pett told a very different story to Mallalieu. The moors, he said, were being patrolled night and day: it was believed the fugitive was in hiding in one of the old quarries. Every road and entrance to Norcaster, and to all the adjacent towns and stations, was watched and guarded. There was no hope for Mallalieu but in the kindness and contrivance of the aunt and the nephew, and Mallalieu recognized the inevitable and was obliged to yield himself to their tender mercies.

25. NO FURTHER EVIDENCE

While Mallalieu lay captive in the stronghold of Miss Pett, Cotherstone was experiencing a quite different sort of incarceration in the detention cells of Norcaster Gaol. Had he known where his partner was, and under what circumstances Mallalieu had obtained deliverance from official bolts and bars, Cotherstone would probably have laughed in his sleeve and sneered at him for a fool. He had been calling Mallalieu a fool, indeed, ever since the previous evening, when the police, conducting him to Norcaster, had told him of the Mayor's escape from the Town Hall. Nobody but an absolute fool, a consummate idiot, thought Cotherstone, would have done a thing like that. The man who flies is the man who has reason to fly—that was Cotherstone's opinion, and in his belief ninety-nine out of every hundred persons in Highmarket would share it. Mallalieu would now be set down as guilty—they would say he dared not face things, that he knew he was doomed, that his escape was the desperate act of a conscious criminal. Ass!—said Cotherstone, not without a certain amount of malicious delight: they should none of them have reason to say such things of him. He would make no attempt to fly—no, not if they left the gate of Norcaster Gaol wide open to him! It should be his particular care to have himself legally cleared—his acquittal should be as public as the proceedings which had just taken place. He went out of the dock with that resolve strong on him; he carried it away to his cell at Norcaster; he woke in the morning with it, stronger than ever. Cotherstone, instead of turning tail, was going to fight—for his own hand.

As a prisoner merely under detention, Cotherstone had privileges of which he took good care to avail himself.

Four people he desired to see, and must see at once, on that first day in gaol—and he lost no time in making known his desires. One—and the most important—person was a certain solicitor in Norcaster who enjoyed a great reputation as a sharp man of affairs. Another—scarcely less important—was a barrister who resided in Norcaster, and had had it said of him for a whole generation that he had restored more criminals to society than any man of his profession then living. And the other two were his own daughter and Windle Bent. Them he must see—but the men of law first.

When the solicitor and the barrister came, Cotherstone talked to them as he had never talked to anybody in his life. He very soon let them see that he had two definite objects in sending for them: the first was to tell them in plain language that money was of no consideration in the matter of his defence; the second, that they had come there to hear him lay down the law as to what they were to do. Talk he did, and they listened— and Cotherstone had the satisfaction of seeing that they went away duly impressed with all that he had said to them. He went back to his cell from the room in which this interview had taken place congratulating himself on his ability.

"I shall be out of this, and all'll be clear, a week today!" he assured himself. "We'll see where that fool of a Mallalieu is by then! For he'll not get far, nor go hidden for thirty years, this time."

He waited with some anxiety to see his daughter, not because he must see her within the walls of a prison, but because he knew that by that time she would have learned the secrets of that past which he had kept so carefully hidden from her. Only child of his though she was, he felt that Lettie was not altogether of his sort; he had often realized that she was on a different mental plane from his own, and was also, in some respects, a little of a mystery to him. How would she take all this?— what would she say?—what effect would it have on her?—

he pondered these questions uneasily while he waited for her visit.

But if Cotherstone had only known it, he need have suffered no anxiety about Lettie. It had fallen to Bent to tell her the sad news the afternoon before, and Bent had begged Brereton to go up to the house with him. Bent was upset; Brereton disliked the task, though he willingly shared in it. They need have had no anxiety, either. For Lettie listened calmly and patiently until the whole story had been told, showing neither alarm, nor indignation, nor excitement; her self-composure astonished even Bent, who thought, having been engaged to her for twelve months, that he knew her pretty well.

"I understand exactly," said Lettie, when, between them, they had told her everything, laying particular stress on her father's version of things. "It is all very annoying, of course, but then it is quite simple, isn't it? Of course, Mr. Mallalieu has been the guilty person all through, and poor father has been dragged into it. But then—all that you have told me has only to be put before the—who is it?—magistrates?—judges?—and then, of course, father will be entirely cleared, and Mr. Mallalieu will be hanged. Windle—of course we shall have to put off the wedding?"

"Oh, of course!" agreed Bent. "We can't have any weddings until all this business is cleared up."

"That'll be so much better," said Lettie. "It really was becoming an awful rush."

Brereton glanced at Bent when they left the house.

"I congratulate you on having a fiancée of a well-balanced mind, old chap!" he said. "That was—a relief!"

"Oh, Lettie's a girl of singularly calm and equable temperament," answered Bent. "She's not easily upset, and she's quick at sizing things up. And I say, Brereton, I've got to do all I can for Cotherstone, you know. What about his defence?"

"I should imagine that Cotherstone is already arranging his defence himself," said Brereton. "He struck me during that talk this morning at Tailington's as being very well able to take care of himself, Bent, and I think you'll find when you visit him that he's already fixed things. You won't perhaps see why, and I won't explain just now, but this foolish running away of Mallalieu, who, of course, is sure to be caught, is very much in Cotherstone's favour. I shall be much surprised if you don't find Cotherstone in very good spirits, and if there aren't developments in this affair within a day or two which will impress the whole neighbourhood."

Bent, visiting the prisoner in company with Lettie next day, found Brereton's prediction correct. Cotherstone, hearing from his daughter's own lips what she herself thought of the matter, and being reassured that all was well between Bent and her, became not merely confident but cheerily boastful. He would be free, and he would be cleared by that day next week—he was not sorry, he said, that at last all this had come out, for now he would be able to get rid of an incubus that had weighted him all his life.

"You're very confident, you know," remarked Bent.

"Not beyond reason," asserted Cotherstone doggedly. "You wait till tomorrow!"

"What is there tomorrow?" asked Bent.

"The inquest on Stoner is tomorrow," replied Cotherstone. "You be there—and see and hear what happens."

All of Highmarket population that could cram itself into the Coroner's court was there next day when the adjourned inquest on the clerk's death was held. Neither Bent nor Brereton nor Tallington had any notion of what line was going to be taken by Cotherstone and his advisers, but Tallington and Brereton exchanged glances when Cotherstone, in charge of two warders from Norcaster, was brought in, and when the Norcaster solicitor and the Norcaster barrister whom he had retained, shortly afterwards presented themselves.

"I begin to foresee," whispered Tallington. "Clever!—devilish clever!"

"Just so," agreed Brereton, with a sidelong nod at the crowded seats close by. "And there's somebody who's interested because it's going to be devilish clever—that fellow Pett!"

Christopher Pett was there, silk hat, black kid gloves and all, not afraid of being professionally curious. Curiosity was the order of the day: everybody present—of any intelligent perception—wanted to know what the presence of Cotherstone, one of the two men accused of the murder of Stoner, signified. But it was some little time before any curiosity was satisfied. The inquest being an adjourned one, most of the available evidence had to be taken, and as a coroner has a wide field in the calling of witnesses, there was more evidence produced before him and his jury than before the magistrates. There was Myler, of course, and old Pursey, and the sweethearting couple: there were other witnesses, railway folks, medical experts, and townspeople who could contribute some small quota of testimony. But all these were forgotten when at last Cotherstone, having been duly warned by the coroner that he need not give any evidence at all, determinedly entered the witness-box—to swear on oath that he was witness to his partner's crime.

Nothing could shake Cotherstone's evidence. He told a plain, straightforward story from first to last. He had no knowledge whatever of Stoner's having found out the secret of the Wilchester affair. He knew nothing of Stoner's having gone over to Darlington. On the Sunday he himself had gone up the moors for a quiet stroll. At the spinney overhanging Hobwick Quarry he had seen Mallalieu and Stoner, and had at once noticed that something in the shape of a quarrel was afoot. He saw Mallalieu strike heavily at Stoner with his oak stick—saw Mallalieu, in a sudden passion, kick the stick over the edge of the quarry, watched him go down into the quarry and eventually leave it. He told how he himself had gone after the stick, recovered it, taken it home, and had eventually told the police where it was. He had never spoken to Mallalieu on that Sunday—never seen him except under the circumstances just detailed.

The astute barrister who represented Cotherstone had not troubled the Coroner and his jury much by asking questions of the various witnesses. But he had quietly elicited from all the medical men the definite opinion that death had been caused by the blow. And when Cotherstone's evidence was over, the barrister insisted on recalling the two sweethearts, and he got out of them, separately (each being excluded from the court while the other gave evidence), that they had not seen Mallalieu and Cotherstone together, that Mallalieu had left the quarry some time before they saw Cotherstone, and that when Mallalieu passed them he seemed to be agitated and was muttering to himself, whereas in Cotherstone's manner they noticed nothing remarkable.

Brereton, watching the faces of the jurymen, all tradesmen of the town, serious and anxious, saw the effect which Cotherstone's evidence and the further admissions of the two sweethearts was having. And neither he nor Tallington—and certainly not Mr. Christopher Pett—was surprised when, in the gathering dusk of the afternoon, the inquest came to an end with a verdict of *Wilful Murder against Anthony Mallalieu.*

"Your client is doing very well," observed Tallington to the Norcaster solicitor as they foregathered in an ante-room.

"My client will be still better when he comes before your bench again," drily answered the other. "As you'll see!"

"So that's the line you're taking?" said Tallington quietly. "A good one—for him."

"Every man for himself," remarked the Norcaster practitioner. "We're not concerned with Mallalieu—we're concerned about ourselves. See you when Cotherstone's

brought before your worthies next Tuesday. And—a word
in your ear!—it won't be a long job, then."

Long job or short job, the Highmarket Town Hall was
packed to the doors when Cotherstone, after his week's
detention, was again placed in the dock. This time, he
stood there alone—and he looked around him with
confidence and with not a few signs that he felt a sense of
coming triumph. He listened with a quiet smile while the
prosecuting counsel—sent down specially from London to
take charge—discussed with the magistrates the matter
of Mallalieu's escape, and he showed more interest when
he heard some police information as to how that escape
had been effected, and that up to then not a word had
been heard and no trace found of the fugitive. And after
that, as the prosecuting counsel bent over to exchange a
whispered word with the magistrates' clerk, Cotherstone
deliberately turned, and seeking out the place where Bent
and Brereton sat together, favoured them with a peculiar
glance. It was the glance of a man who wished to say "I
told you!—now you'll see whether I was right!"

"We're going to hear something—now!" whispered
Brereton.

The prosecuting counsel straightened himself and
looked at the magistrates. There was a momentary
hesitation on his part; a look of expectancy on the faces of
the men on the bench; a deep silence in the crowded
court. The few words that came from the counsel were
sharp and decisive.

"There will be no further evidence against the
prisoner now in the dock, your worships," he said. "The
prosecution decides to withdraw the charge."

In the buzz of excitement which followed the voice of
the old chairman was scarcely audible as he glanced at
Cotherstone.

"You are discharged," he said abruptly.

Cotherstone turned and left the dock. And for the
second time he looked at Bent and Brereton in the same

peculiar, searching way. Then, amidst a dead silence, he walked out of the court.

26. THE VIRTUES OF SUSPICION

During that week Mallalieu was to learn by sad experience that it is a very poor thing to acquire information at second hand. There he was, a strictly-guarded—if a cosseted and pampered—prisoner, unable to put his nose outside the cottage, and entirely dependent on Chris Pett for any and all news of the world which lay so close at hand and was just then so deeply and importantly interesting to him. Time hung very heavily on his hands. There were books enough on the shelves of his prison-parlour, but the late Kitely's taste had been of a purely professional nature, and just then Mallalieu had no liking for murder cases, criminal trials, and that sort of gruesomeness. He was constantly asking for newspapers, and was skilfully put off—it was not within Christopher's scheme of things to let Mallalieu get any accurate notion of what was really going on. Miss Pett did not take in a newspaper; Christopher invariably forgot to bring one in when he went to the town; twice, being pressed by Mallalieu to remember, he brought back *The Times* of the day before—wherein, of course, Mallalieu failed to find anything about himself. And it was about himself that he so wanted to hear, about how things were, how people talked of him, what the police said, what was happening generally, and his only source of information was Chris.

Mr. Pett took good care to represent everything in his own fashion. He was assiduous in assuring Mallalieu that he was working in his interest with might and main; jealous in proclaiming his own and his aunt's intention to get him clear away to Norcaster. But he also never ceased dilating on the serious nature of that enterprise, never wearied in protesting how much risk he and Miss Pett were running; never refrained from showing the captive how very black things were, and how much blacker they would be if it were not for his present gaolers' goodness. And when he returned to the cottage after the inquest on Stoner, his face was unusually long and grave as he prepared to tell Mallalieu the news.

"Things are looking in a very bad way for you, Mr. Mallalieu," he whispered, when he was closeted with Mallalieu in the little room which the captive now hated fiercely and loathingly. "They look in a very bad way indeed, sir! If you were in any other hands than ours, Mr. Mallalieu, I don't know what you'd do. We're running the most fearful risks on your behalf, we are indeed. Things is—dismal!"

Mallalieu's temper, never too good, and all the worse for his enforced confinement, blazed up.

"Hang it! why don't you speak out plain?" he snarled. "Say what you mean, and be done with it! What's up now, like? Things are no worse than they were, I reckon."

Christopher slowly drew off one of the black kid gloves, and blew into it before laying it on the table.

"No need to use strong language, Mr. Mallalieu," he said deprecatingly, as he calmly proceeded to divest the other hand. "No need at all, sir—between friends and gentlemen, Mr. Mallalieu!—things are a lot worse. The coroner's jury has returned a verdict of wilful murder—against you!"

Mallalieu's big face turned of a queer grey hue—that word murder was particularly distasteful to him.

"Against me!" he muttered. "Why me particularly? There were two of us charged. What about Cotherstone?"

"I'm talking about the inquest" said Christopher. "They don't charge anybody at inquests—they only inquire in general. The verdict's against you, and you only. And—it was Cotherstone's evidence that did it!"

"Cotherstone!" exclaimed Mallalieu. "Evidence against me! He's a liar if——"

"I'll tell you—all in due order," interrupted Chris. "Be calm, Mr. Mallalieu, and listen—be judicial."

But in spite of this exhortation, Mallalieu fumed and fretted, and when Christopher had told him everything he looked as if it only required a little resolution on his part to force himself to action.

"I've a good mind to go straight out o' this place and straight down to the police!" he growled. "I have indeed!— a great mind to go and give myself up, and have things proved."

"Do!" said Christopher, heartily. "I wish you would, sir. It 'ud save me and my poor aunt a world of trouble. Only—it's my duty as a duly qualified solicitor of the High Court to inform you that every step you take from this haven of refuge will be a step towards the—gallows!"

Mallalieu shrank back in his chair and stared at Mr. Pett's sharp features. His own blanched once more.

"You're sure of that?" he demanded hoarsely.

"Certain!" replied Christopher. "No doubt of it, sir. I know!"

"What's to be done, then?" asked the captive.

Christopher assumed his best consultation-and-advice manner.

"What," he said at last, "in my opinion, is the best thing is to wait and see what happens when Cotherstone's brought up before the bench next Tuesday. You're safe enough until then—so long as you do what we tell you. Although all the country is being watched and searched, there's not the ghost of a notion that you're in Highmarket. So remain as content as you can, Mr. Mallalieu, and as soon as we learn what takes place next Tuesday, we'll see about that plan of ours."

"Let's be knowing what it is," grumbled Mallalieu.

"Not quite matured, sir, yet," said Christopher as he rose and picked up the silk hat and the kid gloves. "But when it is, you'll say—ah, you'll say it's a most excellent one!"

So Mallalieu had to wait until the next Tuesday came round. He did the waiting impatiently and restlessly. He ate, he drank, he slept—slept as he had never slept in his life—but he knew that he was losing flesh from anxiety. It was with real concern that he glanced at Christopher when that worthy returned from the adjourned case on the Tuesday afternoon. His face fell when he saw that Christopher was gloomier than ever.

"Worse and worse, Mr. Mallalieu!" whispered Christopher mysteriously when he had shut the door. "Everything's against you, sir. It's all centring and fastening on you. What do you think happened? Cotherstone's discharged!"

"What!" exclaimed Mallalieu, jumping in his chair. "Discharged! Why, then, they'd have discharged me!"

Christopher laid his finger on the side of his nose.

"Would they?" he said with a knowing wink. "Not much they wouldn't. Cotherstone's let loose—to give evidence against you. When you're caught!"

Mallalieu's small eyes began to bulge, and a dull red to show on his cheek. He looked as if he were bursting with words which he could not get out, and Christopher Pett hastened to improve the occasion.

"It's my opinion it's all a plant!" he said. "A conspiracy, if you like, between Cotherstone and the authorities. Cotherstone, he's got the smartest solicitor in Norcaster and the shrewdest advocate on this circuit— you know 'em, Mr. Mallalieu—Stilby's the solicitor, and Gradston the barrister—and it strikes me it's a put-up job. D'ye see through it? First of all, Cotherstone gives evidence at that inquest: on his evidence a verdict of murder is returned against—you! Now Cotherstone's discharged by the magistrates—no further evidence being offered against him. Why? So that he can give evidence before the magistrates and at the Assizes against—you! That is—when you're caught."

"They've got to catch me yet," growled Mallalieu. "Now then—what about this plan of yours? For I'm going to wait no longer. Either you tell me what you're going to do for me, or I shall walk out o' that door as soon as it's dark tonight and take my chances. D'ye hear that?"

Christopher rose, opened the door, and softly called Miss Pett. And Miss Pett came, took a seat, folded her thin arms, and looked attentively at her learned nephew.

"Yes, sir," said Christopher, resuming the conversation, "I hear that—and we are now ready to explain plans and discuss terms. You will, of course, recompense us, Mr. Mallalieu?"

"I've said all along that you'd not lose by me," retorted Mallalieu. "Aught in reason, I'll pay. But—this plan o' yours? I'm going to know what it is before we come to any question of paying. So out with it!"

"Well, it's an excellent plan," responded Christopher. "You say that you'll be safe if you're set down in a certain part of Norcaster—near the docks. Now that will suit our plans exactly. You're aware, of course, Mr. Mallalieu, that my aunt here is about to remove her goods and chattels— bequeathed by Mr. Kitely, deceased—from this house? Very well—the removal's to take place tomorrow. I have already arranged with Mr. Strawson, furniture remover, to send up a couple of vans tomorrow morning, very early. Into those vans the furniture will be placed, and the vans will convey it to Norcaster, whence they will be transshipped bodily to London, by sea. Mr. Mallalieu— you'll leave here, sir, in one of those vans!"

Mallalieu listened, considered, began to see possibilities.

"Aye!" he said, with a cunning glance. "Aye!—that's not a bad notion. I can see my way in that respect. But— how am I going to get into a van here, and got out of it there, without the vanmen knowing?"

"I've thought it all out," answered Christopher. "You must keep snug in this room until afternoon. We'll get the first van off in the morning—say by noon. I'll so contrive that the second van won't be ready to start until after it's dusk. When it is ready the men'll go down to fetch their horses—I'll give 'em something to get themselves a drink before they come back—that'll delay 'em a bit longer. And while they're away, we'll slip you into the van—and I shall go with that van to Norcaster. And when we get to the shed at Norcaster where the vans are to be left, the two men will go away with their horses—and I shall let you out.. It's a good plan, Mr. Mallalieu."

"It'll do, anyhow," agreed Mallalieu, who felt heartily relieved. "We'll try it. But you must take all possible care until I'm in, and we're off. The least bit of a slip——"

Mr. Pett drily remarked that if any slips occurred they would not be of his making—after which both he and his aunt coughed several times and looked at the guest-prisoner in a fashion which seemed to invite speech from him.

"All right then," said Mallalieu. "Tomorrow, you say? All right—all right!"

Miss Pett coughed again and began to make pleats in her apron.

"Of course, Christopher," she said, addressing her nephew as if there were no other person present, "of course, Mr. Mallalieu has not yet stated his terms."

"Oh!—ah!—just so!" replied Christopher, starting as from a pensive reverie. "Ah, to be sure. Now, what would you say, Mr. Mallalieu? How do you feel disposed, sir?"

Mallalieu looked fixedly from aunt to nephew, from nephew to aunt. Then his face became hard and rigid.

"Fifty pound apiece!" he said. "That's how I'm disposed. And you don't get an offer like that every day, I know. Fifty pound apiece!"

Miss Pett inclined her turbaned head towards her right shoulder and sighed heavily: Mr. Pett folded his hands, looked at the ceiling, and whistled.

"We don't get an offer like that every day!" he murmured. "No!—I should think we didn't! Fifty pound apiece!—a hundred pound altogether—for saving a fellow-creature from the gallows! Oh, Mr. Mallalieu!"

"Hang it!—how much money d'ye think I'm likely to carry on me?—me!—in my unfortunate position!" snarled Mallalieu. "D'ye think——"

"Christopher," observed Miss Pett, rising and making for the door, "I should suggest that Mr. Mallalieu is left to consider matters. Perhaps when he's reflected a bit——"

She and her nephew went out, leaving Mallalieu fuming and grumbling. And once in the living-room she turned to Christopher with a shake of the head.

"What did I tell you?" she said. "Mean as a miser! My plan's much the best. We'll help ourselves—and then we can snap our fingers at him. I'll give him an extra strong nightcap tonight, and then...."

But before the close of that evening came Mallalieu's notions underwent a change. He spent the afternoon in thinking. He knew that he was in the power of two people who, if they could, would skin him. And the more he thought, the more he began to be suspicious—and suddenly he wondered why he slept so heavily at night, and all of a sudden he saw the reason. Drugged!—that old she-devil was drugging his drink. That was it, of course—but it had been for the last time: she shouldn't do it again.

That night when Miss Pett brought the hot toddy, mixed according to the recipe of the late Kitely, Mallalieu took it at his door, saying he was arrayed for sleep, and would drink it when in bed. After which he carefully poured it into a flower-pot that graced his room, and when he presently lay down it was with eyes and ears open and his revolver ready to his right hand.

27. MR. WRAYTHWAITE OF WRAYE

Had the Mayor of Highmarket, lying there sullen and suspicious, only known what was taking place close to him at that very moment, only known what had been happening in his immediate vicinity during the afternoon and evening, he might have taken some course of action which would have prevented what was shortly to come. But he knew nothing—except that he was angry, and full of doubts, and cursed everything and everybody that had led to this evil turn in his fortunes, and was especially full of vindictiveness towards the man and woman in the next room, who, as he felt sure, were trying to take advantage of his present helplessness. And meanwhile, not far away, things were going on—and they had been going on all that day since noon.

Brereton, going away from Highmarket Town Hall after the dramatic discharge of Cotherstone, was suddenly accosted by a smart-looking young man whom, at first glance, he knew to be in some way connected with the law.

"Mr. Gifford Brereton?" inquired this stranger. "I have a note for you, sir."

Brereton took the note and stepped aside into a quiet corner: the young man followed and stood near. To Brereton's surprise he found himself looking at a letter in the handwriting of a London solicitor who had two or three times favoured him with a brief. He hastily glanced through its contents:

"THE DUKE'S HEAD HOTEL"
Norcaster.
"DEAR MR. BRERETON,—

"I have just arrived at this place on business which is closely connected with that which you have in hand. I shall be much obliged if you join me here at once, bringing with you the daughter of your client Harborough—it is important that she should accompany you. The bearer will have a car in readiness for you.

Yours sincerely,

"H. C. CARFAX."

Brereton put the note in his pocket and turned to the messenger.

"Mr. Carfax wishes me to return with you to Norcaster," he remarked. "He mentions a car."

"Here, Mr. Brereton—round the corner—a good one, that will run us there in twenty minutes," replied the messenger.

"There's a call to make first," said Brereton. He went round the corner with his companion and recognized in the chauffeur who waited there a man who had once or twice driven him from Norcaster of late. "Ah!" he said, "I daresay you know where Mrs. Northrop lives in this town—up near the foot of the Shawl? You do?—run us up there, then. Are you one of Mr. Carfax's clerks?" he asked when he and the messenger had got into the car. "Have you come down with him from London?"

"No, sir—I am a clerk at Willerby & Hargreaves' in Norcaster," replied the messenger. "Carfax and Spillington are our London agents. Mr. Carfax and some other gentlemen came down from town first thing this morning, and Mr. Carfax got me to bring you that note."

"You don't know what he wants to see me about?" asked Brereton, who was already curious to the point of eagerness.

"Well, sir, I have a pretty good idea," answered the clerk, with a smile, "but I think Mr. Carfax would rather tell you everything himself. We shall soon be there, Mr. Brereton—if the young lady doesn't keep us."

Brereton ran into Northrop's house and carried Avice off with scant ceremony.

"This, of course, has something to do with your father's case," he said, as he led her down to the car. "It may be—but no, we won't anticipate! Only—I'm certain things are going to right themselves. Now then!" he called to the driver as they joined the clerk. "Get along to Norcaster as fast as you can."

Within half an hour the car stopped at the old-fashioned gateway of the Duke's Head in Norcaster market-place, and the clerk immediately led his two companions into the hotel and upstairs to a private sitting-room, at the door of which he knocked. A voice bade him enter; he threw the door open and announced the visitors.

"Miss Harborough—Mr. Brereton, Mr. Carfax," he said.

Brereton glanced sharply at the men who stood in the room, evidently expectant of his and his companion's arrival. Carfax, a short, middle-aged man, quick and bustling in manner, he, of course, knew: the others were strangers. Two of them Brereton instantly set down as detectives; there were all the marks and signs of the craft upon them. They stood in a window, whispering together, and at them Brereton gave but a glance. But at the fourth man, who stood on the hearthrug, he looked long and hard. And his thoughts immediately turned to the night on which he and Avice had visited the old woman who lived in the lonely house on the moors and to what she had said about a tall man who had met Harborough in her presence—a tall, bearded man. For the man who stood there before him, looking at Avice with an interested, somewhat wistful smile, was a tall, bearded man—a man past middle age, who looked as if he had seen a good deal of the far-off places of the world.

Carfax had hurried forward, shaken hands with Brereton, and turned to Avice while Brereton was making this rapid inspection.

"So here you are, Brereton—and this young lady, I suppose, is Miss Harborough?" he said, drawing a chair forward. "Glad you've come—and I daresay you're wondering why you've been sent for? Well—all in good time, but first—this gentleman is Mr. John Wraythwaite."

The big man started forward, shook hands hastily with Brereton, and turned more leisurely to Avice.

"My dear young lady!" he said. "I—I—the fact is, I'm an old friend of your father's, and—and it will be very soon now that he's all right—and all that sort of thing, you know! You don't know me, of course."

Avice looked up at the big, bearded figure and from it to Brereton.

"No!" she said. "But—I think it was you who sent that money to Mr. Brereton."

"Ah! you're anticipating, young lady!" exclaimed Carfax. "Yes—we've a lot of talking to do. And we'd better all sit down and do it comfortably. One moment," he continued, and turned away to the two men in the window, who, after a few words with him, left the room. "Now then—we'll do our first part of the business, Brereton!" he went on, as they all took seats at a table near the fire. "You, of course, don't know who this gentleman is?"

"Not at all," replied Brereton.

"Very good!" continued Carfax, rubbing his hands as if in enjoyment of the situation. "Then you've some interesting facts to hear about him. To begin with, he's the man who, when your client, this young lady's father, is brought up at these coming Assizes, will prove a complete *alibi* on his behalf. In other words, he's the man with whom Harborough was in company during the evening and the greater part of the night on which Kitely was murdered."

"I thought so," said Brereton. He looked reflectively at Mr. Wraythwaite. "But why did you not come forward at once?" he asked.

"My advice—my advice!" exclaimed Carfax hastily. "I'm going to explain the reasons. Now, you won't understand, Brereton, but Miss Harborough, I think, will know what I mean, or she'll have some idea, when I say

that this gentleman is now—now, mind you!—Mr.
Wraythwaite of Wraye."

Avice looked up quickly with evident comprehension,
and the solicitor nodded.

"You see—she knows," he went on, turning to
Brereton. "At least, that conveys something to her. But it
doesn't to you. Well, my dear sir, if you were a native of
these parts it would. Wraye is one of the oldest and most
historic estates between here and the Tweed—everybody
knows Wraye. And everybody knows too that there has
been quite a romance about Wraye for some time—since
the last Wraythwaite died, in fact. That Wraythwaite was
a confirmed old bachelor. He lived to a great age—he
outlived all his brothers and sisters, of whom he'd had
several. He left quite a tribe of nephews and nieces, who
were distributed all over the world. Needless to say, there
was vast bother and trouble. Finally, one of the nephews
made a strong claim to the estate, as being the eldest
known heir. And he was until recently in good trim for
establishing his claim, when my client here arrived on
the scene. For he is the eldest nephew—he is the rightful
heir—and I am thankful to say that—only within this
last day or two—his claim has been definitely recognized
and established, and all without litigation. Everything,"
continued Carfax, again rubbing his hands with great
satisfaction, "everything is now all right, and Mr.
Wraythwaite of Wraye will take his proper and rightful
place amongst his own people."

"I'm exceedingly glad to hear it," said Brereton, with a
smile at the big man, who continued to watch Avice as if
his thoughts were with her rather than with his solicitor's
story. "But—you'll understand that I'd like to know how
all this affects my client?"

"Ye—yes!" said Mr. Wraythwaite, hastily. "Tell Mr.
Brereton, Carfax—never mind me and my affairs—get on
to poor Harborough."

"Your affair and Harborough's are inextricably mixed,
my dear sir," retorted Carfax, good-humouredly. "I'm

coming to the mingling of them. Well," he continued, addressing himself again to Brereton. "This is how things are—or were. I must tell you that the eldest brother of the late Squire of Wraye married John Harborough's aunt—secretly. They had not been married long before the husband emigrated. He went off to Australia, leaving his wife behind until he had established himself—there had been differences between him and his family, and he was straitened in means. In his absence our friend here was born—and at the same time, sad to say, his mother died. The child was brought up by Harborough's mother— Mr. Wraythwaite and Harborough are foster-brothers. It remained in the care of Harborough's mother—who kept the secret of the marriage—until it was seven years old. Then, opportunity occurring, it was taken to its father in Australia. The father, Matthew Wraythwaite, made a big fortune in Australia, sheep-farming. He never married again, and the fortune, of course, came at his death to his only son—our friend. Now, he had been told of the secret marriage of his father, but, being possessed of an ample fortune himself, he concerned himself little about the rest of the old family. However, a year or so ago, happening to read in the newspapers about the death of the old Squire, his uncle, and the difficulty of definitely deciding the real heirship, he came over to England. But he had no papers relating to his father's marriage, and he did not know where it had taken place. At that time he had not consulted me—in fact, he had consulted no one. If he had consulted me," continued Carfax, with a knowing wink at Brereton, "we should have put him right in a few hours. But he kept off lawyers—and he sought out the only man he could remember—his foster-brother, Harborough. And by Harborough's advice, they met secretly. Harborough did not know where that marriage had taken place—he had to make inquiries all over this district—he had to search registers. Now and then, my client—not my client then, of course—came to see Harborough; when he did so, he and Harborough met in quiet places. And on the night on which that man Kitely was murdered," concluded the solicitor, "Harborough was with my client from nine o'clock until half-past four in the morning, when he parted with him near Hexendale railway station. Mr. Wraythwaite will swear that."

"And fortunately, we have some corroboration," observed Brereton, with a glance at Avice, "for whether Mr. Wraythwaite knows it or not, his meeting with Harborough on the moors that particular night was witnessed."

"Capital—capital!" exclaimed Carfax. "By a credible—and creditable—witness?"

"An old woman of exceptional character," answered Brereton, "except that she indulges herself in a little night-poaching now and then."

"Ah, well, we needn't tell that when she goes into the witness-box," said Carfax. "But that's most satisfactory. My dear young lady!" he added, turning to Avice, "your father will be released like—like one o'clock! And then, I think," he went on bustling round on the new Squire of Wraye, "then, my dear, I think Mr. Wraythwaite here——"

"Leave that to me, Carfax," interrupted Mr. Wraythwaite, with a nod at Avice. "I'll tell this young lady all about that myself. In the meantime——"

"Ah, just so!" responded Carfax. "In the meantime, we have something not so interesting or pleasing, but extremely important, to tell Mr. Brereton. Brereton—how are things going? Has any fresh light been thrown on the Kitely murder? Nothing really certain and definite you say? Very well, my dear sir—then you will allow me to throw some light on it!"

So saying, Carfax rose from his chair, quitted the room—and within another minute returned, solemnly escorting the two detectives.

28. PAGES FROM THE PAST

Before the solicitor and his companions could seat themselves at the table whereat the former's preliminary explanation had been made, Mr. Wraythwaite got up and motioned Avice to follow his example.

"Carfax," he said, "there's no need for me to listen to all that you've got to tell Mr. Brereton—I know it already. And I don't think it will particularly interest Miss Harborough at the moment—she'll hear plenty about it later on. She and I will leave you—make your explanations and your arrangements, and we'll join you later on."

He led the way to the door, beckoning Avice to accompany him. But Avice paused and turned to Brereton.

"You feel sure that it is all right now about my father?" she said. "You feel certain? If you do——"

"Yes—absolutely," answered Brereton, who knew what her question meant. "And—we will let him know."

"He knows!" exclaimed Carfax. "That is, he knows that Mr. Wraythwaite is here, and that everything's all right. Run away, my dear young lady, and be quite happy—Mr. Wraythwaite will tell you everything you want to know. And now, my dear sir," he continued, as he shut the door on Wraythwaite and Avice and bustled back to the table, "there are things that you want to know, and that you are going to know—from me and from these two gentlemen. Mr. Stobb—Mr. Leykin. Both ex-Scotland Yard men, and now in business for themselves as private inquiry agents. Smart fellows—though I say it to their faces."

"I gather from that that you have been doing some private inquiry work, then?" said Brereton. "In connexion with what, now?"

"Let us proceed in order," answered Carfax, taking a seat at the head of the table and putting his fingers together in a judicial attitude. "I will open the case. When Wraythwaite—a fine fellow, who, between ourselves, is going to do great things for Harborough and his daughter—when Wraythwaite, I say, heard of what had happened down here, he was naturally much upset. His first instinct was to rush to Highmarket at once and tell everything. However, instead of doing that, he very wisely came to me. Having heard all that he had to tell, I advised him, as it was absolutely certain that no harm could come to Harborough in the end, to let matters rest for the time being, until we had put the finishing touches to his own affair. He, however, insisted on sending you that money—which was done: nothing else would satisfy him. But now arose a deeply interesting phase of the whole affair—which has been up to now kept secret between Wraythwaite, myself, and Messrs. Stobb and Leykin there. To it I now invite your attention."

Mr. Carfax here pulled out a memorandum book from his pocket, and having fitted on his spectacles glanced at a page or two within it.

"Now," he presently continued, "Wraythwaite being naturally deeply interested in the Kitely case, he procured the local newspapers—Norcaster and Highmarket papers, you know—so that he could read all about it. There was in those papers a full report of the first proceedings before the magistrates, and Wraythwaite was much struck by your examination of the woman Miss Pett. In fact, he was so much struck by your questions and her replies that he brought the papers to me, and we read them together. And, although we knew well enough that we should eventually have no difficulty whatever in proving an *alibi* in Harborough's behalf, we decided that in his interest we would make a few guarded but strict inquiries into Miss Pett's antecedents."

Brereton started. Miss Pett! Ah!—he had had ideas respecting Miss Pett at the beginning of things, but other matters had cropped up, and affairs had moved and developed so rapidly that he had almost forgotten her.

"That makes you think," continued Carfax, with a smile. "Just so!—and what took place at that magistrates' sitting made Wraythwaite and myself think. And, as I say, we employed Stobb and Leykin, men of great experience, to—just find out a little about Miss Pett. Of course, Miss Pett herself had given us something to go on. She had told you some particulars of her career. She had been housekeeper to a Major Stilman, at Kandahar Cottage, Woking. She had occupied posts at two London hotels. So—Stobb went to Woking, and Leykin devoted himself to the London part of the business.

"And I think, Stobb," concluded the solicitor, turning to one of the inquiry agents, "I think you'd better tell Mr. Brereton what you found out at Woking, and then Leykin can tell us what he brought to light elsewhere."

Stobb, a big, cheery-faced man, who looked like a highly respectable publican, turned to Brereton with a smile.

"It was a very easy job, sir," he said. "I found out all about the lady and her connexion with Woking in a very few hours. There are plenty of folk at Woking who remember Miss Pett—she gave you the mere facts of her residence there correctly enough. But—naturally—she didn't tell you more than the mere facts, the surface, as it were. Now, I got at everything. Miss Pett was housekeeper at Woking to a Major Stilman, a retired officer of an infantry regiment. All the time she was with him—some considerable period—he was more or less of an invalid, and he was well known to suffer terribly from some form of neuralgia. He got drugs to alleviate the pain of that neuralgia from every chemist in the place, one time or another. And one day, Major Stilman was found dead in bed, with some of these drugs by his bedside. Of course an inquest was held, and, equally of course, the evidence of doctors and chemists being what it was, a verdict of death from misadventure—overdose of the stuff, you know—was returned. Against Miss Pett there appears to have been no suspicion in Woking at that time—and for the matter of that," concluded Mr. Stobb drily, "I don't know that there is now."

"You have some yourself?" suggested Brereton.

"I went into things further," answered Mr. Stobb, with the ghost of a wink. "I found out how things were left—by Stilman. Stilman had nothing but his pension, and a capital sum of about two thousand pounds. He left that two thousand, and the furniture of his house, to Miss Pett. The will had been executed about a twelvemonth before Stilman died. It was proved as quickly as could be after his death, and of course Miss Pett got her legacy. She sold the furniture—and left the neighbourhood."

"What is your theory?" asked Brereton.

Mr. Stobb nodded across the table at Carfax.

"Not my business to say what my theories are, Mr. Brereton," he answered. "All I had to do was to find out facts, and report them to Mr. Carfax and Mr. Wraythwaite."

"All the same," said Brereton quietly, "you think it quite possible that Miss Pett, knowing that Stilman took these strong doses, and having a pecuniary motive, gave him a still stronger one? Come, now!"

Stobb smiled, rubbed his chin and looked at Carfax. And Carfax pointed to Stobb's partner, a very quiet, observant man who had listened with a sly expression on his face.

"Your turn, Leykin," he said. "Tell the result of your inquiries."

Leykin was one of those men who possess soft voices and slow speech. Invited to play his part, he looked at Brereton as if he were half apologizing for anything he had to say.

"Well," he said, "of course, sir, what Miss Pett told you about her posts at two London hotels was quite right. She had been storekeeper at one, and linen-keeper at another—before she went to Major Stilman. There was nothing against her at either of those places. But of course I wanted to know more about her than that. Now she said in answer to you that before she went to the first of those hotels she had lived at home with her father, a Sussex farmer. So she had—but it was a long time before. She had spent ten years in India between leaving home and going to the Royal Belvedere. She went out to India as a nurse in an officer's family. And while she was in India she was charged with strangling a fellow-servant— a Eurasian girl who had excited her jealousy."

Brereton started again at that, and he turned a sharp glance on Carfax, who nodded emphatically and signed to Leykin to proceed.

"I have the report of that affair in my pocket," continued Leykin, more softly and slowly than ever. "It's worth reading, Mr. Brereton, and perhaps you'll amuse yourself with it sometime. But I can give you the gist of it in a few words. Pett was evidently in love with her master's orderly. He wasn't in love with her. She became madly jealous of this Eurasian girl, who was under-nurse. The Eurasian girl was found near the house one night with a cord tightly twisted round her neck—dead, of course. There were no other signs of violence, but some gold ornaments which the girl wore had disappeared. Pett was tried—and she was discharged, for she set up an *alibi*—of a sort that wouldn't have satisfied me," remarked Leykin in an aside. "But there was a queer bit of evidence given which you may think of use now. One of the witnesses said that Pett had been much interested in reading some book about the methods of the Thugs, and had talked in the servants' quarters of how they strangled their victims with shawls of the finest silk. Now this Eurasian girl had been strangled with a silk handkerchief—and if that handkerchief could only have been traced to Pett, she'd have been found guilty. But, as I said, she was found not guilty—and she left her place at once and evidently returned to England. That's all, sir."

"Stobb has a matter that might be mentioned," said Carfax, glancing at the other inquiry agent.

"Well, it's not much, Mr. Brereton," said Stobb. "It's merely that we've ascertained that Kitely had left all he had to this woman, and that——"

"I know that," interrupted Brereton. "She made no concealment of it. Or, rather, her nephew, acting for her, didn't."

"Just so," remarked Stobb drily. "But did you know that the nephew had already proved the will, and sold the property? No?—well, he has! Not much time lost, you see, after the old man's death, sir. In fact, it's been done about as quickly as it well could be done. And of course Miss Pett will have received her legacy—which means that by this time she'll have got all that Kitely had to leave."

Brereton turned to the solicitor, who, during the recital of facts by the two inquiry agents, had maintained his judicial attitude, as if he were on the bench and listening to the opening statements of counsel.

"Are you suggesting, all of you that you think Miss Pett murdered Kitely?" he asked. "I should like a direct answer to that question."

"My dear sir!" exclaimed Carfax. "What does it look like? You've heard the woman's record! The probability is that she did murder that Eurasian, girl—that she took advantage of Stilman's use of drugs to finish him off. She certainly benefited by Stilman's death—and she's without doubt benefited by Kitely's. I repeat—what does it look like?"

"What do you propose to do?" asked Brereton.

The inquiry agents glanced at each other and then at Carfax. And Carfax slowly took off his spectacles with a flourish, and looked more judicial than ever as he answered the young barrister's question.

"I will tell you what I propose to do," he replied. "I propose to take these two men over to Highmarket this evening and to let them tell the Highmarket police all they have just told you!"

29. WITHOUT THOUGHT OF CONSEQUENCE

Everything was very quiet in the house where Mallalieu lay wide-awake and watchful. It seemed to him that he had never known it so quiet before. It was quiet at all times, both day and night, for Miss Pett had a habit of going about like a cat, and Christopher was decidedly of the soft-footed order, and stepped from one room to another as if he were perpetually afraid of waking somebody or trusting his own weight on his own toes. But on this particular night the silence seemed to be unusual—and it was all the deeper because no sound, not even the faint sighing of the wind in the firs and pines outside came to break it. And Mallalieu's nerves, which had gradually become sharpened and irritated by his recent adventures and his close confinement, became still more irritable, still more set on edge, and it was with difficulty that he forced himself to lie still and to listen. Moreover, he was feeling the want of the stuff which had soothed him into such sound slumber every night since he had been taken in charge by Miss Pett, and he knew very well that though he had flung it away his whole system was crying out for the lack of it.

What were those two devils after, he wondered as he lay there in the darkness? No good—that was certain. Now that he came to reflect upon it their conduct during the afternoon and evening had not been of a reassuring sort. Christopher had kept entirely away from him; he had not seen Christopher at all since the discussion of the afternoon, which Miss Pett had terminated so abruptly. He had seen Miss Pett twice or thrice—Miss Pett's attitude on each occasion had been that of injured innocence. She had brought him his tea in silence, his supper with no more than a word. It was a nice supper— she set it before him with an expression which seemed to say that however badly she herself was treated, she would do her duty by others. And Mallalieu, seeing that expression, had not been able to refrain from one of his sneering remarks.

"Think yourself very badly done to, don't you, missis!" he had exclaimed with a laugh. "Think I'm a mean 'un, what?"

"I express no opinion, Mr. Mallalieu," replied Miss Pett, frigidly and patiently. "I think it better for people to reflect. A night's reflection," she continued as she made for the door, "oft brings wisdom, even to them as doesn't usually cultivate it."

Mallalieu had no objection to the cultivation of wisdom—for his own benefit, and he was striving to produce something from the process as he lay there, waiting. But he said to himself that it was easy enough to be wise after the event—and for him the event had happened. He was in the power of these two, whom he had long since recognized as an unscrupulous woman and a shifty man. They had nothing to do but hand him over to the police if they liked: for anything he knew, Chris Pett might already have played false and told the police of affairs at the cottage. And yet on deeper reflection, he did not think that possible—for it was evident that aunt and nephew were after all they could get, and they would get nothing from the police authorities, while they might get a good deal from him. But—what did they expect to get from him? He had been a little perplexed by their attitude when he asked them if they expected him to carry a lot of money on him—a fugitive. Was it possible— the thought came to him like a thunderclap in the darkness—that they knew, or had some idea, of what he really had on him? That Miss Pett had drugged him every night he now felt sure—well, then, in that case how did he know that she hadn't entered his room and searched his belongings, and especially the precious waistcoat?

Mallalieu had deposited that waistcoat in the same place every night—on a chair which stood at the head of his bed. He had laid it folded on the chair, had deposited his other garments in layers upon it, had set his candlestick and a box of matches on top of all. And everything had always been there, just as he had placed things, every morning when he opened his eyes. But—he had come to know Miss Pett's stealthiness by that time, and ...

He put out a hand now and fingered the pile of garments which lay, neatly folded, within a few inches of his head. It was all right, then, of course, and his hand drew back—to the revolver, separated from his cheek by no more than the thickness of the pillow. The touch of that revolver made him begin speculating afresh. If Miss Pett or Christopher had meddled with the waistcoat, the revolver, too, might have been meddled with. Since he had entered the cottage, he had never examined either waistcoat or revolver. Supposing the charges had been drawn?—supposing he was defenceless, if a pinch came? He began to sweat with fear at the mere thought, and in the darkness he fumbled with the revolver in an effort to discover whether it was still loaded. And just then came a sound—and Mallalieu grew chill with suspense.

It was a very small sound—so small that it might have been no more than that caused by the scratch of the tiniest mouse in the wainscot. But in that intense silence it was easily heard—and with it came the faint glimmering of a light. The light widened—there was a little further sound—and Mallalieu, peeping at things through his eyelashes became aware that the door was open, that a tall, spare figure was outlined between the bed and the light without. And in that light, outside the door, well behind the thin form of Miss Pett, he saw Christopher Pett's sharp face and the glint of his beady eyes.

Mallalieu was sharp enough of thought, and big man though he was, he had always been quick of action. He knew what Miss Pett's objective was, and he let her advance half-way across the room on her stealthy path to the waistcoat. But silently as she came on with that cat-like tread, Mallalieu had just as silently drawn the revolver from beneath his pillow and turned its small muzzle on her. It had a highly polished barrel, that revolver, and Miss Pett suddenly caught a tiny scintillation of light on it—and she screamed. And as she screamed Mallalieu fired, and the scream died down to a queer choking sound ... and he fired again ... and where Christopher Pett's face had shown itself a second before there was nothing—save another choking sound and a fall in the entry where Christopher had stood and watched.

After that followed a silence so deep that Mallalieu felt the drums of his ears aching intensely in the effort to catch any sound, however small. But he heard nothing—not even a sigh. It was as if all the awful silences that had ever been in the cavernous places of the world had been crystallized into one terrible silence and put into that room.

He reached out at last and found his candle and the matches, and he got more light and leaned forward in the bed, looking.

"Can't ha' got 'em both!" he muttered. "Both? But——"

He slowly lifted himself out of bed, huddled on some of the garments that lay carefully folded on the chair, and then, holding the candle to the floor, went forward to where the woman lay. She had collapsed between the foot of the bed and the wall; her shoulders were propped against the wall and the grotesque turban hung loosely down on one shoulder. And Mallalieu knew in that quick glance that she was dead, and he crept onward to the door and looked at the other still figure, lying just as supinely in the passage that led to the living-room. He looked longer at that ... and suddenly he turned back into his parlour-bedchamber, and carefully avoiding the dead woman put on his boots and began to dress with feverish haste.

And while he hurried on his clothes Mallalieu thought. He was not sure that he had meant to kill these two. He would have delighted in killing them certainly, hating them as he did, but he had an idea that when he fired he only meant to frighten them. But that was neither here nor there now. They were dead, but he was alive—and he must get out of that, and at once. The moors—the hills—anywhere....

A sudden heavy knocking at the door at the back of the cottage set Mallalieu shaking. He started for the front—to hear knocking there, too. Then came voices demanding admittance, and loudly crying the dead woman's name. He crept to a front window at that, and carefully drew a corner of the blind and looked out, and saw many men in the garden. One of them had a lantern, and as its glare glanced about Mallalieu set eyes on Cotherstone.

30. COTHERSTONE

Cotherstone walked out of the dock and the court and the Town Hall amidst a dead silence—which was felt and noticed by everybody but himself. At that moment he was too elated, too self-satisfied to notice anything. He held his head very high as he went out by the crowded doorway, and through the crowd which had gathered on the stairs; he might have been some general returning to be publicly fêted as he emerged upon the broad steps under the Town Hall portico and threw a triumphant glance at the folk who had gathered there to hear the latest news. And there, in the open air, and with all those staring eyes upon him, he unconsciously indulged in a characteristic action. He had caused his best clothes to be sent to him at Norcaster Gaol the previous night, and he had appeared in them in the dock. The uppermost garment was an expensive overcoat, finished off with a deep fur collar: now, as he stood there on the top step, facing the crowd, he unbuttoned the coat, threw its lapels aside, and took a long, deep breath, as if he were inhaling the free air of liberty. There were one or two shrewd and observant folk amongst the onlookers—it seemed to them that this unconscious action typified that Cotherstone felt himself throwing off the shackles which he had worn, metaphorically speaking, for the last eight days.

But in all that crowd, no one went near Cotherstone. There were many of his fellow-members of the Corporation in it—councillors, aldermen—but none of them approached him or even nodded to him; all they did was to stare. The news of what had happened had quickly leaked out: it was known before he came into view that Cotherstone had been discharged—his appearance in that bold, self-assured fashion only led to covert whispers and furtive looks. But suddenly, from somewhere in the crowd, a sneering voice flung a contemptuous taunt across the staring faces.

"Well done, Cotherstone!—saved your own neck, anyway!"

There was a ripple of jeering laughter at that, and as Cotherstone turned angrily in the direction from whence the voice came, another, equally contemptuous, lifted itself from another corner of the crowd.

"King's evidence! Yah!—who'd believe Cotherstone? Liar!"

Cotherstone's face flushed angrily—the flush died as quickly away and gave place to a sickly pallor. And at that a man who had stood near him beneath the portico, watching him inquisitively, stepped nearer and whispered—

"Go home, Mr. Cotherstone!—take my advice, and get quietly away, at once!"

Cotherstone rejected this offer of good counsel with a sudden spasm of furious anger.

"You be hanged!" he snarled. "Who's asking you for your tongue? D'ye think I'm afraid of a pack like yon? Who's going to interfere with me, I'd like to know? Go home yourself!"

He turned towards the door from which he had just emerged—turned to see his solicitor and his counsel coming out together. And his sudden anger died down, and his face relaxed to a smile of triumph.

"Now then!" he exclaimed. "Didn't I tell you how it would be, a week since! Come on across to the Arms and I'll stand a bottle—aye, two, three, if you like!—of the very best. Come on, both of you."

The solicitor, glancing around, saw something of the state of affairs, hurriedly excused himself, and slipped back into the Town Hall by another entrance. But the barrister, a man who, great as his forensic abilities were, was one of those people who have no private reputation to lose, and of whom it was well known that he could never withstand the temptation to a bottle of champagne, assented readily, and with great good humour. And he and Cotherstone, arm in arm, walked down the steps and across the Market Place—and behind them the crowd sneered and laughed and indulged in audible remarks.

Cotherstone paid, or affected to pay, no heed. He steered his companion into the Arms, and turned into the great bow-windowed room which served as morning meeting-place for all the better class of loungers and townsmen in Highmarket. The room was full already. Men had come across from the court, and from the crowd outside; a babel of talk arose from every corner. But when Cotherstone and the well-known barrister (so famous in that circuit for his advocacy of criminals that he had acquired the nickname of the Felons' Friend) entered, a dead silence fell, and men looked at this curious pair and then at each other with significant glances.

In that silence, Cotherstone, seizing a waiter, loudly demanded champagne and cigars: he glared defiantly around him as he supplemented the order with a command for the best box of cigars in the house, the best champagne in the cellars. A loud laugh from some corner of the room broke the silence, and the waiter, a shrewd fellow who saw how things were, gave Cotherstone a look.

"Come into the small parlour, Mr. Cotherstone," he whispered. "Nobody in there—you'll be more comfortable, sir."

"All right, then," responded Cotherstone. He glared once more at the company around him, and his defiance suddenly broke out in another fashion. "Any friend of mine that likes to join us," he said pointedly, "is welcome. Who's coming, like?"

There was another hoarse laugh at this, and most of the men there turned their backs on Cotherstone and began to talk loudly. But one or two of the less particular and baser sort, whom Cotherstone would certainly not have called friends a week before, nudged each other and made towards the door which the waiter held invitingly open—it was not every day that the best champagne and the best cigars were to be had for nothing, and if Cotherstone liked to fling him money about, what did it matter, so long as they benefited by his folly?

"That's the style!" said Cotherstone, pushing the barrister along. "Bring two—bring three bottles," he cried to the waiter. "Big 'uns!—and the best."

An elderly man, one of Cotherstone's fellow-members of the Corporation, came forward and caught him by the arm.

"Cotherstone!" he whispered. "Don't be a fool! Think of what's only just over. Go home, like a good fellow—go quietly home. You're doing no good with this—you'll have all the town talking!"

"Hang the town, and you too!" snapped Cotherstone. "You're one of them that shouted at me in front of the Town Hall, curse you! I'll let you and all Highmarket see what I care for you. What's it to you if I have a quiet glass of wine with my friends?"

But there was no quiet drinking of a glass of wine in the parlour to which Cotherstone and his cronies retired. Whenever its door opened Cotherstone's excited tones were heard in the big room, and the more sober-minded of the men who listened began to shake their heads.

"What's the matter with him?" asked one. "Nobody ever knew him like this before! What's he carrying on in that fashion for?"

"He's excited with getting off," said another. "And that bit of a scene outside there threw him off his balance. He should ha' been taken straight home. Nice lot he's got with him, too! We all know what yon barrister chap is— he can drink champagne like water, they say, and for the others—listen to that, now!" he added as a burst of excited talking came through the opened door. "He'll be in a fine fit state to go home to that daughter of his, I know, if that goes on."

"It mustn't go on," said another, and got up. "I'll go across to Bent's and get him to come over and take

Cotherstone away. Bent's the only man that'll have any influence with him."

He went out and crossed the Market Place to Bent's office. But Bent was not there. By his advice Lettie had gone to stay with some friends until the recent proceedings were over in one way or another, and Bent himself, as soon as Cotherstone had left the court, had hurried away to catch a train to the town in which she was temporarily staying in order to tell her the news and bring her home. So the would-be doer-of-good went back disappointed—and as he reached the hotel, Cotherstone and the barrister emerged from it, parted at the door with evident great cordiality, and went their several ways. And Cotherstone, passing the man who had been to Bent's, stared him in the face and cut him dead.

"It's going to be war to the knife between Cotherstone and the town," remarked the ambassador, when he re-entered the big room and joined his own circle. "He passed me just now as if I were one of the paving-stones he trod on! And did you see his face as he went out?— egad, instead of looking as if he'd had too much to drink, he looked too sober to please me. You mind if something doesn't happen—yon fellow's desperate!"

"What should he be desperate about?" asked one of the group. "He's saved his own neck!"

"It was that shouting at him when he came out that did it," observed another man quietly. "He's the sort of man to resent aught like that. If Cotherstone thinks public opinion's against him—well, we shall see!"

Cotherstone walked steadily away through the Market Place when he left the barrister. Whatever the men in the big room might have thought, he had not been indulging too freely in the little parlour. He had pressed champagne on the group around him, but the amount he had taken himself had not been great and it had pulled him together instead of intoxicating him. And his excitement had suddenly died down, and he had stopped what might have developed into a drinking bout by

saying that he must go home. And once outside, he made
for his house, and as he went he looked neither to right
nor left, and if he met friend or acquaintance his face
became hard as flint.

Cotherstone, indeed, was burning and seething with
indignation. The taunts flung at him as he stood on the
Town Hall steps, the looks turned in his direction as he
walked away with the convivially inclined barrister, the
expression on the faces of the men in the big room at the
Highmarket Arms—all these things had stung him to the
quick. He knew, whatever else he might have been, or
was, he had proved a faithful servant to the town. He had
been a zealous member of the Corporation, he had taken
hold of the financial affairs of the borough when they
were in a bad way and had put them in a safe and
prosperous footing; he had worked, thought, and planned
for the benefit of the place—and this was his reward! For
he knew that those taunts, those looks, those half-
averted, half-sneering faces meant one thing, and one
thing only—the Highmarket men believed him equally
guilty with Mallalieu, and had come to the conclusion
that he was only let off in order that direct evidence
against Mallalieu might be forthcoming. He cursed them
deeply and bitterly—and sneered at them in the same
breath, knowing that even as they were weathercocks,
veering this way and that at the least breath of public
opinion, so they were also utter fools, wholly unable to see
or to conjecture.

The excitement that had seized upon Cotherstone in
face of that public taunting of him died away in the
silence of his own house—when Lettie and Bent returned
home in the course of the afternoon they found him
unusually cool and collected. Bent had come with uneasy
feelings and apprehensions; one of the men who had been
at the Highmarket Arms had chanced to be in the station
when he and Lettie arrived, and had drawn him aside
and told him of what had occurred, and that Cotherstone
was evidently going on the drink. But there were no signs

of anything unusual about Cotherstone when Bent found him. He said little about the events of the morning to either Bent or Lettie; he merely remarked that things had turned out just as he had expected and that now perhaps they would get matters settled; he had tea with them; he was busy with his books and papers in his own room until supper-time; he showed no signs of anything unusual at supper, and when an hour later he left the house, saying that he must go down to the office and fetch the accumulated correspondence, his manner was so ordinary that Bent saw no reason why he should accompany him.

But Cotherstone had no intention of going to his office. He left his house with a fixed determination. He would know once and for all what Highmarket felt towards and about him. He was not the man to live under suspicion and averted looks, and if he was to be treated as a suspect and a pariah he would know at once.

There was at that time in Highmarket a small and select club, having its house in the Market Place, to which all the principal townsmen belonged. Both Mallalieu and Cotherstone had been members since its foundation; Cotherstone, indeed, was its treasurer. He knew that the club would be crowded that night—very well, he would go there and boldly face public opinion. If his fellow-members cut him, gave him the cold shoulder, ignored him—all right, he would know what to do then.

But Cotherstone never got inside the club. As he set his foot on the threshold he met one of the oldest members—an alderman of the borough, for whom he had a great respect. This man, at sight of him, started, stopped, laid a friendly but firm hand on his arm, and deliberately turned him round.

"No, my lad!" he said kindly. "Not in there tonight! If you don't know how to take care of yourself, let a friend take care of you. Have a bit of sense, Cotherstone! Do you want to expose yourself again to what you got outside the

Town Hall this noon! No—no!—go away, my lad, go home—come home with me, if you like—you're welcome!"

The last word softened Cotherstone: he allowed himself to be led away along the street.

"I'm obliged to you," he said brusquely. "You mean well. But—do you mean to say that those fellows in there—men that know me—are thinking—that!"

"It's a hard, censorious world, this," answered the elder man. "Leave 'em alone a bit—don't shove yourself on 'em. Come away—come home and have a cigar with me."

"Thank you," said Cotherstone. "You wouldn't ask me to do that if you thought as they do. Thank you! But I've something to do—and I'll go and do it at once."

He pressed his companion's arm, and turned away—and the other man watching him closely, saw him walk off to the police-station, to the superintendent's private door. He saw him enter—and at that he shook his head and went away himself, wondering what it was that Cotherstone wanted with the police.

The superintendent, tired by a long day's work, was taking his ease with his pipe and his glass when Cotherstone was shown into his parlour. He started with amazement at the sight of his visitor: Cotherstone motioned him back to his chair.

"Don't let me disturb you," said Cotherstone. "I want a word or two with you in private—that's all."

The superintendent had heard of the scene at the hotel, and had had his fears about its sequel. But he was quick to see that his visitor was not only sober, but remarkably cool and normal, and he hastened to offer him a glass of whisky.

"Aye, thank you, I will," replied Cotherstone, seating himself. "It'll be the first spirits I've tasted since you locked me up, and I daresay it'll do me no harm. Now then," he went on as the two settled themselves by the hearth, "I want a bit of a straight talk with you. You know me—we've been friends. I want you to tell me, straight, plain, truthful—what are Highmarket folk thinking and saying about me? Come!"

The superintendent's face clouded and he shook his head.

"Well, you know what folks will be, Mr. Cotherstone!" he answered. "And you know how very ready to say nasty things these Highmarket people are. I'm not a Highmarket man myself, any more than you are, and I've always regarded 'em as very bitter-tongued folk, and so——"

"Out with it!" said Cotherstone. "Let's know the truth—never mind what tongues it comes from. What are they saying?"

"Well," replied the superintendent, reluctantly, "of course I get to hear everything. If you must have it, the prevailing notion is that both you and Mr. Mallalieu had a hand in Kitely's death. They think his murder's at your doors, and that what happened to Stoner was a by-chance. And if you want the whole truth, they think you're a deal cleverer than Mallalieu, and that Kitely probably met his end at your hands, with your partner's connivance. And there are those who say that if Mallalieu's caught—as he will be—he'll split on you. That's all, sir."

"And what do you think?" demanded Cotherstone.

The superintendent shifted uneasily in his chair.

"I've never been able to bring myself to think that either you or Mallalieu 'ud murder a man in cold blood, as Kitely was murdered," he said. "As regards Stoner, I've firmly held to it that Mallalieu struck him in a passion. But—I've always felt this—you, or Mallalieu, or both of you, know more about the Kitely affair than you've ever told!"

Cotherstone leaned forward and tapped his host on the arm.

"I do!" he said significantly. "You're right in that. I—do!"

The superintendent laid down his pipe and looked at his visitor gravely.

"Then for goodness sake, Mr. Cotherstone," he exclaimed, "for goodness sake, tell! For as sure as we're sitting here, as things are at present, Mallalieu 'll hang if you don't! If he doesn't hang for Stoner, he will for Kitely, for if he gets off over Stoner he'll be re-arrested on the other charge."

"Half an hour ago," remarked Cotherstone, "I shouldn't have minded if Mallalieu had been hanged half a dozen times. Revenge is sweet—and I've good reason for being revenged on Mallalieu. But now—I'm inclined to tell the truth. Do you know why? Why—to show these Highmarket folks that they're wrong!"

The superintendent sighed. He was a plain, honest, simple man, and Cotherstone's reason seemed a strange—even a wicked one—to him. To tell the truth merely to spite one's neighbour—a poor, poor reason, when there was life at stake.

"Aye, Mr. Cotherstone, but you ought to tell the truth in any case!" he said. "If you know it, get it out and be done with it. We've had enough trouble already. If you can clear things up——"

"Listen!" interrupted Cotherstone. "I'll tell you all I know—privately. If you think good, it can be put into proper form. Very well, then! You remember the night of Kitely's murder?"

"Aye, I should think so!" said the superintendent. "Good reason to!"

"Let your mind go back to it, and to what you've since heard of it," said Cotherstone. "You know that on that afternoon Kitely had threatened me and Mallalieu with exposure about the Wilchester affair. He wanted to blackmail us. I told Mallalieu, of course—we were both to think about it till next day. But I did naught but think—I didn't want exposure for my daughter's sake: I'd ha' given anything to avoid it, naturally. I had young Bent and that friend of his, Brereton, to supper that night—I was so full of thought that I went out and left 'em for an hour or more. The truth was I wanted to get a word with Kitely. I went up the wood at the side of my house towards Kitely's cottage—and all of a sudden I came across a man lying on the ground—him!—just where we found him afterwards."

"Dead?" asked the superintendent.

"Only just," replied Cotherstone. "But he was dead—and I saw what had caused his death, for I struck a match to look at him. I saw that empty pocket-book lying by—I saw a scrap of folded newspaper, too, and I picked it up and later, when I'd read it, I put it in a safe place—I've taken it from that place tonight for the first time, and it's here—you keep it. Well—I went on, up to the cottage. The door was open—I looked in. Yon woman, Miss Pett, was at the table by the lamp, turning over some papers—I saw Kitely's writing on some of 'em. I stepped softly in and tapped her on the arm, and she screamed and started back. I looked at her. 'Do you know that your master's lying dead, murdered, down amongst those trees?' I said. Then she pulled herself together, and she sort of got between me and the door. 'No, I don't!' she says. 'But if he is, I'm not surprised, for I've warned him many a time about going out after nightfall.' I looked hard at her. 'What're you doing with his papers there?' I says. 'Papers!' she says. 'They're naught but old bills and things that he gave me to sort.' 'That's a lie!' I says, 'those aren't bills and I believe you know something about this, and I'm off for the police—to tell!' Then she pushed the door to behind her and folded her arms and looked at me. 'You tell a word,' she says, 'and I'll tell it all over the town that you and your partner's a couple of ex-convicts! I know your tale—Kitely'd no secrets from me. You stir a step to tell anybody, and I'll begin by going straight to young Bent—and I'll not stop at that, neither.' So you see where I was—I was frightened to death of that old affair getting out, and I knew then that Kitely was a liar and had told this old woman all about it, and—well, I hesitated. And she saw that she had me, and she went on,

'You hold your tongue, and I'll hold mine!' she says.
'Nobody'll accuse me, I know—but if you speak one word,
I'll denounce you! You and your partner are much more
likely to have killed Kitely than I am! Well, I still stood,
hesitating. 'What's to be done?' I asked at last. 'Do
naught,' she said. 'Go home, like a wise man, and know
naught about it. Let him be found—and say naught. But
if you do, you know what to expect.' 'Not a word that I
came in here, then?' I said at last. 'Nobody'll get no words
from me beyond what I choose to give 'em', she says.
'And—silence about the other?' I said. 'Just as long as
you're silent,' she says. And with that I walked out—and
I set off towards home by another way. And just as I was
leaving the wood to turn into the path that leads into our
lane I heard a man coming along and I shrank into some
shrubs and watched for him till he came close up. He
passed me and went on to the cottage—and I slipped back
then and looked in through the window, and there he
was, and they were both whispering together at the table.
And it—was this woman's nephew—Pett, the lawyer."

The superintendent, whose face had assumed various
expressions during this narrative, lifted his hands in
amazement.

"But—but we were in and about that cottage most of
that night—afterwards!" he exclaimed. "We never saw
aught of him. I know he was supposed to come down from
London the *next* night, but——"

"Tell you he was there *that* night!" insisted
Cotherstone. "D'ye think I could mistake him? Well, I
went home—and you know what happened afterwards:
you know what she said and how she behaved when we
went up—and of course I played my part. But—that bit of
newspaper I've given you. I read it carefully that night,
last thing. It's a column cut out of a Woking newspaper of
some years ago—it's to do with an inquest in which this
woman was concerned—there seems to be some evidence
that she got rid of an employer of hers by poison. And d'ye
know what I think, now?—I think that had been sent to

Kitely, and he'd plagued her about it, or held it out as a threat to her—and—what is it?"

The superintendent had risen and was taking down his overcoat.

"Do you know that this woman's leaving the town tomorrow?" he said. "And there's her nephew with her, now—been here for a week? Of course, I understand why you've told me all this, Mr. Cotherstone—now that your old affair at Wilchester is common knowledge, far and wide, you don't care, and you don't see any reason for more secrecy?"

"My reason," answered Cotherstone, with a grim smile, "is to show Highmarket folk that they aren't so clever as they think. For the probability is that Kitely was killed by that woman, or her nephew, or both."

"I'm going up there with a couple of my best men, any way," said the superintendent. "There's no time to lose if they're clearing out tomorrow."

"I'll come with you," said Cotherstone. He waited, staring at the fire until the superintendent had been into the adjacent police-station and had come back to say that he and his men were ready. "What do you mean to do?" he asked as the four of them set out. "Take them?"

"Question them first," answered the superintendent. "I shan't let them get out of my sight, any way, after what you've told me, for I expect you're right in your conclusions. What is it?" he asked, as one of the two men who followed behind called him.

The man pointed down the Market Place to the doors of the police-station.

"Two cars just pulled up there, sir," he said. "Came round the corner just now from the Norcaster road."

The superintendent glanced back and saw two staring headlights standing near his own door.

"Oh, well, there's Smith there," he said. "And if it's anybody wanting me, he knows where I've gone. Come on—for aught we know these two may have cleared out already."

But there were thin cracks of light in the living-room window of the lonely cottage on the Shawl, and the superintendent whispered that somebody was certainly there and still up. He halted his companions outside the garden gate and turned to Cotherstone.

"I don't know if it'll be advisable for you to be seen," he said. "I think our best plan'll be for me to knock at the front door and ask for the woman. You other two go round—quietly—to the back door, and take care that nobody gets out that way to the moors at the back—if anybody once escapes to those moors they're as good as lost for ever on a dark night. Go round—and when you hear me knock at the front, you knock at the back."

The two men slipped away round the corner of the garden and through the adjacent belt of trees, and the superintendent gently lifted the latch of the garden gate.

"You keep back, Mr. Cotherstone, when I go to the door," he said. "You never know—hullo, what's this?"

Men were coming up the wood behind them, quietly but quickly. One of them, ahead of the others, carried a bull's-eye lamp and in swinging it about revealed himself as one of the superintendent's own officers. He caught sight of his superior and came forward.

"Mr. Brereton's here, sir, and some gentlemen from Norcaster," he said. "They want to see you particularly—something about this place, so I brought them——"

It was at that moment that the sound of the two revolver shots rang out in the silence from the stillness of the cottage. And at that the superintendent dashed forward, with a cry to the others, and began to beat on the front door, and while his men responded with similar knockings at the back he called loudly on Miss Pett to open.

It was Mallalieu who at last flung the door open and confronted the amazed and wondering group clustered thickly without. Every man there shrank back affrighted at the desperation on the cornered man's face. But Mallalieu did not shrink, and his hand was strangely

steady as he singled out his partner and shot him dead—
and just as steady as he stepped back and turned the
revolver on himself.

A moment later the superintendent snatched the
bull's-eye lamp from his man, and stepped over
Mallalieu's dead body and went into the cottage—to come
back on the instant shivering and sick with shock at the
sight his startled eyes had met.

31. THE BARRISTER'S FEE

Six months later, on a fine evening which came as the fitting close of a perfect May afternoon, Brereton got out of a London express at Norcaster and entered the little train which made its way by a branch line to the very heart of the hills. He had never been back to these northern regions since the tragedies of which he had been an unwilling witness, and when the little train came to a point in its winding career amongst the fell-sides and valleys from whence Highmarket could be seen, with the tree-crowned Shawl above it, he resolutely turned his face and looked in the opposite direction. He had no wish to see the town again; he would have been glad to cut that chapter out of his book of memories. Nevertheless, being so near to it, he could not avoid the recollections which came crowding on him because of his knowledge that Highmarket's old gables and red roofs were there, within a mile or two, had he cared to look at them in the glint of the westering sun. No—he would never willingly set foot in that town again!—there was nobody there now that he had any desire to see. Bent, when the worst was over, and the strange and sordid story had come to its end, had sold his business, quietly married Lettie and taken her away for a long residence abroad, before returning to settle down in London. Brereton had seen them for an hour or two as they passed through London on their way to Paris and Italy, and had been more than ever struck by young Mrs. Bent's philosophical acceptance of facts. Her father, in Lettie's opinion, had always been a deeply-wronged and much injured man, and it was his fate to have suffered by his life-long connexion with that very wicked person, Mallalieu: he had unfortunately paid the penalty at last—and there was no more to be said about it. It might be well, thought Brereton, that Bent's wife should be so calm and equable of temperament, for Bent, on his return to England, meant to go in for politics, and Lettie would doubtless make an ideal help-meet for a public man. She would face situations with a cool head and a well-balanced judgment—and so, in that respect, all was well. All the same, Brereton had a strong notion that neither Mr. nor Mrs. Bent would ever revisit Highmarket.

As for himself, his thoughts went beyond Highmarket—to the place amongst the hills which he had never seen. After Harborough's due acquittal Brereton, having discharged his task, had gone back to London. But ever since then he had kept up a regular correspondence with Avice, and he knew all the details of the new life which had opened up for her and her father with the coming of Mr. Wraythwaite of Wraye. Her letters were full of vivid descriptions of Wraye itself, and of the steward's house in which she and Harborough—now appointed steward and agent to his foster-brother's estate—had taken up their residence. She had a gift of description, and Brereton had gained a good notion of Wraye from her letters—an ancient and romantic place, set amongst the wild hills of the Border, lonely amidst the moors, and commanding wide views of river and sea. It was evidently the sort of place in which a lover of open spaces, such as he knew Avice to be, could live an ideal life. But Brereton had travelled down from London on purpose to ask her to leave it.

He had come at last on a sudden impulse, unknown to any one, and therefore unexpected. Leaving his bag at the little station in the valley at which he left the train just as the sun was setting behind the surrounding hills, he walked quickly up a winding road between groves of fir and pine towards the great grey house which he knew must be the place into which the man from Australia had so recently come under romantic circumstances. At the top of a low hill he paused and looked about him, recognizing the scenes from the descriptions which Avice had given him in her letters. There was Wraye itself—a big, old-world place, set amongst trees at the top of a long park-like expanse of falling ground; hills at the back, the sea in the far distance. The ruins of an ancient tower stood near the house; still nearer to Brereton, in an old-fashioned flower garden, formed by cutting out a plateau on the hillside, stood a smaller house which he knew— also from previous description—to be the steward's. He looked long at this before he went nearer to it, hoping to catch the flutter of a gown amongst the rose-trees already bright with bloom. And at last, passing through the rose-trees he went to the stone porch and knocked—and was half-afraid lest Avice herself should open the door to him. Instead, came; a strapping, redcheeked North-country lass who stared at this evident traveller from far-off parts before she found her tongue. No—Miss Avice wasn't in, she was down the garden, at the far end.

Brereton hastened down the garden; turned a corner; they met unexpectedly. Equally unexpected, too, was the manner of their meeting. For these two had been in love with each other from an early stage of their acquaintance, and it seemed only natural now that when at last they touched hands, hand should stay in hand. And when two young people hold each other's hands, especially on a Springtide evening, and under the most romantic circumstances and surroundings, lips are apt to say more than tongues—which is as much as to say that without further preface these two expressed all they had to say in their first kiss.

Nevertheless, Brereton found his tongue at last. For when he had taken a long and searching look at the girl and had found in her eyes what he sought, he turned and looked at wood, hill, sky, and sea.

"This is all as you described it" he said, with his arm round her, "and yet the first real thing I have to say to you now that I am here is—to ask you to leave it!"

She smiled at that and again put her hand in his.

"But—we shall come back to it now and then— together!" she said.

Resurrected Press Mysteries by J. S. Fletcher

The Orange-Yellow Diamond
When an elderly pawnbroker is murdered in the London parish of Paddington, a young, down on his luck writer is accused of the crime. But then it's found the pawnbroker had had in his possession an extraordinary South African diamond worth over eighty-thousand pounds — a diamond that's now missing. It falls to Melky Rubenstein to unravel the mystery and prove the young man's innocence.

The Middle Temple Murder
When an elderly man's body is found on the steps of chambers in the Midde Temple, one of the Inns of Court, it falls to newspaperman Frank Spargo and Detective-Sergeant Rathbury to solve the crime. The murdered man, for indeed it was murder, was found with no money or identification on his person except for a piece of paper with the name and address of a young barrister. Who is the victim? Why was he killed? Who is the murderer?

Scarhaven Keep
Bassett Oliver, the famed actor, has gone missing. When Oliver fails to show for a rehearsal, aspiring playwright Richard Copplestone finds himself sent to the small village of Scarhaven on the northern coast of England to track down the actors movements. What he finds is mystery. Find the answers as Copplestone unravels the mystery of Scarhaven Keep.

Visit www.resurrectedpress.com

Resurrected Press Mysteries by Fergus Hume

The Green Mummy

Professor Braddock hoped to compare the burial practices of the Egyptians with those of the ancient Peruvians with his latest acquisition, the mummy of the last Inca, Caxas. But on arrival, the packing case proved to hold not the mummy, but the body of his assistant Sidney Bolton. It falls to Archie Hope to discover the murderer if he is to marry the professors step-daughter, Lucy Kendal. Who killed Bolton and where is the mummy? Was it the sea captain Hervey? The mysterious Don Pedro? Cockatoo the Polynesian servant? The professor, himself? And what has become of the emeralds? These are the questions that Hope must answer amongst the secrets of the past in The Green Mummy.

The Mystery of a Hansom Cab

"Truth is said to be stranger than fiction, and certainly the extraordinary murder which took place in Melbourne Friday morning goes a long way towards verifying that saying." Thus opens The Mystery of a Hansom Cab, the best selling mystery of the nineteenth century. When a man is found dead in a hansom cab one of Melbourne's leading citizens is accused of the murder. He pleads his innocence, yet refuses to give an alibi. It falls to a determined lawyer and an intrepid detective to find the truth, revealing long kept secrets along the way. Fergus Hume's first and perhaps most famous mystery... The Mystery Of A Hansom Cab.

Visit www.resurrectedpress.com

Resurrected Press Mysteries from the Dr. John Thorndyke Series

Dr. John Thorndyke - Lecturer on Medical Jurisprudence and Forensic Medicine. Before Bones, before CSI, before Quincy, M.E – there was Dr. John Thorndyke solving the most baffling cases of Edwardian London using the latest tools of medical science. Read about his cases in:

The Eye of Osiris
John Bellingham, noted Egyptologist has vanished not once but twice in the same day. Now Dr, Thorndyke must unravel the tangled claims on his estate, solve the riddle of the missing man and find the "Eye of Osiris".

The Mystery of 31 New Inn
When Dr. Jervis is whisked away in a coach with no windows to an unknown location to treat a man in a coma from undivulged causes it is Dr. Thorndyke who must come up with the solution.

The Red Thumb Mark
The first of Dr. Thorndyke's cases finds him trying to prove the innocence of a young man accused of being a diamond thief despite the fact that his finger print was found at the scene of the crime.

John Thorndyke's Cases
More cases of medical mysteries as told by his trusted assistant Jervis, M.D. Eight stories of crime and deduction in Edwardian London.

Visit www.resurrectedpress.com

Resurrected Press Mysteries by John R. Watson & Arthur J. Rees

The Hampstead Mystery

High Court Justice Sir Horace Fewbanks found shot dead in his Hampstead home, a butler with a criminal past, a scorned lover and a hint of scandal. These are the elements of the Hampstead Mystery that Detective Inspector Chippenfield of Scotland Yard must unravel with the assistance of the ambitious Detective Rolfe. But will he be able to sort out the tangled threads of this case and arrest the culprit before he is upstaged by the celebrated gentleman detective Crewe. Follow the details of this amazing case at it plays out across Hampstead, London and Scotland until it reaches a stunning conclusion in the courts of the Old Bailey.

The Mystery of the Downs

When Harry Marsland was caught in a sudden down pour he sought shelter at Cliff Farm. Met at the door by a young woman clearly expecting someone else he is only too glad to get inside to wait out the storm. When they hear a noise upstairs in the deserted house they investigate only to discover the body of the farm's owner, Frank Lumsden, dead of a gunshot wound. Who then, killed Lumsden, and why? Who was the woman expecting and did she have any roll in the murder? These are the questions that private detective Crewe must answer in The Mystery of the Downs.

Visit www.resurrectedpress.com

Other Resurrected Press Mysteries

Mysteries on a Train

Before the Orient Express there was:

The Rome Express by Arthur Griffiths
A man is found dead in his first class sleeping compartment on the express from Rome to Paris. Who was his murderer? The Countess? The English General? His brother the clergy man? The maid who has disappeared? Is the French justice system up to solving the crime? Read about it in The Rome Express.

The Passenger from Calais by Arthur Griffiths
Colonel Basil Annesley finds he is the only passenger on the train from Calais to Lucerne. That is until a mysterious woman shows up at the last minute to book a compartment. Who is after her? What is her secret? Is she a criminal or a victim? Read about it in The Passenger from Calais

Visit us at www.resurrectedpress.com

About Resurrected Press

A division of Intrepid Ink, LLC, Resurrected Press is dedicated to bringing high quality, vintage books back into publication. See our entire catalogue and find out more at www.ResurrectedPress.com.

About Intrepid Ink, LLC

Intrepid Ink, LLC provides full publishing services to authors of fiction and non-fiction books, eBooks and websites. From editing to formatting, from publishing to marketing, Intrepid Ink gets your creative works into the hands of the people who want to read them. Find out more at www.IntrepidInk.com.